PALE MIDNIGHT

A.C. ARQUIN

WORDS ON THE WIND, LLC

1

The street outside the bar was a technicolor smear, neon letters fuzzy around the edges, half-hidden behind billowing fog. Stephen shivered. He'd been warned the nights were cold in San Francisco, but he hadn't been prepared for this. Especially coming from a scorching midwestern summer. Now he was just another of those tragically unprepared visitors, forced to buy a sweatshirt on Fisherman's Wharf. He might as well wear a blinking sign that said tourist.

At least people were nice to tourists in SF. When you got outside the major tourist trap areas, anyway. Inside of the tourist traps, visitors were all just dollar signs with legs.

Stephen glanced blearily up and down the street, uncertain which direction his hotel was. It was only his second day in the city and everything looked the same. Old Victorian buildings. Rolling San Francisco hills. Shantytowns in rubble-strewn vacant lots in every direction.

He'd just decided the hotel was to his left when a hand fell on his shoulder.

"Not that way, handsome." His friend Malcolm gently turned him in the opposite direction. "Come on, I'll walk you to your door."

Stephen narrowed his eyes, fingering the soft lapel of Malcolm's leopard-print coat. "OK, but don't think you're coming up for a nightcap."

Malcolm laughed. "Stephen, that ship sailed years ago, and we both know it. You're like a pair of comfortable old socks to me."

Stephen's face scrunched up, his carefully trimmed beard bunching around the corners of his mouth. "I'm trying to decide if I should be offended by that remark."

"Think of it as a compliment. There aren't many people I'd rather cozy up with on the couch on a cold night."

Something was wrong with that logic, but Stephen couldn't quite put his finger on what. He shrugged and snuggled against Malcolm's side. "OK, walk me home then."

As they walked, they rehashed old times, as friends who haven't seen each other in a long time do. Stephen and Malcolm had grown up together.

Well, not literally grown up together.

They had met when they were both eighteen, young and unsure and out on their own in the world for the first time. They'd been roommates, and sure, they had slept together once, but they quickly realized that was a bad idea. They were better off just being friends.

A year later, Malcolm had taken off for San Francisco and Stephen had stayed in Chicago. But they'd never lost touch and wrote each other long accounts of their adventures, on real paper and with real ink.

Malcolm had been trying to get Stephen to come visit San Francisco for years. This was the first time Stephen had taken him up on the offer. It was different from Chicago, that was for sure. Stranger and more decadent. Like an aging diva who still appreciates theatricality in her daily life.

Stephen wasn't sure if he liked it or not, but it was good to see Malcolm. Spending time with Malcolm made him feel young, almost like he was eighteen all over again. Even if Malcolm's receding hairline and Stephen's paunch exposed the lie.

"Give me another bump of that stuff," Stephen said.

Malcolm looked at him dubiously. "Are you sure? It might keep you from sleeping."

"I can sleep when I'm dead. Tonight I am alive and in San Francisco and I want drugs." He threw his arms open and whirled around on the sidewalk, imagining himself in a movie.

Malcolm laughed. "I couldn't possibly say no to that."

He pulled out the little vial and put two drops in Stephen's eyes, then in his own.

Stephen shuddered as a fever wave rolled through his skull. Fire followed by ice followed by a tingling thickness. The world went soft around him. Things in his peripheral vision started to drift. The street-lights all had halos, shimmering green and purple.

He looked at Malcolm. His friend's face had gone pale, but he was smiling. Stephen found himself grinning too.

"That's much better." His head felt light. Drifting away on a cloud. "What did you say this stuff was called again?"

"Dream."

"Right." He had to speak carefully; his tongue was thick in his mouth. "Makes sense. I feel like I am in a dream now."

They linked arms and continued down the street, swaying a little. All too soon, Malcolm tugged at Stephen's arm, bringing them to a halt in front of a grand entrance.

"Well, here we are."

Stephen blinked and looked around. The hotel seemed older at night, more weathered. As if the building's accumulated years gathered in the shadows, lurking in every corner. He smiled wryly to himself. That was San Francisco all over. He'd never been in a city that felt more haunted by its past.

"You sure you don't want to come up for a drink?" He worked his eyebrow and put on a come-hither expression.

Malcolm patted the top of his head, then leaned in and kissed him on the cheek. "You're adorable. Don't ever change. Get some sleep and I'll see you tomorrow. TTFN."

Stephen grinned as he watched Malcolm sashay down the sidewalk away from him. "Sweet dreams, Tigger," he called.

"Good night, Rabbit," Malcolm returned without slowing.

Stephen kept grinning as he pushed his way in through the front door. That was an old game they used to play when they were roommates. They'd pick a fictional universe and decide which member of that universe each of their friends was. In A.A. Milne's *Winnie the Pooh* universe, Malcolm was the fun-loving Tigger, and Stephen was the uptight worrywart Rabbit. Despite that, they'd remained best friends. Sometimes opposites really did attract.

Stephen stopped in front of the door to his room, feeling around in his pockets for the key. The door had an electronic card reader on it, but it was vestigial at this point. Electricity was unreliable and at a premium since the Collapse, so hotels had gone back to good old-fashioned physical keys with tumblers.

He checked his front pocket, then his back pocket, then the pockets of his sweatshirt. Then he started the process all over again. Halfway through his third time around, he noticed that the door to his room wasn't locked. In fact, it wasn't even closed all the way. He could see a sliver of darkness separating the door frame from the door.

"That's weird."

He must have forgotten to lock the door on his way out. That wasn't like him, but he had been drinking a lot the last two days. His brain felt spongy and saturated. It certainly wasn't outside the realm of possibility that he had forgotten.

He pushed into the dark room, closed the door behind him, and stumbled into the bathroom to pour himself a glass of water. In the mirror his face was pale and drawn, his eyes bloodshot. He looked like hell.

"You're definitely not eighteen anymore," he told himself. "You're probably going to regret this in the morning."

A wave of exhaustion rolled over him. He realized he was lying on the worn carpet. Vaguely, he thought he should get up. Get into bed. But it was too much effort. He was drifting. Dreamy. His mind floating somewhere above his body.

He was almost asleep, wafting on the edge of consciousness, when he started to see colors behind his eyelids. Green and blue and purple, glowing and shifting.

Stephen smiled, drifting towards the lights in his half-dreaming state. He thought he heard someone calling to him, off in the distance.

The voice was soft and soothing, drawing him in like a balloon at the end of a string. Was there more than one voice?

He started to feel heat. A campfire? He didn't know, but it was bright and getting uncomfortably warm now. Waves of heat pulsed through his body. He tried to back away, but the pull was insistent, drawing him ever forward.

Something else was tugging him in another direction. It was cold that way, ice cold and dark.

The heat was becoming painful. One part of him was burning, the other freezing. Stephen tried to open his eyes, but he couldn't. Was this a nightmare?

He didn't feel like he was dreaming. He felt as though he was still awake and getting more awake with each passing second as the opposing forces pulled on him ever harder. He was caught in a tug of war between the frozen wastes of Antarctica and the fires of hell.

He struggled to open his eyes, to scream, to do something, but he couldn't. All he could do was stretch and freeze and burn.

The voices were getting louder, chanting. Chanting his name? The light seared into him. He felt pressed against a griddle, his mind sizzling. His spirit was getting thinner, stretching into taffy. His soul moving forward while his body remained behind. His world was agony as the connections to his body frayed like overwrought tendons and snapped one by one.

Stephen screamed as the last connection parted. His soul was pulled down into the abyss.

2

Valora Keri startled awake to the roar of the vacuum cleaner. She pulled her pillow over her head. The machine continued to rumble, getting louder as it approached the door to her bedroom. Also, someone was singing. Loudly and off-key.

A glance at the clock told her it was nine a.m. She'd gotten off work at five.

Val crossed her room in two strides and yanked the door open, startling her roommate. Sandra wore baggy sweats, and her ears were covered by large headphones. Her singing stopped mid-note.

Val jerked the vacuum's plug out of the wall. "What the fuck are you doing?" she yelled.

Sandra shrank inside her hoodie. "Vacuuming?" she squeaked.

"At nine a.m.? How many times have we talked about this?"

Her roommate's shoulders came up so high she looked like a turtle retreating into her shell. "Um, I don't know..."

Sandra worked at a coffee shop and woke up early, even on the days when she wasn't working. For someone used to starting work at five a.m., nine probably seemed late in the day.

Val disagreed.

"You know what, Sandra? I don't think this is going to work out.

You're sweet and all, but our schedules are polar opposites. Maybe you need to find another place to live."

Sandra's mouth dropped open. "Wh... What? Are you kicking me out?"

"Look, it's nothing personal. Our schedules just conflict. You wake up around the same time I go to bed. We're not compatible."

Sandra hung her head. "I'm sorry. I understand."

At the hurt look on the girl's face, Val regretted her outburst. She tried to find something kind to say, but Sandra had already dropped the vacuum and turned away. She watched the girl disappear into her bedroom and shut the door.

"That was tactful," Mister E observed. The demon cat floated on his back, blowing candy cigarette smoke rings at the ceiling. *"As if you don't already have enough crises in your life. Might as well throw another log on the fire."*

"Stuff it, furball." Val stomped back into her bedroom and snatched up her gym bag. She was too agitated to go back to sleep. Now she needed to blow off some steam.

Forty minutes later, Val's fist slammed into flesh, her knuckles making a satisfying sound against the bone beneath. She followed the punch with a left cross, then immediately stepped into a straight right.

Her opponent bounced against the ropes and rebounded towards her, his hands up, trying to guard the space. He used his momentum to slip past her, escaping back into the open ring. Val turned, watching him, ready for anything.

"Not a bad punch, Chiquita." Mars winked at her, his eyes bright below the thick ridge of his brow. "Too bad you hit like a girl."

Val advanced cautiously, refusing to take the bait. Mars was trying to make her angry and sloppy. Which wasn't difficult, considering she'd been angry when she got here. She ground her teeth together and tried to maintain control.

She swiveled her hips and launched a snap kick at his ribs. Mars grunted as he absorbed the blow with his bicep. His guard dropped for a moment and Val darted in, snake fast, going for his face with a straight left. His eyes widened and for a second Val thought she had him. Then Mars bared his teeth in a grin and clamped his thick fingers around her wrist, pulling her forward as he pivoted. She hardly had time to gasp in surprise before she was flying through the air, landing with a thud on the mat.

As she lay there catching her breath, his barking laughter rang down around her. "You know, you kick like a girl, too."

Val vaulted back to her feet, her vision turning red. That was it. His ass was going down.

Her opponent's cocky smile slipped a notch as he saw her face. That was all he had time to do before Val was upon him.

Mars wanted to make her mad? Now he'd have to live with the consequences.

Val hit him with a right and a left, then a straight kick to the stomach. A hail of blows came in a wild flurry, almost too fast to follow. Mars tried to rely on technique as she rained blows down on him one after another, overwhelming his defenses with sheer ferocity and power. She caught him with an uppercut and his eyes went glassy. She followed with a roundhouse kick and he toppled like a tree.

She was on him in an instant, pounding him into the mat, blood on her fists, her breath coming in ragged gasps. It wasn't until Mister E showed up that she realized how much she had lost control. The cat demon floated in the air above her shoulder, purring, whispering in her ear. *"Yes. Beat him. Give me blood."*

She came back to herself with a start and jerked away, staring at the blood on her knuckles, then at Mars, lying unconscious on the mat, and his ruined face.

"No no no no no," she whispered, and called across the gym. "George, I need some towels in here."

The old trainer came shuffling out of his office, cocking his head. His pointed ears twitched, the little tufts of gray hair on the top swaying with the movement.

"What's that?" he yelled.

"Towels," Val screamed. "Mars is losing a lot of blood."

George snatched up a couple of towels from the bench outside the office and hobbled stiffly across the gym.

"Gods,Val," he cursed. "What were you doing?"

Val pressed the towels against her opponent's bloody skin. He was motionless, his blocky face looking innocent in unconsciousness.

"Things got out of control, George. I'm sorry."

George sighed. "Again? You keep this up, you're gonna run out of guys willing to spar with you."

"Maybe that wouldn't be the worst thing in the world," Val muttered. "Safer for everyone involved."

She left Mars in George's capable hands and went to hit the showers. Her stomach writhed. What the hell was wrong with her? That was the third time in a month she'd lost control in a training match. Her temper was getting worse, rage slipping over her without warning. If she wasn't careful, she really might kill someone.

"You are a predator," Mister E said lazily. *"Killing is your nature."*

"It's your nature, not mine," she growled.

Mister E's Cheshire Cat smile shone through the clouds of steam filling the air. *"We are one and the same. My nature is your nature."*

"No." She slammed the water shut. "I can't believe that. If I let myself kill people, then I'm no better than the monsters I'm fighting against."

She stared at herself through the steam on the mirror, running her fingers over the tattoos that covered her heart and wrapped up and over her left shoulder. The ink was a patchwork memento mori, with bits for everyone she'd lost, both those she'd accidentally killed—like her mother and her best friend Amber—as well as people like Ruby and Shanna, who had died simply because they were near her. It was a mosaic of guilt and regret.

She ground her teeth. Yes, she had accidentally killed, and she'd spent her life trying to balance those scales. But no matter what Mister E said, she was not an intentional killer. She could not, and would not be.

Out on the street, she stood blinking in the sun, her hair still damp over her standard uniform of black jeans, black boots, and a black leather jacket. Her mood had not improved. She still felt groggy from Sandra's unwanted wake-up call, and now she felt guilty about hurting Mars, too. And to put a cherry on top of everything else, it was inventory day at the Alley Cat, and she had to go to work early.

She ground her knuckles into her heavy eyes. Caffeine. She needed caffeine in her system before she went down to the Alley Cat. Fortunately, her local shop was only a couple of blocks away.

Val pushed through the door to Zombie Coffee—Coffee strong enough to wake the dead!—and breathed in the rich aroma. The smell of coffee always made her feel better. After ordering her customary butterscotch latte, she joined the small crowd waiting for their drinks.

The coffee shop was warm and bustling, as always. Caffeine was one of the few things almost everyone could agree on. Her other roommate, Malcolm, had once given her a lecture on what an amazing survival trait the coffee plant had stumbled upon when it made its beans caffeinated. Now an entire planet's worth of caffeine-addicted humans were invested in ensuring that the coffee plant continued to thrive and flourish. Survival of the fittest, indeed.

Val had never seen any evidence of a capital-G God, but things like that did make her wonder. Sometimes it felt like the pieces of the natural puzzle fit together a little too neatly to be coincidence. Though she did know for a fact that there were plenty of little-g gods running around, so maybe one of them was to blame. In fact, now that she thought about it, it was probably one of the trickster gods. They were no doubt having a good laugh at the way they'd made the entire planet dependent on a single species of plant.

She shuddered as she imagined what would happen if they decided to send a blight to wipe out the coffee bean harvest. The resulting wars would be spectacular.

The barista called her name, and she picked up her coffee from the counter. She blinked at the cup. Instead of a leaf or a cat or some cute foam art, the barista had drawn a frowny face on top of her latte.

"What the hell?" she muttered.

Mister E's mocking laughter filled her ears. "*Reaping what we sow already?*"

"Reaping what I sow? What the hell does that mean?"

"*I wonder. Let's follow the clues, shall we? You kicked your roommate out this morning. Said roommate works in a coffee shop. The barista at your local coffee shop seems to be rather upset with you. How in the world could these events possibly be connected?*"

"Your sarcasm before I've had my coffee is not appreciated," Val grumbled. "But I still don't see how these things are related. Sandra doesn't even work here."

"But this is the closest coffee shop to our flat, and she likes to hang out here when she's not working. If you pull your head out of your ass, you'll see that she's sitting at a table in the corner right now."

Val swore under her breath. Sure enough, Sandra was bent over her sketchpad with her headphones on, determinedly not looking in Val's direction.

She took a sip of her latte and sighed. Even the butterscotch tasted like it was frowning.

"Why are people so complicated? I just want us all to get along. Is that too much to ask?"

The spirit-cat's laughter rang out again.

"Oh, child. People have been failing to get along since the dawn of time. Put any two people together for any length of time and they will invariably argue. Lock one person alone in a room and they'll argue with themselves, for that matter. Humans are a very contrary race. It's a miracle you've survived this long without killing each other."

Val grimaced as she pushed back out onto the street.

"Yeah, well it certainly hasn't been for lack of trying."

Her conversation was interrupted when a familiar face popped up in front of her. Malcolm's face was ashen and he was panting, as if he'd just run a long way.

"Val," he gasped. His bottom lip trembled. Tears filled his eyes. "You have to help me. Something's happened to Stephen."

3

The Alley Cat was bumping. The crowd was lively, the music was loud, and the drinks were flowing. Malina bobbed to the beat in the DJ booth. Jewel spun around the stage, her dancer's legs locked around the metal pole, torso perpendicular to the ground, arms extended as if she were flying. A naked angel full of grace.

Val hardly noticed any of it. All she could see was Malcolm's tear-streaked face. His oldest friend was dead, and instead of helping Malcolm find out what happened, Val was stuck cutting limes behind the bar of the Alley Cat because she'd just lost her temper and kicked Sandra out. She couldn't afford to miss a shift, or they'd all be out on the street.

Still, her thoughts were on Malcolm, and Stephen. It sounded like he might have been murdered. Another dead friend on her watch. Death followed her around like the stench of rancid milk.

Maybe she'd been cursed on the day she'd freed Mister E in exchange for magic. She'd only been six years old, she'd had no idea what he was asking or offering. All she knew was that the bullies were after her again and she wanted them to stop. She wanted the power to stop them.

The cat-demon's power had overwhelmed her. She'd inadvertently killed her mother and another little girl, Katrina. They had been her first victims, but far from the last. There had been many others over the years. Greg and Wanda. Sylvio and Amber. Ruby and Sandra. Some dead by her hand, others, like Stephen, simply dead near her, caught in the swirling vortex of death that followed wherever she went.

Val thought she could fight the darkness. Balance the scales by fighting monsters. Defend humanity from the darkness.

But the deaths kept coming. Maybe they were all her fault. Maybe she should kill herself in order to save everyone else.

If she thought killing herself would help, she would do it. But what if the monsters kept coming? What if removing herself from the equation only removed an obstacle from their path? What if her death actually made things easier for them?

"Val? Are you OK?"

She turned to find Lisa peering at her. Straight blond hair framed the young barback's long face, falling over the shoulders of her vintage Oakland Seals jersey. Her dreamy sculptor's eyes were filled with concern.

Val tried to make her lips curve into a smile. "I'm fine."

Lisa didn't look convinced, but she knew better than to press. "The boss wants to see you," she said, jerking her head towards the office on the other side of the club.

Val rolled her eyes. "Great, just what I need."

Tommy Walker's office was set high above the club to peer down over the floor. From up here, you felt like you were lord of all you surveyed. Which was just the way Tommy liked it.

Val poked her head in the door. "You wanted to see me, boss?"

Walker had greasy hair, sallow skin, and a shiny silk shirt under his sport jacket. His desk was huge and polished, and his leather chair cost more than Val's motorcycle. He looked like the kind of guy you should never buy a used car from.

Tommy barely glanced up from the receipts on his desk. "I've got a job for you. A private party Thursday night."

"A private party?" Val asked. "Here?"

The Alley Cat never had private parties, at least none that Val had ever seen. Tommy always said they had too many regular customers to give the entire club to just one of them.

"No, not here. At the Masonic Temple on Oak."

Val frowned. "I don't work at the Masonic Temple on Oak. I work at the Alley Cat."

Walker glared at her. "You work where I say you work. Thursday, you're working at the Masonic Temple on Oak. They requested you specifically."

"Who is this 'they'?"

Tommy smiled. "You'll find out when you get there. Just dress nice."

Dress nice? Val's eyebrows rose almost to her hairline. She gestured down at the black sleeveless shirt, black jeans, and black boots she customarily wore at the Alley Cat. "This isn't nice enough for your fancy customers?"

"Fuck, no, it's not. Wear a dress and show some cleavage."

Val choked.

Tommy laughed. "I'm just yanking your chain about the dress. Don't take everything so personally. You just need some professional attire. Don't worry, I'll have something delivered to your place tomorrow. Just put it on and show up at the address I tell you to."

Val's eyes narrowed. "What is this event, anyway?"

Tommy put a finger to his lips and winked at her. "It's a big secret. On a need-to-know basis. And you don't need to know. You just need to pour the drinks and keep your mouth shut."

"What if I say no?"

Tommy sat back in his expensive chair. "If you say no, you know where the door is. Don't let it hit you in the ass on the way out."

Val's lips pressed into a tight line. Was it worth her job to turn down this mystery gig? She had no savings and was perpetually one month away from being out on the street. Bartending jobs were hard to come by in the city, and now that she'd kicked Sandra out, she needed this job more than ever. How bad could it be, anyway?

She sighed. "Fine. This had better pay well."

"You'll get a bonus for it, plus tips. And, as I'm sure you've guessed, these people have money." Tommy turned his attention back to the receipts on his desk and waved his fingers at her. "You can go now. Masonic Temple at nine o'clock. Don't be late."

Val lingered in the doorway for a moment, staring at him. She had more questions, but she wasn't going to get any more out of him right now. Finally, she huffed and went back down the stairs.

Back behind the bar, she worked mechanically, pouring drinks and making small talk with customers without really registering any of it. She turned the mystery gig over and over in her head. She hated mysteries, and something about this one stank. Unfortunately, she really didn't have a choice. She needed this job more than it needed her. If she wanted to keep a roof over her head and food in her mouth, she had to stay on Tommy Walker's good side. And if that meant showing up and smiling for a bunch of rich assholes, so be it.

By five a.m. her feet hurt and she smelled like perfume made out of vodka and sweat. Val gratefully locked up the Alley Cat and walked around the silent building to the small lot in the back where she parked the Ural. At least the city around her was quiet. One good thing about getting off work at five a.m.: you practically had the city to yourself. The breeze was cold and salty in her nostrils, swirling the banks of fog that drifted low over the rooftops. She stopped and closed her eyes for second, listening to the silence. As she listened, tiny sounds emerged. The flapping of wings overhead. The yowl of a cat. Paper rustling in the wind.

And something else.

The hair prickled along the back of her neck. Someone was watching her. Val cracked her eyes and peered between her eyelashes to her left, carefully moving only her eyes and not her head.

There. A girl in a long grey skirt and a white peasant's blouse at the far end of the lot, watching Val with grey eyes. Medium height, about eighteen years old. Dark hair and angular features. Then the fog swirled between them, and as the sightline cleared again, the girl was gone.

Val waited a dozen breaths for the girl to reappear, but she didn't. Finally, she opened her eyes and pulled her helmet out of the lockbox. That's when she realized the girl was now standing right beside her.

She jumped. "What the fuck?"

The girl's expression stayed flat. "Hello, Valora. We've been looking for you."

Val swallowed, her pulse ticking upward as a jolt of fear shot through her. She tried to keep her emotions from her face.

"Olga. Did you come all the way out here just for me? You should have called ahead; I'd have made up the guest room for you. Remind me again: Would you want one bed or three?" She tried to keep her voice light. The Three Sisters had found her. If Olga was here, Anastasia and Maria must be nearby. This was not good.

"The Coven misses you," Olga said. "You left us in such a hurry. We did not have a proper chance to say goodbye."

"Sorry about that. I hate goodbyes. It's better to just move on and get on with your new life, don't you think?"

"Moving on..." Olga began.

"... That's a funny concept," a new voice finished from behind Val's left shoulder.

Val suppressed the urge to whirl around. The Sisters were telepathic, and they often finished each other's sentences. It gave the creepy impression they all shared one mind. She glanced behind her casually, as if she'd known the other girl was there all along. This sister looked almost identical to the first, except her skirt was brown.

"Hello, Maria. Or is it Anastasia? I'm never sure which one of you I'm talking to."

"That's because you're talking to all of us." A third girl emerged from the fog directly across from Val. Her skirt was black. She had the same olive skin and flat grey eyes as her sisters.

"Well, that makes it easy then," Val smiled. "Why bother with names at all? Maybe I'll just call you the Three Blind Mice."

"The Three Fates would be more appropriate..." Olga started.

"... in the current circumstance," one of the others finished.

"You have harmed the Coven," the third put in.

Val suppressed a shudder. The notes of the sisters' voices blended into an eerie minor chord.

"You have killed," Olga continued.

"and you must answer..."

"... for your crimes."

Guilt hung heavy around Val's neck. They were talking about Amber and Sylvio. The weight she'd been carrying for years.

"It was an accident," she said softly. "I didn't mean to hurt them."

"Yet they are dead all the same," Olga said.

"And Paula says..."

"...you must answer..."

"... for your crimes," the sisters repeated.

Ice crept down Val's spine. Paula was an old witch who had taught Val some ritual magic while she lived in the abandoned warehouse in Brooklyn they called the Emerald City. She was also the head of the Coven.

Her fingers strayed to the memento mori over her heart. Val had been dreading this moment for a long time. Years ago, she'd killed her best friend and her lover in a fit of despair and jealousy. She hadn't meant to. She'd caught them together and her emotions had over-whelmed her. The magical whirlwind that tore them apart had simply been an outward manifestation of her inner turmoil. She hadn't meant to hurt anyone. It just happened.

But her intentions didn't matter to her former friends. Amber and Sylvio were just as dead either way.

She'd known this day would come. For years, she'd be running. Hiding. Living in fear.

But the guilt had always come with her. It was graven into her soul like the ink of her tattoos.

Val squared her shoulders and looked Olga in the eye. Maybe it was time to stop running.

"You're right. So do we do this here, or what?"

"You will appear before a tribunal..."

"... at midnight,"

"… three nights hence."

"You will stand before your peers..."

"... and you will..."

"... be judged."

Val shivered. She felt like her entire body was coated in ice.

Still, she managed to form the words: "I'll be there."

4

The Queen Anne Hotel had seen better days. Built in 1890, it was originally a girls' boarding school, and later narrowly survived the great San Francisco earthquake of 1906. The grand Victorian's once colorful paint was gray and faded, its windows coated with grime. Tourism was down significantly since the Collapse and many hotels had folded entirely. That the Queen Anne soldiered on was a testament to the landmark's enduring popularity.

So it was no surprise that Malcolm's friend Stephen had chosen to stay there. It had a lot of distinctive San Francisco charms and was representative of the city's rich history. In a town chockfull of old Victorians, staying in a Victorian-era hotel was a must if you really wanted an authentic taste of the city.

Unfortunately for Stephen, his choice hadn't worked out so well in the end.

Sneaking into the Queen Anne turned out to be easier than Val expected. The lobby was deserted, and a beautiful glass chandelier cast light over a quaint Victorian sitting area, complete with beautifully patterned carpet and wallpaper, and hardwood chairs upholstered with plush covers. The chairs and carpet were threadbare in places, but the bones of their grand history were still clearly visible. The night clerk was nodding off over his book and didn't even look up as she went past.

Mister E appeared over her shoulder, or at least his wide Cheshire Cat smile and glowing eyes did. The rest of his body was missing, though she could faintly see his tail lashing.

"I smell ghosts," he growled. *"They make my nose itch."*

Val wasn't surprised. The Queen Anne had long been rumored to be haunted. Mister E's itchy nose only confirmed it.

They ascended the stairs, passed the second floor and moved on to the third.

She recalled what Malcolm had told her that afternoon.

"I left him at the front door last night. He was drunk. We'd been out having a good time. He asked me to come up for a nightcap, but I turned him down." Tears ran down his cheeks. "I came by this morning to pick him up. We were supposed to go get some brunch. I had them call up from the front desk, but he didn't answer his phone. I came up and knocked on his door. Still no answer. Finally, I talked house-keeping into opening the door for me. I found Stephen lying on the floor, still wearing the clothes he wore last night. He was lying on his back, staring up at the ceiling. His eyes were open, and he wasn't breathing."

"Were there any signs of forced entry?" Val asked.

"No, nothing that I saw."

She scanned the door frame, and what she observed matched Malcolm's words. There were no marks on the frame, no indication of a busted latch. The door was locked and had police tape across it, but that wasn't an impediment to Val. A few seconds with a lock pick and the bolt clicked open. She was in.

"Ah, the fruits of a misspent youth," Mister E purred, striding into the room with his tail in the air.

"It was either that or starve. Picking locks was a pretty practical skill for a homeless teen to have."

"I still think it was a waste of your time. You could have simply killed people and taken what you needed. Much simpler and cleaner."

"You have a strange definition of 'simpler and cleaner'," Val muttered.

She frowned as she studied the small room. No bloodstains, no bodily fluids stained the carpet. If it wasn't for the taped outline of Stephen's body, she would have no idea where he'd even died.

She knelt and ran her fingers over the carpet, hoping to detect some resonance of his spirit. There was nothing.

"Well, shit. This death was too clean. I don't know if I can even detect anything here."

"Clean deaths are so boring," Mister E complained. *"What's the point of even killing someone if you aren't going to paint the walls red with blood?"* He perched on the edge of the bed and disdainfully started cleaning himself.

Val ignored him. "I suppose all I can do is try."

She pulled chalk out of her bag and drew a circle and pentagram around the outline of the body. Then she lit candles at the five corners of the star and sat in the center, crossing her legs.

Ritual magic wasn't her strong suit, but she'd had pretty good luck with this ritual on her last case. Of course, she'd literally been sitting on a puddle of the victim's blood that time. Blood magic was the most direct way to get in touch with a dead soul. Without blood, finding the soul would be a lot more difficult.

Still, she had to try. Malcolm was her friend, and Stephen had been like family to him. She'd never be able to look Malcolm in the eye again if she didn't at least give it her best shot.

Val closed her eyes and let her breathing become deep and strong, stoking her energy as she dropped into a meditative trance. She tried to fix Stephen in her mind, but the truth was she hardly knew the man. She'd only met him once, very briefly, when he and Malcolm had stopped by the flat for a minute before they went out to hit the bars. He'd had a kind face and an absentminded air. Brown hair. A close-cropped beard. She dredged up every detail, fleshing out his image in her mind as best she could.

When she felt she had a firm grasp on him, Val gathered her power and breathed out a seeking. She wasn't overly hopeful. Seeking spells generally needed a physical component to be effective. Preferably the victim's blood or other bodily fluids. Even hair or flakes of skin could work.

But the police had gone over the room with a fine-toothed comb, and that stuff had been gathered for evidence. All she had left was the idea of Stephen, and the hope that his spirit was still lingering somewhere in the vicinity of his death.

For a long minute, nothing happened. Val felt the energy of her spell swirling around the circle, trying to locate something to latch on to. Finding nothing, the energy began to dissipate, leeching away into the atmosphere. Val swore. So much for step one.

Then she felt a jerk, and the buzz of energy in the room surged. Her spell had found something.

She clamped down on the excitement pulsing through her veins. Ritual magic required control and focus. If she broke her trance, the spell would evaporate in an instant.

Val focused on her breathing, keeping it slow and deep as she followed the line of her spell. It led down through the floor, to a ball of energy so far below it might even be underneath the hotel. It was hard to say. You couldn't really measure spiritual distances against the physical plane.

But the ball of energy was a spirit, she was sure of it. It had the unique flavor of a human spirit, and as she got a better sense of it, she was sure the person had not died happily.

"Stephen?" She thought the question at the spirit, pushing the word along the line of her spell.

She felt the spirit register her presence, sensed the humming energy turn to regard her.

"Stephen?" She thought again, pushing a little more energy into the word this time. "This is Val. Malcolm's friend. I need to ask you a few questions."

The energy shifted as the spirit seemed to consider this. Val felt the corners of her mouth quirk up into a smile. It was working. She had the spirit's attention. She was going to get some answers about Stephen's death.

But as she opened her mouth to speak, the energy shifted. She felt anger. Rage. The temperature in the room plummeted as the spirit rushed up the line of her spell, shrieking towards her.

Val tried to sever the connection, but the spirit was on her in an instant. Bursts of color exploded behind her eyelids. She could feel the spirit invading her mind, surrounding her body. She had invited the connection, so her circle did nothing to protect her.

She had an impression of strength and pain and rage. Whatever this spirit was that she had found, it wasn't Stephen. This spirit was old and powerful. Far more powerful than Val was in the narrow magical space carved out by the ritual.

It wrapped around her like a python and began to squeeze.

5

Val couldn't move. Couldn't speak. Couldn't breathe. The lights behind her eyelids intensified, splashes of green and blue and copper, filmed over by a wash of red and black as her body started to suffer from lack of oxygen. She struggled, but this was a type of fight she couldn't possibly win. Her magic was strong in the physical realm. But here in the spirit realm, she was weak as a kitten.

Val's body was going numb. She couldn't feel her arms. Her body felt heavy and thick. Even breathing was a struggle.

She was cold. So cold.

Her heart was slowing, each beat a massive effort of will.

Black water and silence closed over her.

She sank without a ripple.

For a time, there was nothing. No light. No heat. No sound or movement. Just cold and black forever and ever and ever.

She felt disappointment. She'd never believed in heaven, per se, but she thought that something interesting would happen when she died. Not this cold black nothing. Was this all there was?

Then something moved in the corner of her eye. The black water swirled. A flash of color pierced the murk.

Golden eyes. A Cheshire smile. Mister E was there.

The cat-demon grabbed her by the scruff of the neck and yanked upward. The water swirled around them, bubbling and frothing. She could feel the spirit's agitation.

Mister E bared his teeth and lashed out with his claws. The water drew back. Val saw light above them.

She surfaced with a gasp, her eyes snapping open as light and heat flooded her senses. She found herself sprawled inside the pentagram, her limbs arranged so that she was lying inside the tape outline where Stephen's body had been.

She scrambled to her feet, shuddering. "What the fuck was that?"

"Something old and powerful. Something that was not pleased to see you." Mister E wound around her feet, rubbing his back against her shins and purring.

"You saved me?"

"Somebody had to do it." She could feel his mental shrug. *"I didn't see anyone else lining up to volunteer."*

"Thank you." She wrapped her arms around her stomach and hugged herself as the shivers intensified. "That thing almost killed me."

Mister E leapt up onto the dresser and started to clean himself. *"Well, we couldn't have that. I waited thousands of years to find a host. I couldn't let you die on me so soon."*

"Right." Val shook feeling back into her sluggish limbs and packed away the candle stubs. She scrubbed the chalk from the carpet with a focused blast of wind. "I guess we found out what killed Stephen."

"Perhaps."

"What do you mean, perhaps? That thing almost killed me. Of course it killed Stephen." She stepped out into the hallway and closed the door behind her. Morning sunlight was streaming through the windows, and she could hear other guests waking and moving about. It was time to make herself scarce.

As she exited the front entrance, two cops were getting out of a SFPD cruiser. The nearer one turned to face her and Val winced.

"Keri. What the hell are you doing here?" Detective Chen looked tired. In Val's experience, he always looked tired. Wrinkles gathered at the corner of his eyes, and his clothes were so rumpled he might have been sleeping in them.

The other cop was a young woman with coke-bottle glasses, a beak nose, and a white lab coat. Obviously some sort of technician. She glanced up at Val but didn't stop working.

"Detective Chen. How nice to see you again."

"I wish I could say the same." He crossed his arms over his chest. "Are you going to tell me what you're doing here? Or am I going to have to arrest you for interfering with an investigation?"

"The victim was a friend," Val said simply.

Chen swore. "Another dead friend of yours? At this rate, I'm surprised you have any friends left, Keri. You don't strike me as the type that makes friends easily."

"You'd be surprised, Detective. I'm the life of the party."

Chen laughed sourly. "Sow that bullshit somewhere else, Keri. I'm sure people call you a lot of things, but the life of the party isn't one of them. Are you going to answer my question? What are you doing here?"

"I told you, the victim was a friend."

"That still doesn't answer the question. Friend or not, you've got no business here. I told you to stay out of my investigations."

"And I told you that there are some things the police aren't equipped to handle. I'm not going to stay away when my expertise is needed."

"This is a crime scene, Keri. You've got no place here. Get lost before I charge you with obstruction."

Val scowled but turned and moved away down the sidewalk. She was parked around the corner, and she'd already gotten what she needed. Antagonizing the SFPD wouldn't help find Stephen's killer.

Chen called after her, "Don't let me catch you interfering in my investigation again, Keri. Don't think I won't haul your ass down to the station."

Val pulled her helmet out of the lockbox and fired up the Ural.

"What did you mean, *perhaps*?" She pressed Mister E. "Clearly that thing I encountered killed, Stephen."

"Not necessarily. You went looking for something and you found a spirit that was better left undisturbed. There's no guarantee the spirit killed

Stephen. It might have been slumbering peacefully until you went poking at it with your ritual stick."

"Flying toads. So how do we find out?" She raised a hand, cutting him off. "Don't tell me. I know what you're going to say. We have to question Stephen's spirit directly. And to do that, we need a physical connection to his body." She sighed. "Which means we have to break into the SFPD morgue."

Mister E grinned from ear to ear.

Val sighed and pulled the big motorcycle around the corner, onto a dark side street. She glanced in the rearview mirror at the Queen Anne as she drove. Chen stood out on the sidewalk, scowling as he watched her ride away. If the detective didn't like her showing up at the Queen Anne, he really wasn't going to be happy about what she had to do next.

6

"I can't believe I have to wear this thing." Val tugged at the black dress, scowling at herself in the mirror.

"At least you fill it out," Lisa said. The barback unhappily adjusted her own dress. "I look like a twig in a sleeve."

They were setting up the bar for the party at the Masonic Temple, plucking at the dresses Tommy Walker had insisted they wear. Around them, other staff moved about in black dresses and tuxedos. The party was definitely of the fancy-dress variety.

Val was only half paying attention. Her mind was still on Stephen, and Detective Chen, and the dark presence that had tried to kill her. She'd stopped to check out the SFPD station that housed the morgue on her way home. In the twenty minutes she'd sat parked across the street, she'd watched thirty cops go in and out the main doors. Walking in through the front doors was out of the question. But if she wanted to talk to Stephen, she had to get inside that station.

Malcolm had of course pounced on her as soon as she stepped through the door to their apartment.

"Val? Did you find the bastard that killed Stephen?" His eyes were puffy. He'd clearly been crying.

"Not yet, but I will," she'd assured him. "I need your help."

"Anything. Tell me what you need."

"This is going to sound strange, but..."

Malcolm cut her off with a short laugh. "Strange? Coming from you? Honey, your picture is in the dictionary next to the word strange."

"You're probably right. I need you to find the blueprints for SFPD's central station and the blocks surrounding it. Concentrate on the underground levels. Basements and sewers. Maintenance tunnels. I need to get into the morgue to see Stephen's body."

Malcolm was silent for a long moment. Then he cleared his throat.

"Well, you certainly don't shrink from a challenge, do you?"

"Go big or go home," Val confirmed. "Can you do it?"

He sucked in a breath, his face contorting this way and that. "I think so. They should be in the public records. Give me a few hours."

Val released a breath she didn't know she'd been holding.

"Take all the time you need. Be careful. And thank you."

"It's the least I can do," he said. "Stephen would have done the same for me. I'll let you know when I've got something."

"Don't worry, you look great," Lisa said, pulling her out of her thoughts.

"I'm just glad you're here with me," Val tugged the shoulder of her dress up, pushed it down, then pulled it back up again. She huffed in exasperation. "I can't remember the last time I had to wear a dress."

"Well, I'm serious. With those lean muscles you've got, you look like an exotic animal. A panther or something."

Val laughed. "OK, Lisa. I know you're trying to make me feel better, but you don't have to lay it on quite so thick. Are you ready? We were supposed to be up and running five minutes ago."

Lisa sighed and tucked a stray strand of hair behind her ear with a manicured nail. Today her nails were lime green with white tips.

Val had no idea how Lisa maintained nails like that. Her own were always jagged and bitten down to nubs. She supposed her fighting didn't help.

The barback put on her game face. "Ready as I'll ever be. Here, I brought you a present." She pulled out a pair of butterscotch candies from her pocket and tossed one over.

Val grinned as she popped the butterscotch into her mouth. "You're the best. At least the night isn't a total loss. Now let's go pour drinks for some assholes."

They were assigned to a bar at one end of a massive ballroom. The ballroom was gorgeous: polished hardwood floors, crystal chandeliers hanging on thick chains, and heavy velvet curtains flanking massive glass doors that opened onto a marble terrace. Beyond the terrace, the lights of downtown shone.

"This place is amazing," Lisa breathed. "No wonder they wanted us wearing dresses."

"I'm still waiting to find out who the mysterious 'they' are," Val said, eyeing the guests who were starting to trickle into the ballroom.

The guests wore elaborate masks, with feathers flaring at the corners and gemstones embedded in the fabric. Their outfits shone and sparkled. Apparently, the party was a masquerade.

"Well, now I feel naked," Lisa complained. "Why didn't we get masks?"

"*Because the help go naked before the nobility.*" Mister E appeared on the edge of the bar, digging his claws into the white tablecloth as he stretched. "*It helps to keep you in your place.*"

As more guests filtered in, Val had a feeling Mister E had hit the nail on the head. That was exactly why she was here. Somebody wanted to put her in her place.

The first guests made a beeline for the bar, and soon Val was too busy to worry about anything but pouring drinks as fast as she could. She and Lisa fell into their familiar rhythm: Dark strip club or fancy ballroom, a bar was a bar, and alcohol poured into a glass the same everywhere.

Time passed quickly, as it always does during a bar rush, and the next time Val looked up, the ballroom was full. Masked people in expensive fabrics as far as the eye could see.

"It's like an ocean of silk," she muttered to Lisa.

"Do you think this is what they mean by the Silk Road?" Lisa wondered.

Val snorted. "I'm pretty sure that's got something to do with smuggling and drugs. Though there's probably a lot of that going on here as well."

"*There's always a lot of that going on,*" Mister E added. "*As long as humans have existed, people have been finding ways to alter their state of consciousness. With alcohol being one of the oldest and most reliable.*"

Val rolled her eyes. "Alcohol hardly counts as a drug. It's been legal forever."

"*So legal status is the thing that defines something as a drug? I see you've got a bright future ahead of you as a pharmaceutical company publicist,*" Mister E sneered. "*Besides, everything is legal these days. By your definition, there are no drugs.*"

"Everything is available these days," Val corrected. "Not legal. Just because the laws are no longer enforced doesn't mean they aren't still on the books. They're like the anti-sodomy laws of the twentieth century. Social norms dictated that they stopped being enforced, but nobody ever bothered to take the actual laws off the books. Even today, there are a lot of places where you could still technically be arrested for consensual sodomy in the privacy of your own home."

"*Consensual sodomy in the privacy of your own home,*" Mister E repeated, baring his crescent-grin. "*Now, there's a catchy phrase. I think you've missed your calling, Val. You could run for mayor with a slogan like that, especially in this city. Consensual sodomy for all!*"

"Don't knock it till you've tried it," Val shot back.

"*Oh, I've tried it plenty.*" Mister E gave her a wicked grin.

Val shuddered as her mind immediately went there.

"Great. Now I'm going to have that image stuck in my head all night."

"I hate to interrupt your conversation with yourself," a smoky voice cut in from behind her, "But I'd like a drink."

Val's cheeks burned. She'd gotten carried away talking to Mister E and forgotten she was in public. She probably looked like a madwoman muttering to herself.

Her breath caught in her throat as she turned to find the eyes of Melinda Pearl.

7

The queen of San Francisco's vampire cabal was pale and thin, with black hair cut in a razor line level with her chin. Her lips were the red of a winter sunset. Even with half her face hidden behind a black silk mask, there was no mistaking her. The woman crackled with energy.

Val quickly averted her eyes, focusing on Pearl's sharp cheekbones instead. Meeting a vampire's gaze for long was never a good idea.

She tightened her grip on the glass she was holding, ready to smash it against the vampire's face if Pearl came at her. Melinda Pearl was the head of Royal Construction, which was little more than a front for a powerful cabal of vampires. The last time Val had encountered Pearl, she'd fought the vampire high over the chilly waters of the bay. Melinda Pearl had been in the form of a giant bat at the time, and they'd both been in pursuit of the Scepter of Sutro. Val had stabbed the vampire over and over until Pearl had finally broken off her attack and flown away. She hadn't seen the woman since.

She suspected Melinda Pearl was the type to hold a grudge.

But the vampire didn't come flying over the bar, fangs bared. Instead, the woman gave a cold smile that didn't touch her dark eyes.

"I'll have a dirty gin martini. With two olives."

Val stood frozen for a long moment, unwilling to turn her back on the woman.

Pearl's laugh was mocking. "If I was going to harm you, I would have done so already. Make the drink, Keri."

Val swallowed and reluctantly did as she was told. She could feel the vampire's eyes burning into her back the entire time as she poured the gin and vermouth. Still, she stamped a professional smile on her face as she slid the drink across the bar.

"On the house. No hard feelings, eh?"

Melinda Pearl's smile stretched, exposing her sharp fangs.

"Oh, there are definitely hard feelings, Valora Keri. This is a neutral place, and now is neither the time nor the place to express those feelings. But your time of reckoning is coming."

With that parting shot, Melinda Pearl took her drink and melted into the crowd.

Val felt cold as she watched the vampire walk away. Had the vampire queen been the one who demanded her presence at this party?

Lisa's hand came down on her shoulder, making her jump.

"Are you OK?" Lisa's voice was thick with concern.

Val forced a smile. "Yeah, fine."

"Who was that?"

"That was Melinda Pearl, the head of Royal Construction."

"I don't think she likes you very much."

"No, she definitely does not."

As she went back to helping customers, Val turned Pearl's words over in her mind. She'd called this a neutral place. Had she meant the party? Was there some kind of temporary truce in place for the duration of the masquerade? Or had she been referring to the Masonic Temple itself?

Now that she knew Melinda Pearl was here, she scanned the crowd, looking for other players in the local underworld. Their masks were no longer an impediment. The eyes gave the game away every time.

She found Andrei Vasilevski standing in a knot of sharply dressed men in suits. He was a regular at the Alley Cat, and his intense eyes and short, thick build were instantly recognizable. Had he been the one to request her presence? She knew Vasilevski and Tommy Walker did a lot of business. But why would he want her here?

"To put you in your place, of course." Mister E answered her thought.

"But he sees me behind the bar in the Alley Cat all the time," Val objected. "Me serving him is hardly a novel experience."

"It's not for him, it's for everyone else. This room contains some of the most powerful people in the city. People who may have heard about your role in destroying the Scepter of Sutro. I'd wager this little display is to assure them that you are still under control."

"I'm not under anyone's control," she whispered, barely moving her lips, acutely aware that others might be watching her.

"We are all controlled by something," a new voice interrupted.

Val turned to find a tall man in a stylish tuxedo with tails looking down at her, dark skin peeking through his white feathered mask. A purple waistcoat trimmed with gold shimmered beneath his jacket, and his bald pate reflected the light of the chandeliers.

"Excuse me?" Val said.

"We may be controlled by other people, by gods, money, or passion. Every person is driven by something. No man is truly the master of his own ship." His voice had a musical lilt to it. Somewhere in the Caribbean, maybe?

"I don't—" Val began, then stopped, flustered that this man had apparently heard her muttering to Mister E.

"My apologies, I didn't mean to butt in on your conversation. I've got good ears, and I never know when to keep my mouth shut." He smiled, one of his incisors was gold. The guy radiated charm and confidence, and she could tell by the way Mister E's tail was all fluffed that he had some power to back it up.

Val decided she'd better be careful with this one. She quirked an eyebrow and gave him a polite, professional smile.

"I'm sorry. Have we met?"

"No, but I've heard of you, Valora Keri. You've got some people in this town riled up good and proper." The glint of his gold tooth was matched by a flash of amusement in his eyes. She noticed his irises didn't quite match. One was a light coffee-with-cream brown while the other was fresh-roasted black as night. Looking into them made the hairs on the back of her neck stand on end.

"Well, I do aim to please," Val said, forcing herself to hold his uncomfortable gaze. "I'm sorry, I didn't catch your name."

He chuckled. "They were right. You've got some bones in you. I respect that."

He tested his statement by extending his hand to her. A thick gold ring in the shape of a skull wrapped around his middle finger. Tiny rubies flashed in the eye sockets.

"Baron Blood, at your service."

8

Val hesitated, then shook the offered hand. His palm was smooth against hers, his fingers long and bony. An electric jolt of power ran up her arm at the contact, and she had to steel herself to keep from jerking her hand away.

The Baron watched her, weighing her reaction. Then he gave a solemn nod and released her. "Well met, Valora Keri. What brings you to such an auspicious gathering?"

"Auspicious?" Val made a dismissive puff. "All I see is a bunch of self-important socialites preening their feathers."

The Baron frowned. "Be careful, Miss Keri. Some people here do not tolerate disrespect."

"Yeah, well, if they didn't want disrespect, they shouldn't have demanded my presence at this little soiree. Believe me, there are a hundred places I'd rather be tonight."

"You are not here by your own choice? That is interesting." The Baron turned a speculative eye on the crowd. "Which god has compelled the famous Valora Keri to attend to their whim?"

Val snorted. "The same god that compels everyone else. The god of money. My boss made it clear that if I wanted to keep my job, I had to work this event. Ergo, here I am. It's simple, really."

The Baron raised an eyebrow. "And you allow this man to keep living? Why?"

"*I've been asking that same question for months,*" Mister E chimed in. Val ignored him.

"I think you're operating under a misconception of who I am. I'm only a bartender. I've got bills to pay, same as everyone else."

"Only a bartender. Says the woman who defeated a seraph and destroyed the Scepter of Sutro." The Baron laughed long and loud.

Val scowled at him. She'd had enough of this exchange.

"Look, can I get you a drink or not? I've got other customers waiting."

The Baron was still chuckling. "You truly are a treat. I think you know what drink I want."

"Bloody Mary?" she guessed.

She had to fight not to roll her eyes at the Baron's nod. Of course that was his drink.

As she slid the Bloody Mary over, the Baron pushed a card back across the bar. Val quirked an eyebrow at him.

"We have much to discuss, Valora Keri. Call me when you wish to speak of gods and monsters." He bared his gold tooth at her and nodded, his unsettling eyes liquid pools behind the white feathered mask.

"Sure. Maybe I will." She slid the card into her pocket and turned to help another customer. When she looked back a moment later, Baron Blood was gone.

Her night fell into the typical pattern after that. Pour drinks, take money, make small talk, pocket tips, rinse and repeat. Despite the high society status of the masquerade attendees, they got drunk just like anyone else.

Val watched the high rollers clump together to exchange quiet words. There really were an extraordinary number of powerful people in the room. In addition to Vasilevski, Melinda Pearl, and Baron Blood —who was obviously some kind of big shot in his own right—Val recognized several important business owners and political figures, including the mayor and the new district attorney. It probably didn't say great things about the state of the city that such high-profile government figures were openly exchanging pleasantries with gangsters and monsters.

"Have you noticed how pale Thomas Wilkins looks?" Lisa remarked.

Val followed Lisa's gaze and found the man standing in a small circle with the mayor. Thomas Wilkins was old San Francisco money. Val had no idea what his family did, but she knew he wielded enormous influence in local politics. Now that she was paying attention, she saw that Lisa was right: the man's face was ashen.

"Maybe he's sick," Val said.

"That's what I thought at first," Lisa said, biting her lip. "But then I noticed some of the other people are really pale, too."

Val looked where Lisa indicated. Indeed, a number of San Francisco's rich and powerful were as white as milk.

"Maybe they're powdering their faces," Val guessed. "French Renaissance fashion is coming back around. Or perhaps they're going goth. It's hard to keep up with all the weird fashion trends that sweep through the rich."

She watched as Thomas Wilkins pulled out a small vial and put one drop of liquid into each eye. She recognized it instantly; she'd seen plenty of vials like that at the Alley Cat over the last month.

"There's your culprit," she said. "It looks like Wilkins is taking Dream. I guess the rich have gotten swept up in the new drug craze, too. Either way, I don't see how it has anything to do with us."

"Maybe you're right." Lisa agreed, but her face remained troubled.

Another bar rush put an end to their conversation, and time blurred as more drinks were poured.

The next time Val had a chance to take a breath, hours had passed. Her feet hurt and her skin itched from the unfamiliar fabric of the dress. It was well after midnight when a feminine voice whispered in her ear.

"Valora Keri, I need your help."

She turned toward the sound but didn't see anyone. Then she caught movement in the shadow of the thick curtains hanging beside the windows to her right. Dark pixie-cut hair and black-rimmed glasses. Pale skin and ruby-red lips. Up on the liquor shelf, Mister E hissed.

"Hillary Linscomb," Val said, keeping her voice low. She didn't need to project: The vampire's sensitive ears would pick up her voice just fine. "What can I do for you?"

The young woman regarded her with icy eyes. "Were you serious about helping me?"

When Val first encountered Hillary, the young woman had been working as Melinda Pearl's receptionist at Royal Construction. She'd looked scared and nervous, and Val had deduced that Hillary might be trapped in an abusive relationship. In this case, an abusive relationship with her vampire queen boss. Val had known too many women stuck in similar situations, and she'd immediately offered to help Hillary get out if she needed help. The young woman had turned her down.

But now it seemed the vampire might have changed her mind. Val fought back a groan. As if she didn't already have enough trouble with vampires. One of these days, she was going to learn to keep her big mouth shut.

She forced a tight smile. She had offered to help, and she'd meant it. "Of course I was serious. Do you need help?"

The young woman nodded, the movement jerky and birdlike.

"What kind of help?"

"I want to get out."

"*Tell her to step into the sun,*" Mister E hissed. *"That'll set her free."*

"Not helpful," Val said under her breath.

"What was that?" Hillary's eyes narrowed.

"Nothing. Just talking to myself." She sized up the vampire out of the corner of her eye. Hillary looked thinner than the last time Val had seen her, and her pale skin was shading towards an unhealthy gray. "What do you need from me?"

"Sanctuary. A place where I can hide from my master."

"Today must be one of those 'Do six impossible things before break-fast' kind of days," Val muttered.

"Can you help me or not?"

"I said I would, and I keep my word." She eyed the vampire speculatively. "I'm guessing someplace out of the sun. Underground maybe?"

"That would be acceptable."

Val checked the clock. She still had a few hours before the masquerade ended.

"OK. Meet me in the alley across the street when the party's over. I'll be the one on the motorcycle."

9

Hillary appeared out of the darkness next to Val's Ural. Chilly fog misted low over the alley, obscuring the night sky with heavy cotton. The young vampire looked nervous, starting at every little sound. Her eyes kept darting up and down the alley as if she were afraid she'd been followed.

"Are you going to tell me what this is about?" Val asked. "Did you steal Melinda Pearl's boyfriend or something?"

"Very funny," Hillary snapped. "And no, I'm not going to tell you what this is about. All you need to worry about is getting me away from the cabal. Which you offered to do. Are you going to help me or not?"

Val held up her hands in surrender. "Take it easy. I said I'd help you, and I will. I was just wondering what I'm stepping into."

"If we do this right, you'll never have to know," Hillary assured her. "I can disappear, and no one ever needs to be the wiser."

"I'm afraid it's too late for that," someone called out from the end of the alley.

Val spun to find a pair of vampires sauntering down the narrow defile. She cursed as she recognized Melinda Pearl's lieutenant, Rodrigo.

His black hair came down to a sharp widow's peak above his forehead, and a short-sleeved silk shirt exposed his muscular brown arms despite the nighttime chill. He was flanked by a hulking brute with a shaved head. Somehow, Val didn't think these guys were here to talk.

"*There are more behind us,*" Mister E hissed.

Val risked a quick peek over her shoulder. Sure enough, another pair of thugs were closing in from the far end of the alley. Hillary shrank against the Ural, whimpering.

Val squared her shoulders. "What do you want, Rodrigo?"

"I thought that was obvious. Give us the girl and everyone walks away happy."

"Everyone except the girl," Val corrected.

The vampire lieutenant waved away her concern. "The girl's feelings are not important here. She's part of the cabal. She'll do what's best for the cabal."

"I don't think that's what she wants."

"What she wants is not important," Rodrigo repeated. "The cabal decides what is best. She knew that when she accepted our master's blessing. Immortality isn't free."

Val's eyebrows raised.

"She's an immortal slave? Is that what you're saying?"

"This does not concern you, Keri," Rodrigo hissed like a blade. "For the last time, hand over the girl."

Val cocked her head as if she was thinking and glanced over her shoulder again. There were still just the two vampires behind them, a total of four. But really, how many did they need? Beating even one vampire would be a tall order. Two was borderline impossible. Four of them? Very much not great odds.

The closer they let the vampires get, the worse their chances would become. They had to act now.

Val swung her leg over the Ural and snapped at Hillary, "Get in the sidecar." The young vampire slid in, scrunching down on the seat as if trying to make herself invisible.

"Don't do anything stupid, Keri. Be reasonable. This doesn't have to be unpleasant," Rodrigo called out.

"Reasonable?" Val chuckled. "You really don't know who you're dealing with, do you?"

She cranked the throttle.

The Ural rumbled slowly forward, the ancient Russian motor coughing and spitting. Rodrigo snarled, crouching in anticipation as they rolled towards him. The brute at his side didn't even change expression. He just planted himself directly in the Ural's path, implacable as a tree trunk.

"Flaming toads," Val growled. "Hold on. This could get bumpy." She gunned it and the Ural reluctantly picked up speed. The old motorcycle was built like a tank. It didn't have the fastest acceleration in the world, but once it got going, you didn't want to get in front of it.

A widening of his eyes told her that Rodrigo realized this, but the slab-like vampire standing beside him was impervious. The only concession he made as the Ural drew closer was to spread his arms and take a wider stance.

"He can't seriously think he's going to stop us, can he?" Val asked incredulously.

Hillary's voice was tight with suppressed panic. "That's exactly what he thinks. And the worst part is, he's probably right. That's Jonathan Grey. I once saw him lift an entire engine block like it was nothing."

"Flying toads," Val breathed.

"*We've got company on our asses too,*" Mister E added.

Val glanced back and found the vampires behind them had broken into a run. She cursed again. The Ural wasn't up to speed yet, and the vampires were gaining fast.

"Looks like we're the bologna in a vampire sandwich," she growled. "If we don't move that big guy, we're going to get torn to shreds."

Hillary looked at her like she was insane.

"Move him? Didn't you hear what I said? What are you going to move him with, a crane?"

"Something like that."

Val's eyes shone with golden light as she focused her power. Wind spun out before them, howling down between the brick walls. It slammed into the vampires, forcing Rodrigo to step back or be blown off his feet. He leaned into the gust, snarling, but step by step it forced him back toward the mouth of the alley.

Jonathan Grey was another matter. The massive vampire might have been carved out of stone for all the effect the wind seemed to have. He stayed planted in the center of the alley. There was no way the Ural could get past him. This was going to hurt.

"*Fog,*" Mister E hissed.

"What?" Val asked.

"*Fog. Pull it down from above us. Do it now!*"

Val didn't see what fog would do against a vampire, but she didn't have any better ideas. She concentrated on yanking the clouds down from the sky, sending them flowing toward Jonathan Grey in a churning white torrent.

Grey snarled and lifted a hand to shield his eyes as the pavement grew wet beneath his feet. Val gritted her teeth, doubling the downward force of the wind as she turned the alley into a raging funnel of thick mist. She had created complete white-out conditions now, and the massive vampire was swallowed by the storm, disappearing without a trace.

Val cranked the handlebars hard to the side. The sidecar hit something, the frame ringing like a bell as the impact shivered through the Ural. Val held on grimly as the bike was knocked sideways, skidding and teetering. Her heart jumped into her throat as the pavement came towards her face.

Then gravity finally won the battle against momentum, and the heavy bike thudded back down onto its wheels.

With the wind at their back, the Ural felt jet-propelled as it rocketed clear of the alley. A plume of fog followed them onto the street, a rooster-tail of mist spreading over the night.

Val glimpsed Rodrigo out of the corner of her eye, his hair dripping as he shouted something incoherent. But the Ural was well past him, and they were moving too fast for the vampire to catch as they disappeared into the night.

10

B ringing a vampire home from a party isn't as much fun as you think it is. First of all, you're never quite sure what their ulterior motives might be. Also, your roommates probably won't approve. And God help you if you stay up to watch the sunrise together.

The basement of Val's building was dark, musty, and filled with other people's forgotten possessions. Thick cobwebs draped the ceiling and a layer of dust covered boxes, clothes, furniture, rusty tools and mismatched sporting gear. There was even a half-disassembled Honda scooter underneath a tarp. Val had no idea how someone had gotten a scooter down into the basement. Or how they planned to get it out.

It reminded her a lot of her Aunt Marya's attic, which brought a rush of bittersweet nostalgia. Aunt Marya's house had been the first place she'd lived in America. Little Valora had slept in that attic for most of a year, and had spent many happy hours unearthing buried treasures from old boxes and wooden chests.

The attic had also been the place where she'd first met Mister E. Officially, anyway. He had given her power months earlier, on the day she'd accepted his offer to help her fight back against the children who were bullying her. On that day, she had inadvertently used her new power to kill her mother and another child, which had started the chain of events that ended with her getting shipped off to America for her own protection.

But on that dreadful first day of their partnership, Mister E had been nothing more than a voice in her head and a presence. It hadn't been until months later, in Aunt Marya's attic in America, that Mister E had first appeared in his current form. A cat wearing a top hat and puffing on a candy cigarette had strolled out from between some boxes and asked her if she wanted to play. Valora had named him Mister E, and for years he'd been her only friend.

In many ways, he still was.

Sure, she had other friends. Malcolm, Lisa, Junior. Alain, the shifter who had helped her catch Ruby's killer.

But they were all tied to her through something external. Through work, or sharing a flat, or a shared tragedy, or a thirst for justice. She didn't really have any friends she could simply relax with. People who would come over just to play cards or have dinner. Friends who wanted to spend time with her for nothing more than the simple comfort of her presence.

Val snorted softly to herself. She knew her presence wasn't very comforting.

So, yeah. It was just her and the demon-cat. Same as it ever was.

"Is something funny?" Hillary Linscomb broke into her thoughts.

Val looked away.

"Nope. Just a little trip down memory lane. Let's see if we can get you settled, shall we?"

Having the vampire stay in her basement was not her first choice, but it would have to do until she found somewhere to stash the young woman.

She peeled a dusty sheet back, revealing a long-abandoned couch in the corner. The blue upholstery was worn, and the arms of the couch had a few cigarette burns, but it was otherwise intact.

"It's not much, but you'll be safe down here until I can find a better place."

Hillary wrinkled her nose. "This had better not be for more than a day or two. And what if one of your neighbors comes down?"

"They won't. Nobody ever comes down here. But just in case, you should probably cover the couch with the sheet when you go to sleep."

Hillary eyed the dustcover with distaste. "Seriously?"

"What do you care?" Val snapped. She was rapidly running out of patience. "It's not like you have to breathe under there. You'll be dead to the world."

Hillary's glare shifted to Val. "Undead humor. Funny."

"Are you going to tell me what you're running from?" Val perched on the dusty edge of an old desk.

"I'm running from my master, obviously."

"Yes, but the last time we spoke, you seemed pretty happy with your place there. I mean, you didn't look happy, but that's to be expected, right? I don't know any vampires who look happy. Now that I think about it, that isn't a very convincing testimonial for vampirism, is it? Not happy. Two stars. Would not buy again."

"I told you, my reasons are my own," Hillary snarled. "Ask me again and I'll leave."

"Be my guest. The door is right there." Hillary only scowled and folded her arms over her chest. "That's what I thought. You came to me, remember? Look, I'm happy to help you, but I have to know what I'm getting myself into. Is helping you going to make Melinda Pearl mildly annoyed with me? Or am I going to have every vampire in the city hunting me down? Because those are very different realities, and I have to know which one I'm signing up for."

Hillary scowled harder. Val scowled right back. The silence stretched so long she could hear rats skittering behind the walls.

Finally, Hillary threw up her hands.

"Fine. I'll tell you what I know. I'm probably dead anyway, so I guess sharing cabal secrets isn't going to make me any more dead." She started pacing between the boxes, rubbing her right hand over the left arm of her jacket. "There's a new necromancer in town, named Blood or something."

"Baron Blood?" Val remembered the guy from the masquerade. He hadn't seemed like a necromancer, but then what do necromancers seem like, anyway?

"Maybe. I don't know, I haven't met him personally. But it's not exactly a common name."

"No, it's not." Val's frown deepened. Necromancers were bad news. "What about this necromancer?"

"He's been doing some kind of experiments. Some of my brothers and sisters have gone missing."

"Vampires have gone missing? And Melinda Pearl hasn't torn this guy's head off?"

"That's the thing." Hillary lowered her voice as if the walls had ears. "I think he's got her blessing. I think she's letting him experiment on us."

Val's eyebrows tried to climb into her hair. Melinda Pearl was letting some necromancer experiment on her junior vampires?

"That can't be right."

Vampires were insular and very protective of each other. They were famous for not playing well with others. There was no way Melinda Pearl would let some necromancer experiment on her children. Was there?

"That's what I thought at first, too," Hillary agreed. "Then my best friend disappeared."

"Disappeared?"

"Vanished. Gone without a trace. What the hell do you think 'disappeared' means?"

Val held her hands up in a placating gesture. "I'm only trying to get more details. Disappeared how, exactly? I need some context if I'm going to understand what's going on."

Hillary balanced on the edge of the couch, her face a portrait of misery.

"Lila didn't show up one day. I didn't worry about it because that happens. Sometimes one of us will get swept up with a sweet young thing and not come home for a few days. But when a week passed, I started to get worried, so I asked around. Nobody else had seen Lila either." Unable to contain her nervous energy, Hillary started pacing again. "After a few more days, I finally plucked up the courage to ask Mistress Pearl. You know what she said?"

Hillary's face was stricken. Val nodded encouragingly.

"What did she say?"

"She said I should forget about her. That Lila had been given in service to a greater cause." Hillary's nails dug into her palm. She was visibly fighting to maintain control now. "When I asked her what that meant, she said it was not my place to know such things. That she was the shepherd, and that we shouldn't concern ourselves with the direction of the flock. I think Lila's dead."

Val shook her head, incredulous. "I guess that's what happens when you join a death cult."

In an instant, Hillary was at her throat.

Reflex took over. Val's power lashed out and the vampire was thrown across the room, crashing into the cinder block wall. Grey dust exploded from the impact.

Before the dust had even touched the ground, Hillary was back on her feet and coming again.

Val spun up a whirlwind around her, forming a defensive barrier. It didn't stop the vampire, but it knocked her off balance. Val was able to grab the stumbling vampire's arm and use a judo technique to redirect her momentum away.

"*Well, this is fun,*" Mister E grinned. "*Hold on a minute. I'll make some popcorn.*"

Val ignored him and kept her eyes on Hillary, who looked like she was gathering herself for another charge.

"We can keep doing this if you want, but I'm not your enemy," Val snapped.

"You mock me. You mock my friend's memory," Hillary snarled.

"No... Well, OK, maybe I did mock you a bit," Val conceded. "I'm sorry. I'm an asshole. When I get nervous, I make jokes. Sometimes they're inappropriate jokes. It's more a reflection of me than it is of you. Nobody ever taught me how to deal with things like a grownup."

Hillary was still circling, Val turning with her.

"Look, we can beat up on each other, or we can use this energy in a more positive way and try to figure out what happened to your friend." Inwardly, she winced. Had she just offered to help a vampire track down a necromancer? Didn't she already have enough on her plate with Stephen's death and her plan to break into the SFPD morgue? Not to mention the small matter of the Coven's judgement hanging over her head.

She really had to start thinking before she spoke.

But it was too late to take it back. Hillary was regarding her with a look Val recognized all too well.

"You would help me find Lila's killer?"

Val sighed. In for a penny...

"I said I would, didn't I?" She gestured to the blue couch. "Now why don't we both sit down, and you can tell me everything you know."

The vampire bared her teeth in an almost-smile. Val suppressed a shiver. This hero complex she seemed to be developing was definitely not good for her health.

11

It was five am by the time Val finally dragged herself up the stairs and through the door of her flat. Her mind felt overheated and choking on fumes, like an engine that had been running far too long.

To her surprise, there was a lamp on in the living room. Malcolm sat curled in the worn armchair, his feet tucked under a purple blanket. His eyes were sunken, his lips dry and cracked. He was staring listlessly out the bay window and didn't react when Val stepped into the room.

"Malcolm?"

He started and turned his head towards her, his eyes slowly refocusing. "Val?"

She sank onto the couch beside him. "Yeah, Malcolm. It's me. Are you OK?" Val pushed a glass of water across the end table.

He sipped it gratefully. "Thank you."

Malcolm blinked and sighed, slowly coming back from wherever he'd been. He shifted around in the chair so he could look at her without turning his head.

"Did you talk to Stephen?"

"No, I need the blueprints from you first. Did you get them?"

His gaze drifted off into the distance for a second, then he returned to himself with another start. He shuddered and nodded.

"Yes, I got them. Didn't I send them to you?"

Val made a little shrugging motion with her head. "I don't know. It's been a busy night. I haven't had a chance to check my messages."

"Oh. So what's been happening in the Keri Chronicles?"

"The Keri Chronicles?"

"It's how I think of your life. You're always caught up in some adventure. It sounds good, don't you think?"

Val rolled her eyes.

"No, I don't. My life is not some exotic adventure. It's just me jumping from the frying pan into the fire over and over. Or into increasingly large piles of shit, depending on your choice of analogy." She cracked her neck from one side to the other. "Do you want to continue this conversation in the kitchen? I could go for some pancakes."

Malcolm's smile was weak, but it was definitely a smile.

"Now you're speaking my language. You know I'm always up for pancakes. But you'd better let me make them."

Val gave him the side-eye. "I thought maybe you'd like to relax and let me do the cooking for a change."

Malcolm made a shooing motion with his fingers. "Honey, I've seen you cook. There's no way I could relax while watching you destroy perfectly good pancakes. Trust me, it's better for both of us this way. You can make the coffee."

Val chuckled. "It's a deal."

Half an hour later, with butterscotch-syruped pancakes in her belly and a warm coffee mug in her hand, Val leaned back in the kitchen chair and sighed.

"I haven't felt this relaxed in days. You really are a pancake wizard, Malcolm."

"I know." Malcolm smirked in the chair across from her, cupping his own mug between two hands. "Some people are born with brains, some people get looks. I got pancakes." He looked down into the steam and sighed. "My pancakes couldn't save Stephen, though. Were you able to find anything at the Queen Anne?"

Val waggled her head. "Yes, but I don't know if any of it's useful. The cops cleaned up the crime scene really well, so I didn't have any hairs or drops of Stephen's blood to establish a direct connection to his spirit."

Malcolm choked on his coffee.

"That's really a thing? You can cast spells on people with hair and blood? Damn, I'm going to have to start carrying a dust buster around everywhere I go."

"Relax, Malcolm. It's not like voodoo. I can use those things to establish a connection to someone's spirit, but I can't affect them in any way. It's like... Think of a spirit as a book. If I can establish a connection, I might be able to open it and read a few pages, with any luck. But I can't change the story. What's been written is set in stone."

"That's still creepy. I'm buying dust-buster stock right now." Malcolm took a long sip of his coffee, then caught her eyes over the rim. "No blood, no hair, no connection? Did you find out anything at all?"

Val sipped her own coffee, enjoying the warmth expanding through her body as she considered how much she should share with Malcolm. She didn't see how telling him what had happened at the Queen Anne could endanger him in any way. And Stephen was his oldest friend. He deserved the truth.

"Not a lot, honestly. There is something there. Some kind of powerful... something. I accidentally made contact with it, and it tried to kill me."

"That's the thing that killed Stephen?"

"Not necessarily. Like I said, without something to tie me to Stephen, I was just shouting into the dark. Something answered, but it could simply be something that lives in the Queen Anne. Or it could be something unrelated that happened to be nearby at that moment. I mean, it's a big city. If you open a window and shout, someone's going to hear you. So it's impossible to say. That's why I need to get into the morgue to get Stephen's perspective."

Malcolm chewed his lip. A drop of blood welled up through the cracked skin, but he didn't seem to notice.

"Will you be able to talk to him? I'd like to..."

"No." She knew where Malcolm was going, and Val needed to nip this in the bud. "I can't actually speak to the dead. Forget whatever you think you know about it. This isn't a seance. There's no conversation. Remember what I said before—it's like reading a book. Except this time the book will be written from Stephen's point of view. But all I can do is read it. There's no passing messages back and forth. No actual communication."

Malcolm's face fell and Val's heart went out to him. She had to bite her tongue to keep from telling him that mediums who could talk to the dead did exist—it just wasn't something she could do herself. There was no point in getting his hopes up.

In her experience, speaking with the dead was never a good idea. The dead had their own perspective on things, and it was very different from the lens through which the living viewed the world. People who wanted to have one final conversation with their dead loved ones were looking for some kind of closure. In Val's experience, they invariably came away disappointed, and usually left the session more troubled than they'd started.

No, it was best to let the dead lie. The line between life and death was there for a reason, and it was better for everyone if it was never crossed.

"Let's take a look at the map, shall we?" Val said, turning the conversation to more concrete matters. It was best to focus on what they could do, not the things they couldn't.

Malcolm pulled up the map on his phone and swiped the projection onto the kitchen table. Val bent over the image. It was a maze of differently colored lines, many of them overlapping.

"What exactly am I looking at here?"

Malcolm leaned forward so he could point out features as he talked. "The black lines indicate the station's walls, and also the walls of the surrounding buildings. The red show utility tunnels—electricity, gas, water, etc. The green lines are the sewer system, with the teal showing new pipes that were added during the expansion in the twenties."

"And why differentiate the new pipes from the old?"

"They're different sizes. The older ones are smaller and a lot of the time they're plugged up with centuries of storm runoff."

"Meaning the new ones are the ones to use if you want to get around underground."

"Yes and no. They're newer and bigger, but they also have a much better security system. The new tunnels are full of sensors and cameras."

"Do we have locations for those?"

"The security cameras? Yes, they're these little boxes with the slashes through them."

Val steepled her fingers under her chin, her golden eyes intent. She studied the scale of the map.

"It looks like there's a camera every five hundred feet or so, is that right?"

Malcolm thought for a minute before nodding. "I think that's right."

"Where's the nearest access point for this tunnel?" She put her finger on the map, tracing a blue line that appeared to run directly underneath the police station.

"Ummmm... Right here." He tapped a spot half a block away.

"Hmmm, that might be too close. Where's the next one?"

"Here." Malcolm tapped a spot on the next street over.

"Really? It runs over from the next block?" Val leaned forward, her mind racing as she traced the tunnel with her eyes. It looked like it ran beneath several of the neighboring buildings before reaching the station. If she accessed the tunnel from the next block over, the odds of anyone in the station noticing were small. "How many security sensors in that stretch of tunnel?"

Malcolm did a quick count, his fingers dancing over the map. "It looks like six... no, seven."

A tired smile crept across Val's face. "OK, I think I've got my plan of attack."

"I want to go with you."

Val blinked. "That's not a good idea. I might not be able to protect you."

"Protect me from what? Sewer rats?"

"No, it's not that. We'll be breaking and entering, Malcolm. Into a police station. If something goes wrong, I may not be able to get you out."

Her roommate folded his arms over his chest. "Stephen is my friend and you're doing this for me. If you're taking the risk, I should too."

Val ground her knuckles into her eye sockets. "Malcolm..."

"Please, Val. I need to help. And I have to see him one last time."

"Flying toads, Malcolm. You don't know what you're asking."

"Yes, I do. I'm an adult and I know the risks. Please. Stephen is my oldest friend." His eyes were brimming over. A tear slid down his cheek.

Val sighed. "Fine. I've got to work first, so meet me on the corner of 5th and Bryant at 4 a.m. Don't be late, or I'm going in without you."

Malcolm smiled through his tears.

"Thank you, Val. You won't regret it, I promise."

"I regret it already." She stretched and yawned. "Now I need to get some sleep. If anyone tries to wake me up before noon, I will not be responsible for the ensuing destruction."

Her roommate laughed. "At least Sandra won't be vacuuming."

Val winced. "Yeah. Sorry about that."

Malcolm shrugged. "You're the one who's on the hook for double rent if we don't find a new roommate before the first of the month."

"Don't remind me," Val groaned as she stood and slipped through the doorway. She stopped and stuck her head back into the kitchen.

"Oh, I almost forgot. Whatever you do, don't go down in the basement today."

"The basement? What's wrong with the basement?"

"Just trust me on this one."

Malcolm shook his head as he gathered the breakfast plates.

"You know, living with you is like living with a magic eight ball. Every answer only raises more questions."

12

V al was leaning against a brick building on the corner of 5th. It was 3:55 a.m., and there was no sign of Malcolm.

"Maybe he won't show up," she muttered.

"*You don't believe that for a second.*" Mister E blew candy smoke rings at her. "*You only have two types of luck: bad and worse. In no version of the future does your fortune allow the chocolate queen to be a no-show tonight.*"

"The chocolate queen? Really?" Val wrinkled her nose. "You're revealing your age with the offensive stereotypes there."

"*It's not a stereotype if it's true,*" Mister E said primly. "*Besides, I'm not the one choosing the stereotype. Malcolm is proud of who he is. You should be too.*"

Val rolled her eyes and let it go. There was no point in arguing. If you think your grandparents are set in their ways, you should try changing the mind of an entity thousands of years old.

She tried to focus on the job instead, going over the map one more time in her mind. The manhole cover she wanted to access was in the middle of the street, about twenty yards to her right, which was bad luck. Fortunately, four a.m. was probably the quietest hour in the city, and she'd only seen one car drive past in the ten minutes she'd been waiting here. Hopefully, she'd be able to get into the sewer unobserved.

She checked the time. 3:59. She'd warned Malcolm that she wouldn't wait for him. If he missed the boat, it was his own fault. Anyway, this job would be a lot easier on her own. She didn't relish the thought of having to babysit Malcolm while she broke into a police station.

As she was straining to pry up the heavy manhole cover with the lifting hook, a shout made her freeze.

"Val! I'm here!"

She sighed as Malcolm came running down the block.

"You're late," she growled.

"Sorry, there were cops in front of the station and I freaked out and had the pedicab driver drop me off three blocks away. Then I had to run around the long way." He panted, out of breath from his little sprint.

"What are you wearing?"

He grinned at her. "You like it?"

Malcolm had on a tight black outfit, complete with turtleneck, beanie cap, and black leather gloves. He looked like he'd stepped straight out of an old Pink Panther movie.

But that wasn't the most ridiculous part.

On his back, he carried a black backpack big enough for an expedition to the Himalayas. Its metal frame stretched all the way over his head.

"It's certainly... something. Were you planning on staying underground indefinitely?"

Her roommate looked embarrassed. "I wanted to be prepared, so I started packing a fanny pack. That wasn't big enough, so I switched to a messenger bag. Then I filled that too and..." He gestured helplessly at the monstrosity on his back. "This was the result."

"You could stash it in the alley, if you want," Val offered.

Malcolm looked scandalized. "After I spent all that time packing it? Not a chance, girl. Everything I've got in here is absolutely essential. You'll see. All of this is going to come in handy."

"Uh-huh." Val was not convinced. "Anyway, are you ready to go?

We shouldn't stand here in the middle of the street with the manhole cover open."

"I'm as ready as a biscuit fresh from the oven."

"That's..." Val opened her mouth to say something sarcastic but decided to take the high ground. "That's just great. In you go."

Malcolm carefully lowered himself into the manhole. The opening was bigger than Val had expected, and even with his gargantuan backpack he fit through quite easily.

"Don't forget to turn on your headlamp."

"Oh, right."

A tiny pool of light sprang into being, and Val watched it descend the metal rungs. She waited until Malcolm was a good ten feet down before bending toward the hole herself.

"I'm coming in after you. Don't look up, you don't want to get dirt in your eye."

She lowered herself onto the ladder and used the metal tool to pull the manhole cover back into place above her. The heavy disc clanged down over her head, shockingly loud in the enclosed space.

"Don't worry, I didn't need those eardrums," Mister E complained. His golden eyes shone in the near-total darkness.

"Well, that makes one of us," Val grumbled. Her own ears were still ringing.

She clicked on her light, which was hanging around her neck, and carefully followed Malcolm down. When she got to the bottom, he eyed her skeptically.

"Really, Val? That's your light? You don't have some magic pendant or fairy light or something?"

"I can use magic to see in the dark if I really need to, but this is easier than trying to maintain a spell. And I haven't got a clue how to make a magic pendant."

He shook his head sadly. "I thought you'd be better at this."

"I'm sorry to disappoint you. Shall we?"

The tunnel was bigger than Val expected, a high arching expanse over thirty feet across. A narrow cement walkway ran alongside a canal filled with brown water. She tried not to think about what was in the water, but the bits of toilet paper floating by made it pretty obvious. That and the stench. She breathed through her mouth, which only helped a little.

Val coughed and spat. "I swear I can taste the filth on my tongue."

"You didn't bring nose plugs? Mine are working great."

She shone her light on Malcolm and found two white plugs sticking out of his nostrils. A laugh burst out of her.

"You look ridiculous."

"But I can breathe," he replied, arching a manicured eyebrow. "Who looks ridiculous now?"

"Touché. You didn't bring an extra pair, did you?"

Malcolm rolled his eyes. "Of course I did. But you'd better take care of them, because I've only got one pair to give you. If you lose them, you're on your own."

"Yes, Mom."

"All right, let me dig them out. Give me a hand with this?"

She helped Malcolm take off his monstrous backpack and watched while he rummaged through half a dozen different zipper pockets. Finally, he handed a pair of nose plugs to Val. She eyed the package dubiously.

"These are ear plugs, Malcolm."

"Ear plugs, nose plugs, it makes no difference. They're all little holes in our heads that need to be plugged. Do you want them or not?"

"I suppose they're better than nothing." She sighed and inserted the foam pellets into her nostrils. They felt funny as they expanded, but, she had to admit, they did seem to help. "Huh, I guess they work. Thanks, Malcolm."

"Oh, ye of little faith."

She helped him back into his backpack and they started forward again. As they came to a bend in the tunnel, Val held up her hand.

"Stop for a minute. The first security camera is around this corner."

"Are you going to put a hex on it or something?"

"I've got a more low-tech solution in mind." She pulled a square of cloth and a can of black spray paint out of her jacket. She coated the cloth with paint.

Malcolm gave her the side-eye. "I didn't know you were a juvenile delinquent."

Val grinned. "Oh, I definitely was. I spent more time in juvie facilities than I did foster homes. Now be quiet and let me concentrate."

She closed her eyes and whispered, "I need your eyes."

Mister E grinned in response.

Her point of view shifted, and she found herself drifting about fifteen feet in the air. Her mind was inside Mister E, looking out through his glowing eyes. The magical cat's night vision was superb, and the interior of the tunnel now looked almost as bright as day.

Mister E drifted higher, moving toward the security camera. She could see it now, mounted against a support beam. Right where it was supposed to be.

Val split her focus and flexed her power, gently lifting the cloth toward the camera with an updraft. As it got close, a little spotlight flashed on, illuminating the floating cloth clearly.

"Flaming toads," Val cursed and quickly draped the cloth over the lens, blacking it out with the paint.

"What?" Malcolm whispered.

"The cameras have motion sensors. If anyone checks this recording, they're going to wonder what a black painted cloth is doing floating through the sewers."

"As long as we stay out of range ourselves, they'll only have the cloth, right?"

"Right. But I was hoping I'd be able to black them out before they even got that much. The motion detectors are more sensitive than I thought."

"Do you think it tripped an alarm?" Malcolm's eyes widened.

"I doubt it. They wouldn't want an alarm sounding every time a rat tripped the motion sensor. But someone might check the recording later to see what it was."

"And that would be bad?" His voice squeaked a little at the end.

"It will if they can trace the floating cloth back to us. If they can't, I guess it'll just be a little mystery to keep them up at night." She grinned wickedly.

"*I believe I'm finally rubbing off on you. That smile was positively feline,*" Mister E put in.

Val's smile became a scowl. "When you've got somebody living inside your head, you're bound to pick up a few bad habits."

The cat only laughed.

Val had to deal with three more cameras before they came to a large circular chamber where the tunnel intersected with an older sewer line. Mister E's eyes showed her something there that made her stop so abruptly Malcolm almost walked right into her.

"What is it?" he whispered.

"There are four cameras in the intersection just ahead."

"Is that too many for you?"

"No." Val peered around the corner, her brow furrowed.

Malcolm waited for an explanation. When none came, he said, "What's the issue?"

"They've all been disabled already."

"Wait, what? Someone else is blacking out the sewer cameras with spray paint?"

"No, not spray paint. The wires have been cut on a couple of the cameras. The others are missing."

Now it was Malcolm's turn to look worried. "What do you mean, missing?"

"I mean, the entire camera housing is missing. The mounts are still there, so I can see where the cameras used to be. But the cameras themselves are just gone."

"Okayyyy... Maybe the cops replaced them? Maybe those are old mounts and they didn't bother to take them down when they put in the new cameras?"

Val shook her head. "I don't think so. The mounts don't look any older than the mounts on the other cameras. No, I think someone—or some thing—physically removed those security cameras."

"In the sewer? Why?"

Val tensed as she saw a flicker of motion in one of the other tunnels.

"I think the better question is: who? And I'm afraid we're about to find out."

13

M alcolm screamed as a mountain of teeth and claws came charging out of the darkness.

Val reacted instinctively, stepping in front of him and punching a blast of air at their attacker. The creature looked like a cross between a man and a crocodile: a thick, powerful body that was all scales and sharp teeth. Her blast knocked it off the walkway and into the filthy water with a splash.

But there were more where that came from.

"What are they?" Malcolm squeaked.

"Morlocks. They're a tribe that lives under the city. The sewers are technically their territory."

"And you didn't think to mention this before we came down here?"

"I was hoping we wouldn't run into them." Val blasted another Morlock into the water. This one was covered in short black fur.

"Are they animals?" Malcolm cowered behind her. Not that she'd expected him to be much help if they ran into trouble. At least he wasn't hysterical.

"Not exactly. Some are shifters. Some are gene-splices gone wrong. Some are..." She paused to punch another one off the walkway. The first one, the crocodile hybrid, was pulling his thick body out of the water, so she turned and shoved him back in again. "I don't know what they are. I only know that they're fierce. And very territorial."

"Wonderful," Malcolm moaned. "Can't we reason with them? Tell them we're just passing through?"

Val grunted as she hit another Morlock with her magic. Sweat dampened her hair. She had a lot of power, but she didn't usually have to sustain her magic for very long. She was already starting to get tired.

"Sure, be my guest. Reason away. Whatever you do, keep your headlamp pointed at them. Their eyes are really sensitive and they hate bright light."

Val kept blasting the Morlocks, but it quickly became obvious that it was a losing battle. There were too many of them. For every one she knocked into the water, two more took its place. The creatures were coming at them from both sides of the circular chamber now, streaming out of the dark tunnel mouths. She had to shift her blasts back and forth between them, and every time she turned her attention to one, the other group crept closer. The closest Morlocks were now less than twenty feet away. She had only seconds before she and Malcolm would be within reach of their claws and fangs.

Val panted, reaching deep as her power flagged. Magic was like a muscle, and you could only flex it so many times before you needed to rest. She was rapidly reaching her limit, and still the Morlocks kept coming. This was going to get ugly.

Nearly exhausted, she drew her knife and retreated a few steps down the walkway, taking a defensive stance and waiting for the first Morlock to close with her. The narrowness of the walkway worked in her favor. The creatures would have to come at her one at a time.

"Thank heaven for small miracles," she murmured.

"*I doubt heaven is listening. But I am.*"

"That's not reassuring."

The lead Morlock was a wiry creature, with scales mottled red and brown. A spiky crest ran down the center of its head. It hissed at her, baring a double row of razor-sharp fangs.

Val bared her teeth right back, brandishing her long knife. She snarled.

"Come and get it."

The Morlock sprang forward, jaws gaping. Val ducked and got a forearm against the thing's neck, keeping those teeth from tearing into her face. She brought the knife up in two quick jabs. Green blood spurted over the hilt, warm on her fingers. The creature folded and she heaved it into the canal.

Her daily training at the gym paid off as her body fell into the familiar rhythms of hand-to-hand combat. Val hit the next one with a right and a left, then a straight kick to the stomach. She caught him with an uppercut and followed with a roundhouse kick. The creature toppled into the water like a tree.

The Morlocks kept coming. She lost count after the second one, but it didn't matter how many there were, how many came before, or how many came after. Blocking, twisting, punching. All that mattered was the creature directly in front of her. Then the one after that. And the one after that.

The relentless onslaught began to take its toll. One creature slashed open her bicep. Another tore a gash across her forehead. Blood ran down into her eye, burning and obscuring her vision.

Val felt herself start to slow as fatigue and blood loss took their toll. And still the Morlocks came in never-ending waves.

Stepping back, she slipped on a pool of blood. Her back foot skidded out from under her. She caught herself before she fell, but the slip caused her to drop her guard for a second. She recovered almost instantly, but the opening was enough.

A Morlock covered in black fur burst past her defenses, pitching its weight against her, pushing her back. Val's foot slid again and she fell on her back, the creature's teeth inches from her face, stinking breath hot on her skin.

She stabbed upward and the creature shuddered. She kicked its limp form off her, but the damage was done. She was down and vulnerable. A scaled Morlock crashed on her chest, and a scream ripped out of her as it sank its fangs into her shoulder.

Val stabbed again. Her magic was spent. On her death bingo card, she'd never circled "torn apart by Morlocks in a sewer tunnel." Guess she was just unlucky.

She kept stabbing. If she was going down, she was taking as many of the creatures with her as she could.

Suddenly, the Morlock on her chest hissed and flinched away, closing its eyelids tight against a blinding white light that flooded the tunnel, shining right into its face. Pained shrieks went up from all the Morlocks and they retreated, skittering away as the sewer lit up as bright as day.

Val spun around, squinting at the light shining right behind her.

"Malcolm? Is that you?"

She couldn't see him, but she could hear the satisfaction in her housemate's voice.

"Damn straight it's me."

"What the hell is that thing?"

"It's a mobile spotlight. Eight hundred thousand candelas of awesomeness."

"What the hell do you need that for?"

"Oh, you know, I keep it on hand in case I need to repel any Morlocks."

"Seriously?"

"No, it's actually for mobile dance parties. Hang a disco ball from a pole and hit it with this baby—boom, instant party."

"I can see that. I'm impressed. I hate to admit it, but your dramatic flair has paid off."

"And my massive backpack," Malcolm added smugly.

"And your massive backpack," Val conceded.

He knelt beside her and pulled out a big roll of gauze.

"Also, medical supplies." He grimaced as he surveyed the damage. "Yuck. You look like you just spent the afternoon at a toddler's birthday party—you're covered in sticky stuff from head to toe. It's a good thing this blood is color-coded, or I wouldn't know what was yours and what was theirs. Now hold still while I get you cleaned up."

Val sagged against the wall of the tunnel, too exhausted to argue.

14

An old rusty door connected the sewer pipe to the basement morgue of the SFPD.

"Why do they have a door leading to the sewer?" Malcolm asked.

Val knocked lightly on the door and cocked her head, trying to gauge the thickness of the metal by the sound.

"I don't know, but I'm glad they do." She frowned at the thick rust flaking off the hinges. "It looks like it hasn't been used in years."

"Can you blame them? There are Morlocks down here. If I had a door to the sewer in my basement, I'd weld it shut." Malcolm flashed his spotlight up and down the tunnel nervously. The Morlocks hadn't come back, but he'd kept the brilliant light in his hand. He wasn't taking any chances.

"Well, let's hope SFPD is less paranoid than you are."

Val laid her palm flat against the door, trying to sense... something. She wasn't sure exactly what. Her powers were mostly intuitive, and this was one of those situations where her usual bag of tricks wasn't very helpful. She put her palm against the door and let a trickle of power flow through her, hoping the solution would magically come.

It didn't.

"*There's a limit to everything, even magic.*" Mister E floated on his back above the doorframe, head tilted back, giving his upside-down smile. *"If you'd let me train you properly, you might have a way around this door. But using the pull-and-pray method? Not a chance."*

"I could just knock it out of its frame," Val responded truculently.

"You could," the cat acknowledged with a nod. *"But you'd make such a racket that even the half-asleep skeleton crew upstairs would hear you and come running."*

She sighed and squatted on her haunches, examining the ancient lock dubiously. "I don't like the look of this lock at all. It's so full of rust that even if I can get my picks inside, I doubt I could get it to turn. It's probably rusted through."

"Need some lube?" Malcolm asked, offering her a slim cylinder.

Val looked at it skeptically. "Do I want to know why you brought this?"

"A girl has to be prepared." He gave her a saucy wink. "But alas, it's not what you think. This is industrial lubricant, good for unbinding gears and such. It's like WD40 on steroids. And you definitely do not want to be putting this stuff on your squishy bits."

Val took the cylinder. "Magic backpack?"

"Magic backpack," Malcolm agreed.

"I really need to get one of those."

"What for? You've got me."

"True. But a backpack would be easier to cart around in the Ural's lockbox."

She gave the cylinder a shake and squirted a stream of lubricant into the keyhole. "How long do we wait?"

"It shouldn't be more than a minute or two. That stuff'll unblock you faster than a ginger-ale enema."

Val gave him the side-eye. "A what, now?"

Malcolm brushed away her question. "It's just a figure of speech."

While the lube worked its magic, Val pulled her lock picks out of her pocket and unrolled the dirty cloth. Nearly a dozen picks stared up at her, each in their own tiny pocket. Her current kit was a lot fancier than the bent piece of wire with which she'd learned to pick locks as a teenager. The professional kit hadn't been cheap, either. But it had saved her life more than once over the years, and was worth every

penny. Lock-picking was an art, and like any art it was a lot easier if
you had the right tools for the job.

She selected a pick and inserted it into the lock. Wiggling it around,
she carefully probed the positions of the tumblers. Then she put it back
and selected a different pick. Wiggled that one a bit, then tried a third.
Yes, that was the one.

Val went to work on the lock in earnest, poking and twisting,
grunting and muttering under her breath. After several minutes, she
sat back in defeat.

"I don't think even your super-lube is going to unbind this thing.
It's been corroding down here too long. As far as I can tell, it's become
one solid mass of rust."

"What about liquid nitrogen?"

She snorted. "Yeah, that might work. If I happened to have a
canister of liquid nitrogen..." she trailed off as Malcolm produced a
small silver thermos bottle from his backpack and handed it to her.
"You've got to be kidding me. Is there anything you didn't bring?"

"Well, I didn't have room for the chainsaw or the sledgehammer.
But I did bring a ball-peen hammer and some chisels. I think you
might be able to shatter the lock with them if you freeze it first."

Val stared at him with her mouth open. "I think you might be my
new hero, Malcolm."

Malcolm struck a superhero pose, and she snorted.

She carefully poured liquid nitrogen into the lock and watched
frost cover the surface as the temperature of the metal plummeted.
"How do I know if it's cold enough?"

Malcolm shrugged. "I have no idea, but I think it works pretty fast.
Sixty seconds or so ought to do it."

Val kept pouring a slow stream of liquid nitrogen into the keyhole.
White smoke boiled up the outside of the door.

She picked up the hammer and chisel. "Here goes nothing."

She placed the chisel against the lock and rapped the hammer on
the back of it smartly. After a couple of blows, the metal started to
crack.

"Holy funky shorts. I think it's working."

A few more sharp blows, and the crack split the face of the lock. Val twisted the door handle and the locking mechanism fell apart.

"Malcolm, you're an evil genius."

"Thank you," he said, taking a bow. "That's Evil Super Genius to you."

Val gave an experimental tug on the door. The rusted hinges resisted. Val went back to the lube bottle and squirted them down. Waited a minute. Tried again. This time, they shrieked in protest, but grudgingly started to move.

She gave Malcolm back his things and grinned as she helped him into his backpack. "Ready to go in?"

"Am I ready to break into a police station to contact the ghost of my dead friend?" There was fear in his eyes, but his voice was flippant, like he did this every day. He grinned back at her. "Of course. Do you even have to ask?"

15

F inding a specific body in a morgue isn't as easy as you might think. The morgue was dark and silent, lit only by Malcolm's ridiculous spotlight and Val's tiny flashlight. Every little noise made Val freeze and look toward the door, afraid one of the police officers on duty was about to burst in on them. There were dozens of stainless-steel drawers for bodies, stacked up the wall like a refrigerated filing cabinet.

"Do we just start pulling out drawers?" Malcolm asked, shuddering at the thought. Seeing Stephen's body would be bad enough. He hadn't counted on having to search through a bunch of other dead bodies too.

"We could do that. Or we could look through the logbook and figure out which drawer he's in first." Val bent over the coroner's desk and started flipping through a three-ring binder.

Malcolm laughed nervously. "I like your idea better."

"What's Stephen's last name?"

"Hughes. Stephen Hughes."

"Here he is. B-3."

"You sank my battleship," Malcolm said weakly. Neither of them laughed.

They slid the drawer out and unsealed the body bag. Stephen looked cold and pale, eyes closed as if he were merely sleeping.

Malcolm whimpered and a tear slid down his cheek.

Val put an awkward hand on his shoulder. To her surprise, he turned into her arms and laid his head against her collarbone, sobbing unselfconsciously. She held him gingerly, patting his back while he got it all out.

She wasn't good with emotional displays. As a child, moving from foster home to foster home, she hadn't had time to develop close friendships and had never really been able to let her guard down. Mister E had been her only stable confidant, and he was the opposite of sympathetic. She'd quickly learned to swallow her tears.

Malcolm's naked grief was new territory for her. She held him gently, as if he were fragile and she was afraid of damaging him further. She didn't know what to do or say, so she said nothing, stiffly patting his back while he wet the shoulder of her jacket. She felt like a voyeur, seeing something she wasn't supposed to, so she did her best to make herself invisible. This was Malcolm's moment. She just happened to be there.

Eventually, Malcolm cried himself out. He took a deep breath as he stepped back. Mascara tracks ran down his cheeks.

"Thank you." He rummaged in his backpack and came up with a small pack of tissues and a compact mirror. "I must look frightful."

"No. You look human," Val said softly, surprising herself.

Malcolm chuckled, then pinched his mouth as he peered into the mirror. "OK, a frightful human then. I could give Frankenstein's monster a run for his money."

"Well, if you need some replacement body parts, you've come to the right place."

Both laughed. Gallows humor for the win.

"What now?" Malcolm asked. He'd wiped away the worst of the mascara and blotted his puffy eyes as best he could.

"Now we need to put him onto one of the examination tables."

Malcolm blanched. "You're not going to cut him open, are you?"

"No. But I do need to be able to walk all the way around him. I can't do that if he's in this drawer."

"Right." He wiped his palms nervously on his pants. "How do you want to do this?"

They got on opposite sides of him and lifted Stephen's body bag between them. He was surprisingly heavy.

"What did you expect? Dead bodies don't suddenly lose weight," Mister E snarked. *"Unless they've been drained dry by a vampire, of course. All that liquid weighs a ton."*

Once they'd gotten the body settled, Val and Malcolm cleared away the other tables, creating a wide space around Stephen. Val pulled out her chalk and drew a pentagram on the cement floor, with Stephen's body in the center.

She placed candles at the corners of the pentagram and lit them.

"I'm going into a trance now. I need you to keep watch. If anyone comes, do your best to keep them out of the room. Interrupting the spell could have unforeseen consequences."

"What kind of consequences?"

"I don't know, Malcolm. That's why they're unforeseen. Trust me, it's better if we don't find out."

Malcolm glanced nervously at the clock mounted over the door. It was already five o'clock. "How long will this take?"

"I don't know. It'll take as long as it takes. Sometimes spirits are easy to contact. Sometimes not so much." She gestured impatiently. "Enough questions. The sooner I get started, the sooner we can get out of here."

Malcolm looked like he wanted to say more, but he only swallowed, nodded, and moved towards the door.

Val sat on a chair next to the examination table and pulled out her knife. "You might not want to watch this part."

She pricked Stephen's forearm and pushed down on the body until a drop of blood welled out of the wound. Val rubbed the blood between her fingers and dabbed it onto her forehead before closing her eyes and painting her eyelids as well. She kept the fingers of her left hand on Stephen's arm. The more points of contact she had with the body, the better.

She started to chant softly, no more than murmured nonsense syllables, really. The words weren't important. The intention behind them was important, and the lulling, focusing effect their rhythm had upon her. Her breathing slowed as the words took her into a magical trance. Watching with wide eyes, Malcolm saw the candles at the corners of the pentagram dance and sputter despite the stillness of the air in the morgue.

Something shifted, and between one breath and the next, Val felt her soul leave the morgue. She moved through a sparse wood, populated by fog and dark shadows. A skeletal branch brushed the skin of her arm and she flinched away from the icy chill.

Now came the dangerous part. She hadn't been entirely truthful when she'd told Malcolm that she couldn't talk to spirits directly. Sometimes she could, but she had to cross the threshold into the spirit realm to do so, and she was vulnerable on this side of the barrier. To communicate with a spirit, she had to exist as a spirit, the same as the other denizens. Which meant that they could touch her just as easily as she could touch them.

Dark shapes moved in the surrounding fog. Amorphous things vaguely man-shaped. These were spirits of the newly dead. They would linger on this plane for about a week—sometimes as long as a month—before losing their corporeal shape and moving on to the next stage of their journey. Val had no idea what that next stage might be, or even if there was a next stage at all. For all she knew, the spirits simply dissolved back into the stuff of dreams.

So this was the place where she had to catch Stephen's shade if she wanted to talk to him, and the sooner she did so the better. Every hour that passed carried with it a bit more of his humanity, and if she waited too long, he would no longer have any memory of his life remaining at all.

With that in mind, Val took a deep breath, pictured him clearly in her mind, and shouted, "Stephen Hughes!"

A wind sprang up around her, stirring the branches of the skeletal trees. The shades swirled like autumn leaves, whispering and rustling.

No shade stepped forward, so she shouted again, "Stephen Hughes! I bid you to come to me!"

The spirits of the dead gathered, darkening the fog with their presence, drawn by the strength of her summoning. She stood in the center of a crowd now, and though they had no faces, she could feel their eyes upon her.

Still, no shade separated itself from the crowd. None was Stephen Hughes.

Val licked her lips, eyes flicking over the gathering dead. She'd never had a spirit resist her call before. Maybe Stephen's shade had moved on already?

Unlikely. Only two days had passed since his death. Spirits never moved on that quickly.

She focused her will. There was no avoiding it. She would have to use the nuclear option.

"Stephen Hughes! Three times I summon thee. Come to me. Come to me now!"

Val focused on Stephen's blood. Felt it on her forehead. Looked through it on her eyelids. Breathed in the iron tang.

She felt his flesh beneath her fingertips and used the body's natural affinity to call to Stephen's shade. Three was a powerful number and she was confident no spirit could resist a triple summoning.

There.

Her persistence was rewarded as she felt Stephen's shade. It was distant, though, tugging at her like a kite on a string—but no matter how hard she pulled, she could not reel it in.

Val frowned. "What the hell is this?"

"His spirit is bound," Mister E replied, his golden eyes shining like lamps in the fog. *"Something prevents him from answering your call."*

"How can that be?"

"Spirits may be bound in a number of ways. Just as my spirit is bound to you, so Stephen's spirit is bound elsewhere."

"He's bound to a person?"

"Not necessarily. Spirits can be bound to objects, locations. Any number of things."

Val hissed in frustration.

"But why? Stephen was just a normal person. There wasn't any special power in him. Why would someone want to bind his spirit?"

"Spirits have power, even mundane ones. A witch or a necromancer may capture and use shades for any number of reasons."

"A necromancer." Val scowled, remembering what Hillary had told her. "Could it be the same necromancer who's been experimenting on the vampires?"

Mister E shrugged, rolling over in lazy circles as he floated through the fog. *"Perhaps. Perhaps not. It isn't obvious how the two things could be related. Vampires and mundane shades are very different things. If I had to guess, I would say the two are not related."*

"Thanks for nothing."

Val grimaced as she focused on the thread of power connecting her to Stephen's spirit. She could feel the shade struggling, so Mister E was right. He was definitely trapped. But trapped by what?

She slid her mind down the thread, following it out through the forest. The amorphous shades parted to let her pass, closing in again behind her as she floated through the fog. This was dangerous. By traveling outside her summoning circle, she was making herself vulnerable. But she had to know.

As she followed the thread through a misty meadow, the grass painted dewy streaks against her knees. Beyond it was a dark hollow and an enormous fallen tree, its skeletal root cluster looming over her like a crown. Mushrooms and moss grew thick upon the ancient wood, and shadowy ferns lifted feathery leaves.

At the base of the root cluster was a dark hollow as big as a bear's burrow. It was entirely opaque and black as tar. Val gasped when her eyes fell on it. A malevolent energy radiated from the hollow. She took an involuntary step back as she sensed an intelligence in the darkness. Whatever was in there, it was watching her. And it hated her.

The trail of Stephen's spirit led directly into this hollow.

"What the hell is that?" she whispered.

Mister E didn't have an immediate answer. He drifted over the root cluster, keeping a careful distance from the dark maw. He turned this way and that, golden eyes blazing, fur puffing out in all directions, tail twitching in agitation.

"Whatever it is, it's old," he finally said.

"How old?"

"Let's just say it's been here a lot longer than you have."

Val's brow furrowed.

"What is it?"

The demon-cat pulled out a candy cigarette and started blowing smoke rings.

"I don't know."

"Why does it have Stephen?"

"I don't know."

"Then what good are you?" she snapped, her eyes blazing to match his.

Mister E blew another smoke ring.

"I don't know."

"Fine. I'll figure it out myself," Val snarled. She reached a hand toward the darkness.

"I wouldn't do that if I were you."

"Well, it's a good thing you're not me then, isn't it?"

She set her jaw, took a deep breath, and touched the darkness.

Val disappeared.

16

The first thing Val felt was cold. Glacier cold. A cold that hadn't seen the sun in years. Centuries. It clamped around her like a fist, stealing the breath from her lungs, paralyzing her in an instant.

Val fought to breathe, to move, but she was frozen in place. She struggled like a fly caught in a web. The more she fought, the more she was entwined.

There were other things in there with her. In the dark. Other people? She could sense them watching her.

"Stephen?" She wasn't sure if she spoke the name or only thought it, but she felt the darkness shift around her. "Stephen?"

She felt attention flicker toward her. Had he heard her?

"Stephen! Answer me!"

What came to her wasn't an answer.

And she was pretty sure it wasn't Stephen.

A feeling of warmth oozed over her skin. A cocoon of safety. After the incredible cold, the sudden heat was overwhelming. At first, the contrast was too great, and her skin prickled and itched. Then it made her drowsy. She felt her eyelids droop, sagging closed. Colored lights danced behind them. Yellow and green starbursts. Blue and red swirls. The patterns were hypnotizing, ever-shifting kaleidoscopes, and as she watched them move and change, she forgot why she was there. Forgot who she was.

Time passed, though she couldn't say how much. Maybe hours, maybe minutes. There was nothing outside of the moment. Only this place existed.

"Valora!"

A voice called in the distance, but she paid it no mind. Whoever the voice was calling, it wasn't her.

"Valora!"

The voice was louder this time, insistent. A frown creased her face. She just wanted to watch the lights. Was that too much to ask?

"Valora!"

A pair of golden eyes joined the lights. As she watched, they grew brighter and brighter, becoming twin suns, pushing away the colors and patterns, burning away the darkness.

Val opened her eyes with a gasp.

She was back in the morgue, sitting in the chair beside the examination table. Her limbs were stiff, her throat dry, as if she hadn't moved in a long time. The candles at the corners of the pentagram were little more than nubs.

"Oh, thank the Bob you're back."

She looked up to find Malcolm standing on the other side of the table, wringing his hands.

"How long was I gone?" she croaked.

"Too long. I've been freaking out. It's almost seven o'clock." He paced nervously, gesturing as he talked. "Every time I hear footsteps, I think we're about to get busted."

Val blinked. She tried to swallow and grimaced at the sandpaper in her throat.

Malcolm handed her a bottle of water.

"Thank you."

She tried to stand and had to clutch at the table for support. Everything hurt. Her muscles felt like she'd been beaten with a quarterstaff.

Malcolm was at her side in an instant, taking her arm to steady her. Val tried to summon up a smile, but it was ninety percent grimace.

"Thanks again."

"Did you find Stephen?" he asked anxiously.

"Yes and no."

"What does that mean?"

Val's back popped as she straightened up. She felt ancient, like she hadn't moved in years. She took a deep breath before answering.

"His spirit is safe. Well, it's whole anyway," she corrected herself. "Something's got him trapped."

"Something bad?"

"I don't know. It's hard to say. I went in after him, but it trapped me too. I got the impression there were other souls in there. I don't know how many. It was cold, freezing. But then it got warm, and there were lights and colors. Hypnotic patterns."

"But did you see Stephen? Did you talk to him?"

She scrubbed her hands over her face and sighed.

"No, not directly. But he was definitely in there with me."

"Can you get him out?"

Val stared down at Stephen's body on the examination table. Her mouth twisted as she touched his cold flesh with her fingertips.

"I don't know," she finally admitted. "But now that I know where he is, I'm sure I can get back to that place again. I'll be better prepared next time, now that I know what I'm up against."

"I thought you said you didn't know what it was?"

"I don't. I meant... I know what I'm up against in a general sense. Figuring out the specifics is going to take some research."

Malcolm grinned. "My specialty."

"Yeah, that and gigantic backpacks." Val laughed. "Come on, help me get this stuff all cleaned up. We need to get out of here before the coroner comes in for the morning shift."

A new voice rang out across the room: "It's a little late for that."

Val whirled to find Detective Chen standing in the doorway. His pistol was drawn and leveled at the center of her chest.

"Put your hands on your head and kneel down on the ground, nice and slow." He pulled out a pair of handcuffs and shuffled towards her. The gun barrel never wavered. "Valora Keri, you are under arrest."

17

The inside of the SFPD holding cell was worse than Val expected. Streaks of mold stained the cement walls and little piles of rust mounded at the bases of the bars. The mattress smelled like the previous occupant had urinated on it and the toilet was a clogged pool of brown filth. It reminded her of the sewer they'd traversed that morning, actually. The cops had taken Malcolm to a different cell in another part of the precinct. She hoped his cell was in better shape than hers. It certainly couldn't be any worse.

This wasn't Val's first time inside a jail cell. Over the course of her turbulent childhood, she'd been arrested for shoplifting and trespassing and assault and even for petty theft. She did her best to take her booking in stride, allowing Detective Chen to process her without difficulty.

But she was freaking out on the inside. She'd never broken into a police station before, and she'd never drawn a pentagram around a corpse in the SFPD's morgue. Something told her this was more serious than juvenile shoplifting.

Chen hadn't given her a chance to explain before locking her in the cell, and really, what would she say? The truth sounded absurd and the lies she came up with sounded even worse. She'd been caught performing a ritual inside a pentagram with a corpse in SFPD's own basement. It didn't get much more red-handed than that.

So Val sat and waited. And waited. And waited.

There were no windows in her cell and no clocks on the wall, but it felt like she'd been there all day. Her empty stomach rumbled, grumpily agreeing with that assessment.

"Hey!" she called down the hall.

She couldn't see any guards, but she assumed they had to be monitoring her somehow, right?

"Hey, I need to know what time it is. Don't I get a phone call? I'm supposed to work tonight. If I'm going to miss my shift, I need to at least call in and let them know."

There was no response. She cursed and looked around for something to bang on the bars with. In the movies, they always had a tin cup or something. Unfortunately for her, the cops had taken everything she might be able to use as a weapon or to do herself harm. That meant all the metal she had on her, including her rings. They'd even taken the shoelaces out of her boots.

Her boots did still have a couple of metal buckles on them, but she'd have to tear the leather to get them off, and she wasn't ready to start destroying her footwear just yet. Besides, they were still caked in mud and shit from their little jaunt through the sewers. Things would have to be pretty dire before she was ready to tear them apart with her bare hands. She kicked at the bars but couldn't get them to ring loud enough to be effective.

Hours passed. She did her best to stay alert, working up a sweat by shadowboxing and doing burpees. She considered doing some crunches on the stinky mattress, but she wasn't that desperate yet. Though examining the mattress did make her seriously wonder whether she'd be better off sleeping on the cement floor when the time came. Pushing it up with the toe of her boot made her realize it didn't just smell bad: the mattress was literally moist.

"Maybe someone did piss on it," she muttered. "I can't say I blame them. Judging by the state of the toilet, it'll probably overflow if I try to use it."

"Think of it as a human litter box." Mister E smiled. Val noticed that

though he was insubstantial, he didn't touch the mattress either, floating several feet in the air above it. *"It's extra absorbent."*

"Funny. It's a good thing I haven't had my coffee today, or we'd find out just how absorbent it really is."

"You not having your coffee is never a good thing," Mister E contradicted. *"In fact, that's probably the reason they've kept you isolated for so long. Your police file clearly states that you become homicidal when you haven't had caffeine. 'Suspect is bitchy and extremely dangerous.'"*

"They're not wrong. It definitely makes me want to kill someone." She bared her teeth as she paced back and forth.

"You're a real caged tiger. I swear I can see your tail twitching."

Exhaustion eventually overtook her and she slumped against the rusty bars, the cement floor cold beneath her legs. The darkness behind her eyelids was lit by visions of drifting lights and kaleidoscope patterns.

Naturally, the police came to get her as soon as she fell asleep.

They manhandled her out of the cell and into a stark interrogation room, where they shoved her into an orange plastic chair and handcuffed her to the table. Val blinked sandpaper eyelids and groggily took in the strip light overhead, the cheap wood paneling, the institutional linoleum floor, and the large one-way mirror set into the wall across from her. She waved at the cops she assumed were watching from behind it.

After a few minutes, Chen walked in, slapped a manila folder and a notepad on the table, and slid into the seat across from her. The bastard was drinking coffee and Val had to fight the urge to dive across the table and wrestle the cup from his hands. He noticed the hunger in her eyes.

"Coffee drinker?"

Val glared at him, and he smirked.

"I'd offer you some, but the station coffee here is like drinking water straight from the bay. This stuff, though..." Chen held his cup up under his nose and inhaled the steam, sighing with satisfaction. "This is from Madam Wu's coffee cart at Yerba Buena Gardens. Best coffee in the city." He took a long, slurping sip to underscore his point.

His eyes met Val's again and he laughed.

"If looks could kill, I'd be a pile of ash right now."

"How perceptive," she ground out between clenched teeth. "No wonder they made you a detective."

"It doesn't always take miraculous powers of deduction," he agreed. "Sometimes people are so dumb they walk into the station and break laws right in front of us. It's like they want to be caught." He paused and regarded her. "Did you want to be caught, Ms. Keri?"

Val rolled her eyes. "Yeah, I heard about the plush accommodations in the cells and couldn't wait to check them out myself."

"If you didn't want to be caught, why did you break into our morgue?"

"I needed to ask someone a question. That person was in your morgue."

"I assume that person was Stephen Hughes? You are aware that he's dead?"

"No, I hadn't noticed," Val said dryly.

Chen made a note on his pad. "Putting the impossibility of this aside for a second, you thought breaking into a police station was the best way to approach this? Did it ever occur to you to call me first? I know I gave you my number."

Val laughed. "Right. Call you and ask for permission to speak to one of the bodies in your morgue. I'm sure that conversation would have gone well."

"Maybe it would have, maybe it wouldn't. But we'll never know because you didn't take the time to find out."

Chen's brown eyes regarded her as he took another sip of his coffee. Val noticed that he drank it black. Definitely not her first choice, but she'd take it any way she could get it right now. Even instant coffee sounded good.

"I'm not your enemy, Keri. But I could be if you keep treating me like one."

"Oh, please. You're so full of shit right now your eyes are brown. What did you tell me at the Queen Anne? That you'd haul my ass down to the station and charge me with obstruction if you caught me poking around your investigation?" Val spread her hands, indicating their current environment. "Looks like I saved you the trouble by coming to you."

Chen pressed his lips into a thin frown. He scrubbed his hand back through his salt-and-pepper hair.

"Did you find the answers you were looking for?"

"I thought you didn't believe in the supernatural."

"What I believe is immaterial. I'm asking what you believe. Do you believe you spoke with Stephen Hughes?"

Val narrowed her eyes, glancing at the one-way mirror over his shoulder. Was she being recorded? Was he trying to make her look crazy?

Chen noticed her hesitation.

"You can speak freely, Ms. Keri. No one's behind that mirror right now. It's just us."

Val cracked her knuckles one by one, weighing his words. The detective could easily be lying. It was well known the police were allowed to lie when interrogating subjects. She'd be a fool to take what he said at face value.

Still, Chen seemed earnest enough. And he'd always struck her as a straight shooter.

"He's telling the truth," Mister E said, sticking his face through the mirror. *"There's nobody in the next room."*

His back half stayed in the interrogation room, tail sticking straight up into the air, giving her a perfect view of his pucker. She grimaced and looked down at the table.

Fuck it. Chen already thought she was crazy. What did she have to lose?

She raised her gaze to the detective's.

"No. I didn't speak to Stephen Hughes."

"You broke into our morgue and got arrested for nothing? There are easier ways to get locked up, you know."

"Not for nothing," she clarified. "I may not have spoken to Stephen, but I did find out where he's being held."

"When you say he's being held, what do you mean? Is he some kind of hostage?"

"You know, he just might be." Val tapped a finger against her lips, considering. "I assumed he was a prisoner, but if he's a hostage, that opens up a whole new realm of possibilities."

"And when you say 'he,' what are you talking about exactly?"

"His spirit. His soul. Whatever you want to call it."

"Whatever I want to call it? Aren't you supposed to be the expert here?"

Val sighed. "Look, a lot of this stuff is just guesswork. I'm doing my best to figure it out as I go along."

"Guesswork? Didn't you journey to a misty mountaintop to learn magic from Gandalf or Yoda or someone?" Chen smirked. "Don't you have to get a license to practice magic? I mean, come on. You've got to at least have a certificate from a community college."

Val winced as she remembered her summons to face judgment. The witches and wizards of the Coven were the closest thing to mentors she'd ever had. They'd taken her into the Emerald City and offered her shelter and community. For the first time in her life, she'd been around other magic users. People who accepted her for what she was. And she'd repaid them with violence and blood.

She frowned. Events had been piling up, one atop the other, making the days run together. Had it been two days since she received the Coven's summons? Or had it been three?

"Is the conclave tonight?" she whispered under her breath.

"*Indeed it is,*" Mister E confirmed. "*You've been summoned. Midnight at the top of Twin Peaks. Be there or be square.*"

"Shit."

"Is there a problem?" Chen asked.

"No, no problem. Everything's fine. Can you tell me what time it is?"

"It's time for you to answer my questions." He leaned forward in his chair. "Now when you say Stephen's spirit is being held, what does that mean, exactly?"

"I'm happy to cooperate, detective, but I need to know what time it is."

"You got a hot date?"

"Something like that. Look, I'll tell you anything you want, but I need to know what time it is."

"And if I tell you what time it is, you'll answer my questions?"

"Yes." Chen scowled at her as if she was playing some trick on him, so she added, "Please."

The detective sighed and checked his phone. "Fine. It's six thirty."

She would be judged in less than six hours. She shivered and tried to clamp down on her rising anxiety.

"Thank you. If I answer your questions, you'll let me go?"

Chen laughed. "Really, Keri? You think you can break into the SFPD morgue and draw a pentagram around a dead body and walk out the same day? Not happening."

"But I have to go. If I'm not... I have to be somewhere tonight. Somewhere important."

"Not happening," he repeated. "If you're really helpful, I'll see what I can do about getting you released on bail. But you're going to have to stay here overnight, minimum."

"You can't!" Chen jumped as Val jerked on her cuffs. "I have to get out of here!"

The detective's face became stony.

"Not. Going. To. Happen. Actions have consequences, Keri. You made your bed, now you have to lie in it. If your bed stinks, it's your own fault." He gathered his things and stood up. "I'll tell you one thing, free of charge. Stephen Hughes wasn't killed by a ghost. Toxicology is still working on the report, but we do know he had large amounts of Dream in his system. That's probably what caused his death."

Val hardly heard him. What would the Coven do if she didn't show up to face their judgment? They'd tracked her from New York, chased her all the way across the country. To say they'd be unhappy would be an understatement.

She only had one choice. She had to break out of the SFPD jail. And she had to do it within the next five hours.

18

V al paced her cell. All her options were bad. She was trying to decide which of her choices was the least terrible.

"Do I want the Coven hunting me or the SFPD?" she muttered.

"Why not have both?" Mister E offered. He was weaving in and out of her cell, rubbing his back against the bars.

"Both? What are you talking about?"

"I'm just saying, don't set your sights so low. Why stop at pissing off one powerful organization when you could piss them all off?"

"Very funny. I feel like a frog trying to cross the highway. I'm screwed no matter which way I jump."

"A strange comparison, but I can see how frogs crossing highways would not have a great success rate. So I take your meaning. But I'm not joking. Why do you need to play by their rules at all? You are stronger than them; they should be groveling at your feet. If there's one thing I've learned over the centuries, it's this: If you kill enough people, they'll learn to leave you alone eventually." His golden eyes gleamed wickedly. *"Stop playing by the rules of lesser beings. Let me show you how to be a real goddess."*

Val stared at him. "You know, every time I start to believe that cute feline facade, you go and say something like that. Thanks for reminding me what you really are."

Mister E hissed. *"It's you who are mistaken. Pound for pound, cats are the most efficient killing machines on the planet. This cute feline facade, as you put it, in no way disguises my true nature. You simply refuse to recognize the truth."*

Val rolled her eyes. "Be that as it may, killing people is not an option. We need a plan B."

Mister E flopped down onto his side dramatically. *"I really miss the witches of old. Why can't you be one of those women who lives in a small hut in the woods and turns anyone foolish enough to disturb her into a toad? Those were the good old days."*

"Just because you're old doesn't mean you have to live in the past," Val shot back. "Now, can you stop being nostalgic for a minute and help me?"

"I'm a fan of action, personally. Why let this cell hold you when you can break out of it? Besides, the Coven is the more formidable foe. If you have to choose between enemies, always choose the lesser."

"You make a disturbing amount of sense. I might be able to live with having the SFPD mad at me. The worst they're going to do is lock me up, right? Who knows what the Coven will do." She chewed her lip and started pacing again. "Of course, the flip side of that argument is there's no guarantee the Coven won't murder me even if I do show up on Twin Peaks. I did kill Sylvio and Amber in New York, after all. They could be here to demand an eye for an eye. And frankly, I deserve whatever punishment they want to dish out."

"Let them demand all they wish." Mister E started cleaning himself. *"None of them has a fraction of your power. If they try to take your eye, you kill them."*

"I already said killing them is not an option. And I'm not convinced I could take them out even if I wanted to. If I was fighting them one at a time, maybe I'd stand a chance. But I have no idea how many of them are in town. All I've seen so far are the three sisters, and they're pretty powerful by themselves. I doubt I could take them on together."

"It really is criminal the way you underestimate yourself. Let me say it again: You can be a goddess. People should tremble in fear of your wrath, not the other way around. If you'd let me teach you instead of constantly trying to deny your power..."

"It's funny how your 'teaching' always seems to involve you taking control of my body. The last time I let you do that, I woke up in a different state with a blank space in my memories almost a week long. I told you that was the last time, and I meant it."

"It's easier to show you than to tell you. Taking control of your body is the most efficient method of showing," Mister E replied, unruffled by her accusation. *"Think of it as hands-on training."*

"You can keep your hands to yourself," Val growled. She walked over to the back wall of her cell and put her hand against the cinder blocks. "Do you think this is an outside wall?"

"Wouldn't it have a window if it was?"

"It would if they wanted their prisoners to be comfortable. Which I don't think is high on their priorities list."

She closed her eyes and let her power flow into the wall. The cinder blocks were porous, so it was easy to suck air in through the cracks. She sniffed at it as it entered her cell.

"The air beyond this wall smells moist. I bet it's the fog. It must be the outside."

"Elementary, my dear Watson," Mister E agreed. He yawned, exposing his sharp fangs. *"Now may we leave this place? I'm weary of the smell of urine."*

"I'm with you there." She glanced at the surveillance camera across the hall. "I wish we had some of that black spray paint."

"And if wishes were fishes, the whole world would eat. Get on with it already."

"Fine, I will."

Val examined the wall, considering her options. She'd never tried to break through a cement wall before. Assuming she could even do it, what would be the best way?

The weak spots were the mortar lines between the cinder blocks. She knew people cleaned brick walls by sandblasting them, peeling away the outer layer to expose the clean brick below. Maybe she could try something similar?

She bent and scooped up some tiny stones from the base of the wall. If she wanted to hide what she was doing from the security camera, she'd have to keep it very small and focused. It would require a much higher degree of control than anything she'd ever done before.

Keeping her back to the security camera, she summoned a palm-sized whirlwind. It scooped up the rocks in her hand and swirled them around in a tight circle. So far, so good. Now for the hard part.

She took a deep breath. "Here goes nothing."

Val spun the whirlwind as fast as she could, thinning the edge down to a finger's breadth. Sweat sprang up across her forehead. Holding the wind so tightly focused was like trying to wrestle a bull. She carefully moved the little cyclone toward one of the mortar joints in the wall. The moment the whirlwind hit the mortar, grey dust exploded into the air.

A coughing fit shook Val as she sucked in a lungful of dust. Her concentration evaporated and the whirlwind disappeared.

When the fit finally subsided, she wiped the tears from her eyes and examined her handiwork.

"Flying toads, it worked," she breathed. She ran her finger over a clear line where the mortar had been worn away. It was only a scratch about the length of her palm, but her little whirlwind had definitely done some damage. Now that she had her proof of concept, it was time to scale up this operation.

Val summoned the whirlwind again, scooping even more grit, whirling it fast and tight. This time when the whirlwind hit the mortar, she was ready for the dust cloud it produced and corralled the dust with her little cyclone, keeping it contained. This had the extra benefit of making her whirlwind even grittier, which helped it wear away the mortar even faster.

Breathing hard, she paused to check her progress after a minute, funneling down the dirt to settle on the floor at her feet. She whistled as she saw the clear, deep line she'd made in the mortar.

"How have I never down this before? This is even better than power tools." She ran her finger along the gap, which was now the length of an entire cinder block and a couple of inches deep. She squatted to peer into it. "Damn, these blocks are thick. I'm going to have to cut really deep to free this block. Getting enough of them loose to escape is going to take a long time."

Mister E leapt onto the bed, landing on a cushion of air a foot above the soiled mattress. He curled up, wrapping his tail around his nose, and watched her with his golden eyes.

"Then I suggest you get to work. If you need me, I'll be over here supervising."

"You mean napping."

The cat gave his crescent moon smile. *"Isn't that what I said?"*

Val snorted, cracked her knuckles, and got to work.

It took hours, and by the time she was done, Val was exhausted. She'd never used her magic for such an extended time before. She cracked her neck and ran a hand through her sweat-soaked hair.

"This feels less like magic and more like work."

"That's because you haven't trained properly," Mister E reminded her.

"Would you stop with the nagging? You're worse than my grandmother."

"You mean the one you haven't seen since you were six years old? What a remarkable memory you have."

"I may have been young, but believe me, she made a lasting impression. Just like I plan to make on this cell."

Val surveyed the wall. She'd blasted out most of the mortar around a strip of cinder blocks several feet high. One good strong blow should knock them all out at once, creating a gap in the wall big enough for her to squeeze through. As she'd worked, the dust had gotten to be a problem, and she'd surreptitiously created a second funnel that had sucked it all away under the bed. Now there was a large pile of grey dust back there against the wall. Hopefully, no one would notice. At least not until after she was long gone.

"Do I really want to do this?"

Doubt twisted her stomach. If she went through with it, she'd become a fugitive, hunted by the SFPD. Her life in San Francisco would be over. She'd have to quit her job. Leave town. Take to the road again.

She'd spent most of her teens and early twenties in similar situations. Over and over, her powers got her into trouble and she was forced to flee. She'd seen so many towns in her rearview mirror. So many people had come and gone from her life that she'd given up on ever putting down roots. Having friends or an address that lasted longer than a few months were simply not things for her, it seemed.

San Francisco had changed all that. The city was big enough, and weird enough, that for the first time Val was able to blend in. She had a job she liked well enough, friends, and an apartment she'd been able to keep for almost two years. She'd finally started to relax. Finally stopped waiting for the other shoe to drop, for the day it would all fall apart again.

Maybe the only one she'd been fooling was herself.

The Coven had tracked her down. Her past mistakes had caught up with her. And in order to face them, she might have to burn down the life she'd so carefully built up. Even if she survived the Coven's judgment on Twin Peaks, breaking out of jail to get there would ensure that her life in San Francisco was over. She'd never see the Alley Cat again. Never get to say goodbye to Junior and Lisa and Malina and all the girls. She'd never see Tommy Walker or Vasilevski again either, though in their case that was probably a good thing.

Hell, she'd never even get to say goodbye to Malcolm. She'd be leaving him with the unsolved murder of his oldest friend and a breaking and entering charge to boot. Some friend she was.

Hopefully her little escape act would prove to the SFPD that their little B&E that morning was all her doing, and they'd let Malcolm off easy.

Hopefully.

She sighed. It looked like hope was all she had left at this point.

"I'm sorry, Malcolm," she muttered.

She raised her hands, gathering her power. One good gust and the cinder blocks would burst free like children's blocks.

Chen's voice came from behind her.

"That's enough, Keri. Keep your hands up and get down on your knees."

Val whirled around and found herself staring down the barrel of Detective Chen's pistol. She hesitated. Could she knock Chen down, blow out the wall, and escape?

The click of the detective's hammer cocking was loud in the small cell.

"Last chance, Keri. Get down on your knees. Don't make me shoot you."

Val's mind raced, calculating furiously. She couldn't outrun a bullet, and she doubted her wind could hit Chen fast enough to disrupt his aim before he fired.

With a sigh, she dropped to her knees and let her power go.

The bleakness of her situation crashed down on her. On the one hand, she supposed she wouldn't be a fugitive from the SFPD now, but there was no way she was getting to Twin Peaks by midnight. And not showing up to face the Council's judgment was as good as admitting her guilt.

The Coven would be hunting her before sunrise. And this time, they wouldn't be content with talking. This time they'd be coming for blood.

19

Val didn't think she'd ever be able to sleep in the jail cell. Even after Chen undid her hours of labor by moving her to another cell, the new mattress still stank of urine, and her thoughts were whirling far too much for sleep.

So it was a shock when a stocky female cop pulled her out of restless dreams by beating on the bars of her cell with her truncheon.

"Rise and shine, Keri. Let's go. You're getting out of here."

"... What?"

Val groggily tried to wrap her brain around this information. Chen had told her he was going to hold her until she was formally charged, and that she wouldn't be getting out for a few days at least. But here it was, the morning after the crime, and they were releasing her already?

"Is it morning?" she asked, realizing she was making an assumption. There were no windows or clocks in the cell block, so it could still be the middle of the night for all she knew.

"Yup, bright and early. Come on, I haven't got all day."

Val numbly followed the officer down the hall and into the station.

"I don't understand. Am I not being charged?"

"Oh, you're being charged all right," the cop glared at her. "You're going to pay for your little stunt in the morgue. Desecrating dead bodies. You're a real piece of work, lady."

"I didn't desecrate..."

"Save it for the judge. I don't want to hear your sob story." The cop opened a door and held it for her. "Through there. You can get your clothes back at that window. Then you're free to go."

"I don't understand. If I'm being charged, why am I being released?"

A new voice spoke behind her: "Because I bailed you out."

Val whirled to find Vasilevski standing there in a long wool trench coat. Her first reaction was shock. Her second, suspicion.

"What are you doing here?"

"I just answered that question."

She glared at the mobster. "You know what I mean."

His smile didn't touch his eyes. "Come, we can talk once we're outside. There are too many ears here."

Val took two steps and stopped. She turned back to the cop.

"Wait. Where's Malcolm?"

"Your little accomplice is still inside. Nobody bailed him out. I guess he doesn't have the same kind of friends you do."

She whirled back to Vasilevski.

"You need to bail out my friend, too."

He raised an eyebrow. "I don't need to do anything. You should be grateful I am bailing you out."

Val ground her teeth. "I am grateful. Thank you. But I'm not leaving without my friend."

Vasilevski shrugged. "That is not my problem. There is a bail bonds across the street if you wish to free your friend."

"Look. I assume you want something from me. That's why you're here: to put me in your debt. Fine. But my price includes Malcolm's bail. Either he walks or I do."

The Russian gave her a flat stare, but finally nodded. "Agreed."

He paid Malcolm's bail, and they stepped outside to wait for her housemate's release. Vasilevski's silver limo sat at the curb in front, a big driver with a scar along his jaw glaring at anyone who got too close. The driver held the back door open for them.

"Please, sit. We will talk while we wait for your friend," Vasilevski commanded.

The back seat of the limo was immaculate, with black leather seats and a mini bar.

"Drink?" the gangster offered.

"At this time of the morning?"

Vasilevski shrugged. "If you have to watch the sunrise, you should do it with a toast."

"You go ahead. I'd kill for some coffee, though."

He smiled. "I can make that as well."

She watched in silence as he boiled water in an electric kettle, ground fresh beans, and filled a small French press. His movements were meticulous, almost dainty. Not at all what she would have expected.

"Milk? Sugar?"

"You don't have any butterscotch syrup, do you?"

The gangster's composure faltered for a moment, his face contorting in a grimace. "Butterscotch syrup?"

"Never mind, it was a longshot. Yes, milk and sugar."

When the coffee was in her hand at last, she buried her face in the steam, took a big sip, and sighed. "You have no idea how much this means to me. I had to survive the whole day yesterday with no coffee. Bunch of barbarians in there."

Vasilevski said nothing, watching her with his dark eyes.

After a couple more sips, Val felt the caffeine start to work its magic. She raised her eyes to meet his.

"What's the catch?"

"I have a job for you."

"I already have a job."

"Yes, but I have a better one."

"Oh? Are you going to tell me about what a great dental plan you've got?"

"No." Vasilevski did not look amused. "This is a contract job, not a permanent position. Though if you do well, maybe we can talk some more later."

Val's smile became strained.

"Look, Mr. Vasilevski, I'm flattered. But I've already got too much on my plate."

Vasilevski's expression didn't change. "This is not a request. I have an important package that needs to be delivered tonight. You must deliver it for me."

An incredulous laugh burst from her throat. "Package delivery? Seriously? Don't you have a hundred other guys that can deliver packages?"

"Yes, I do. None of them can do what you do. This package is very important to me. It requires special protection. I will pay you very well for your services."

"I don't care what you're paying, it's not..."

Vasilevski named a figure and Val's voice cut off in a squeak. That was more money than she made in the Alley Cat in a month. Maybe two months. And thanks to the Sandra fiasco, she might be on the hook for double rent.

Mister E laughed. "*Everyone has their price.*"

Val tried not to scowl as she cleared her throat. She needed to reassert control of the situation.

"That's a very generous offer. But money isn't everything. There are things I won't do, no matter how much you pay me."

The gangster leaned back in his chair, nodding. "Of course. I understand you have a moral code, Val Keri. That is one of the reasons I want you for this job. You are honorable. If you agree to a job, I know you will do it. You have my word, there is nothing illegal about this delivery."

Val drummed her fingers on her knee, thinking. She was intrigued despite herself. It was an awful lot of money. And Vasilevski had just gotten her out of jail. If there wasn't anything illegal about the job...

"What's the package then?"

"Not what. Who."

"Who?"

"Precisely." Vasilevski leaned forward, folding his hands. His tone dropped, so that Val had to lean in to catch his next words. "You will escort my niece to a party. You will keep an eye on her all evening. You will bring her home safe."

"What's the catch?"

"No catch. You complete this simple job, and you get paid. That is all."

"And why can't one of your boys escort her?"

"I need you to agree to the job before I tell you more details. Confidentiality. You understand."

Val took a deep breath and blew it out through her nose. She knew she didn't really have a choice. Vasilevski had made sure of that by bailing her out and putting her in his debt. And the gangster's offer was very generous. How bad could it be?

She squared her shoulders. "Fine. I'll take the job."

Vasilevski nodded as if this was obvious. "*Da*. Good."

"Now, why can't one of your boys escort her?"

"Because they would not stand a chance against the creatures that will be present. You will."

She narrowed her eyes. All of a sudden, this was sounding like less of a good deal.

"Creatures?"

Vasilevski's smile didn't touch his eyes.

"It is a vampire's ball."

20

Vasilevski kicked her out of the limo when Malcolm finally emerged from the station. Her roommate seemed surprisingly unfazed by his time in the lock up, chattering away about the experience and complaining about the state of his cell while Val put him in the sidecar of the Ural and drove home. Then she collapsed into bed.

Several hours later, the scent of coffee roused her from troubled dreams. She stumbled out to the kitchen, noting that the sun was already setting outside.

"Good evening, Vampira." Malcolm smiled as she entered the kitchen.

Pouring herself some coffee, Val winced, remembering Hillary down in the basement. "Don't even joke about that."

"Well, somebody's got her grumpy pants on today."

"Not before coffee, Malcolm. Give me time for the caffeine to hit my bloodstream, then you can be as chipper as you want."

Val took her cup into the living room, ending the conversation. Malcolm huffed but knew better than to chase her down. She stared out the dirty bay windows, sipping her coffee, allowing her sluggish thoughts to find their own path.

Red and orange streaked the sunset sky, silhouetting the rooftops in stark relief. The sounds of the city filtered in: teenagers laughing, the rumble of an ancient diesel engine, sirens in the distance. She wondered how many of the people out there were aware of the monsters living among them. How many knew the things that went bump in the night were closer than they thought. Did they lie awake at night, hearts racing, rigid with worry? Or was it something they simply tried not to think about, like muggers or car accidents or an incurable disease?

She decided it was most likely the latter. People had a remarkable ability to ignore the things they couldn't face. To pretend they didn't exist.

Val envied them that ability. It was pretty hard to ignore the problems that showed up at her doorstep.

She leaned her forehead against the cool glass. What was she going to do about Hillary, anyway? She couldn't keep her in the basement forever. Thanks to their less than subtle escape from the party, Melinda Pearl already knew Val was helping the young vampire. It was only a matter of time before the hunters tracked them down.

If she could just focus on one problem, she might be able to solve it. But she was being pulled in too many directions at once.

"Do one thing and do it well. Do many things, and do many things poorly," she muttered. "Isn't that some kind of proverb?"

"If it's not, it definitely should be," Malcolm said, sticking his head in the doorway. "Are you starting to feel human again? Can I come in?"

"Sure, Malcolm. Come on in. We've got a lot to talk about." She sank onto the window seat and gestured Malcolm towards the couch.

Case in point, as Val now had to push the vampire question aside and turn her attention to Malcolm and Stephen. She took another sip of coffee to aid the transition.

"First of all, I'm sorry for getting you arrested. It was a risky plan, and I never should have let you come with me," she began.

"Oh, please. I was coming whether you wanted me to or not." Malcolm brushed her words aside. "Besides, now I can say I've been arrested and spent a night in jail. Cross one more thing off the bucket list."

"If we get convicted, we could spend a lot more than one night in jail."

"Maybe. Or maybe you'll solve the case and the SFPD will be so grateful they'll drop all the charges." He looked at her expectantly. "What else have you found out about Stephen's murder?"

Val laughed without mirth. "When do you think I had time to do that?"

"I don't know. Couldn't you call your psychic connection from jail? Or summon up the spirit of Alastair Crowley or Bernadette Peters or something?"

"Bernadette Peters?"

"What? She played the best witch ever on Broadway!"

"You have no idea how this works, do you?"

Malcolm pouted. "You have your goddesses, I have mine."

"Right." Val sighed and turned her gaze back to the window, watching a flock of bicycles hum past on the street below. Just a bunch of normal commuters heading home to one-bedroom apartments and take-out dinners. She envied them.

"Why didn't you tell me Stephen was on Dream the night he died?"

"I didn't know it was important."

"Detective Chen thinks it might be what killed him."

Malcolm's put his hand to his lips. "Oh my god. But I was on it too, and I was fine."

"Things hit different people differently. Have you heard of any other people dying from Dream?"

"No."

"Where did you get it?"

"From a friend." His lip trembled. "Oh god, Val. Did I accidentally kill Stephen?"

She put a hand up to calm him.

"We don't know that. Chen said they weren't sure. And based on that black presence I saw in the morgue, I'm not sure either. It feels like there are a lot of possible causes here. Look, Malcolm, this is going to take some time and some research. Tomorrow we'll go to the Library and see what we can find out." She drained the last of her coffee and headed toward the kitchen. "Right now I need to take a shower and wash the jail-piss smell off, then I have to escort Vasilevski's niece to some fancy ball."

She rinsed out her mug and put it in the dish rack, then stopped in the hall and turned back to Malcom. "I promise we'll find out what happened to Stephen. Tomorrow, OK?"

Malcolm squirmed, his face pinched. "What if I killed him? What if he's suffering? Now his soul is trapped? I feel like I should be doing more."

Val wanted to reach out to him, to comfort him in some way, but she didn't know how. Comfort wasn't something she'd experienced much while growing up. Putting up big, strong walls. Locking her feelings away. Those were the things she was good at.

So she simply sighed and turned away.

"You and me both, Malcolm."

21

It was dark outside by the time Val finished getting ready to go. Vasilevski had sent her home with a sharp black suit, black tie, and black pants. She examined herself in the mirror critically, shrugged, and stepped out into the hallway.

Malcolm whistled. "You look like you're going to a funeral or an assassination. Maybe both."

She tugged at her collar and grimaced. "Is it that bad?"

"No, it's good. You look sharp and deadly. Like a katana in a sheath. It's a good look for you."

"I feel ridiculous."

"Well, you look hot. Take it from me. Nobody's going to fuck with you looking like that."

"I suppose that's the idea."

She gave another tug on her collar and futzed with the waistband on her pants. The clothes fit perfectly—how Vasilevski knew her measurements, she'd rather not know—but despite the immaculate fit, the outfit just felt wrong. These clothes were for someone else, not her. A character in another story. She longed for her simple black jeans and leather jacket.

"Wish me luck."

"You don't need luck. You're going to knock them dead." Malcolm winked at her. "Now go out there and kick some ass."

As she waited at the curb for Vasilevski's car to pick her up, Val felt someone watching her. She stiffened and, without turning her head, let her eyes drift up and down the street. She saw nothing out of the ordinary: a dark street, a few cars parked in puddles of light, a rat dashing into an alley.

A voice in her ear made her jump.

"Nice night for a stroll."

"Hillary." It took all of Val's willpower not to throw the vampire across the street. "I'm surprised to see you out of your basement."

"A girl's got to eat." Hillary's breath was cold on her neck.

"Is that a threat?" Val refused to give the vampire the satisfaction of flinching, though every fiber of her being made her want to run.

"Just an observation." The vampire stepped away from her and leaned against a rusted old sedan that hadn't left the curb the entire time Val lived there. Her voice was sulky. "I'm hungry. I've been stuck in that moldy basement for days. If I hadn't found a box full of comic books, I'd have died of boredom. Did you forget about me?"

"I'm sorry, I haven't forgotten about you. I've just been a little busy."

"You promised you'd take me somewhere safe."

"And I will."

"When?"

"I don't know. I've got a lot of things on my plate right now."

"So I'm supposed to rot in that basement indefinitely?"

Val met the vampire's glare. "You're welcome to try your luck on the street by yourself."

Hillary bared her fangs, and for a moment Val thought she was going to attack. Then the young woman deflated.

"I need to eat, Val. And they'll find me if I go out hunting."

"So... what? You want me to bring you someone to eat? That's not going to happen." Val failed to keep the disgust out of her voice.

"I'm a vampire, not a ghoul. I don't eat people." Hillary sounded almost as disgusted as Val, and for a moment Val was sorry.

But only for a moment.

She'd offered to help Hillary escape her abusive relationship with Melinda Pearl without thinking, and she'd never expected the young woman would take her up on it. She felt bad for Hillary and would honor her offer to help. But that didn't change the fact that Hillary was a vampire. And vampires made Val shudder with revulsion.

"What do you eat? Bags of blood? Cats and dogs?"

Hillary's hands curled into fists, nails digging into her palms.

"Unfortunately, no. It has to be fresh human blood. But it doesn't have to be a lot, and I won't infect them."

Val narrowed her eyes. "You won't infect them? How can you be sure? Do you wear a vampire condom?"

"Funny, Val. No, I won't infect them because it takes many feedings to infect someone, not just a one-night stand. Also, you have to be an elder vampire, which I clearly am not."

Val shrugged. "I'm supposed to know that? It's not like you vampires show your age. You could be a hundred years old for all I know."

"I'm not. I'm barely twenty. It's only been a year since Melinda Pearl turned me."

"Really? What made you want to get into the vampire business?"

Hillary's face became a mask. "That's none of your business. Now, are you going to get me some food or not?"

"There's no way I'm going to bring someone for you to feed off. That's just not happening."

"If you're not going to help me, why did you even offer? I knew I should have stayed with my master, but now I've abandoned my cabal and I'm stuck out here with some witch who doesn't give a shit about me." A single tear ran down her cheek, and she angrily wiped it away. "I should have known better. I guess this is just the latest chapter in my long line of brilliant life choices. Nobody gives a shit about you in this world."

"Hillary..."

But the young vampire was gone, swallowed up by the shadows as if she had never been there.

"... Dammit."

Val tilted her head back and stared up at the fog creeping over the rooftops. Yet another person she was supposed to be helping. Yet another person she was failing.

"I don't know why I even try," she muttered.

"Don't beat yourself up too much." Mister E's voice drifted like the fog. *"It's not as if she paid for your services. If she'd sacrificed a goat, you might have a reason to feel guilty. But verbal contracts are meaningless, and you hardly even have that."*

"Sacrificed a goat?"

His grin curled up to his ears. *"Well, some people would sacrifice their firstborn, but they're extremist wackos. A goat is more traditional."*

Val studied the demon-cat through narrowed eyes. She could never tell when he was pulling her leg.

A black car appeared at the curb in front of her, interrupting her rumination. A square-shouldered driver got out and held open the back door.

"Please get in the car, Ms. Keri."

"Oh boy, here we go. More fun and games," Val muttered under her breath. She straightened her tie, tugged at her collar, and slid into the dark interior.

22

A petite girl with pink hair sat across from Val in the back of the limo. She looked like a miniature doll of a person: tiny hands, tiny feet, a delicately boned face with sharp cheekbones and moss-green eyes. Peach lipstick defined her lips perfectly. She wore a frilled black dress that sparkled when the streetlights hit it and black shoes that looked like ballet slippers. There was no way the girl would be more than five feet tall when she stood up. Vasilevski had said his niece was sixteen, but if Val had seen the girl on the street, she would have thought she was twelve.

The girl eyed Val, her cold, direct gaze eerily reminiscent of Vasilevski's own.

"The famous Val Keri," she said, her voice musical but sharp, like a hammer dulcimer.

Val inclined her head. "Guilty as charged. You must be the girl I'm supposed to babysit tonight."

Rather than become offended, the girl let her peachy lips split into a sly smile. "If you're good, I might even let you change my diaper."

Val looked away, her cheeks growing warm. She was used to plenty of innuendos being directed towards her behind the bar at the Alley Cat, but she'd been caught off guard by this baby-faced girl.

"I like this one already," Mister E whispered. *"I hope you do get to change her diaper."*

"You are not helping," Val muttered under her breath.

To the girl, she said, "I doubt your uncle would find that appropriate. Besides, I don't kiss on the first date."

"Who said anything about kissing?" the girl shot back. The gleam in her eye said she was enjoying Val's discomfort.

Val cleared her throat.

"I think we've gotten off on the wrong foot. You know my name. Maybe you should tell me yours."

The girl's mouth formed a tiny pout. "My uncle didn't even tell you my name?"

"I'm afraid not. Unless you want me to call you Tinkerbell all night, you'll have to fill me in."

"Did you just make a joke about my size? How hilarious. Nobody's ever done that before." The girl's pout became a frown, and she pointedly turned her gaze out the window. "My name is Zoe."

"Nice to meet you, Zoe. I'm sure this wasn't your idea any more than it was mine, so let's play nice and try to get through the night in one piece."

Zoe bit her lip. "Actually, it was my idea. I asked my uncle to get you to go to the ball with me."

Val stared at her. "This was your idea? But... why?"

"Because I wanted to meet you, obviously. I've heard so much about you. I decided it was time to put a face to the name."

"But why would you want to meet me? I'm nobody special."

Zoe laughed, her moss-colored eyes piercing Val's.

"You're either incredibly modest or incredibly dense." She cocked her head, considering. "I'm not sure which one yet."

"I vote for dense," Mister E interjected.

Val bit back a cutting reply. If she was being honest with herself, he was probably right.

Zoe pulled out a vial and dropped some liquid into each eye. She offered the vial to Val. "Dream?"

Val recoiled. "That stuff will kill you."

"It will not."

"Tell that to my dead friend."

Zoe cocked her head. "Your friend was killed by Dream?"

"That's what SFPD told me."

"I don't believe it. I haven't heard of anyone dying from it."

"And you know everything, do you?" Val scoffed.

"When it comes to Dream, yes. I know the woman who makes it."

Val leaned forward in her seat. "Your family makes that stuff? Why am I not surprised? I need to speak to this woman."

Zoe laughed. "You're making demands of me? That's rich."

"Your drug killed my friend. May have," she corrected herself when Zoe open her mouth to protest again.

"I assure you it did not. The maker is an old family friend. She's one of my favorite aunts. If there were harmful side effects, I would know."

"Please, just let me talk to her. I need to find out for myself. I need the truth."

Zoe regarded her through lowered lashes, her mouth quirking up at the corner.

"You're asking for a favor? Favors given for favors owed? Perhaps we can work something out." She leered at Val, sucking in her bottom lip between her teeth.

Val felt her face get hot.

"This assignment is getting worse by the second," she muttered. "It was bad enough being forced to work for Vasilevski, but at least he made it sound like my skills were important to the job. Now I'm dependent on the whim of a sixteen-year-old with boundary issues."

"I am a member of the Vasilevski family. My whims carry more weight than the commands of the mayor."

Val choked out a laugh. "Wow, that's some inflated sense of self-importance you've got there."

"It's not inflated if it's the truth," Zoe replied coldly. "I could have the mayor killed if I wanted to."

"There's a big difference between having the ability to do something and that something being a good idea. Just because you can do something doesn't mean you should. Sure, you might be able to have the mayor killed. But SFPD would launch a retaliatory investigation that would seriously disrupt your family's business. Would any high-ranking family members got to jail? Maybe not. But the disruption would cost you a lot of money, and your uncle cares about that income far more than the life of any one person. On the risk-reward scale, the cost of killing the mayor would far outweigh the reward. If you decided to do something so monumentally stupid, your family would no doubt teach you a very painful lesson in economics." Val shifted in her seat, her golden eyes pinning the girl in the darkness. "Sometimes having power means being wise enough not to use it. Clearly you haven't learned that lesson yet."

"Power is useless if you don't use it," the girl shot back. "A king who doesn't rule is no better than a peasant."

"Strength is the ability to move mountains. Wisdom is knowing there's a better path."

The girl shook her head. "You disappoint me, Val Keri. Everyone told me you're a bad-ass bitch afraid of nothing. And instead of a lion, I find a little mouse who lectures me on strength and wisdom."

"Yeah, well, when you've hurt as many people as I have, you learn that violence should be your last resort." Val rubbed the suit jacket over her left shoulder. She could see the tattoo beneath the fabric in her mind's eye, the memento mori for everyone she'd ever killed. Her guilt was like a lead overcoat.

The Coven's hunters would be coming for her soon. She wondered if she'd even fight them when they did. After all, she deserved their punishment.

"You're too young to have regrets," she said quietly. "You're only thinking of what you can do, not the effects those actions will have. Did you ever hear of the butterfly effect? Every action you take has unexpected consequences, rippling out across the world. You hurt one person and that person takes that violence and passes it on to someone else. And so on and so on. Violence breeds violence. Death leads to more death. Trust me, the more violence you can nip in the bud, the better off you'll be."

To her surprise, Zoe giggled. "You know, that weight-of-the-world-on-your-shoulders thing is super sexy."

Val stared at her in shock. "Sometimes I don't know why I even bother opening my mouth."

"But it's such a cute mouth," Zoe purred.

Val growled and turned her face to the window. She watched the dark streets roll by while the sound of Mister E's laughter rang in her ears.

23

The ball took place in an enormous old mansion on Washington Street, right beside Lafayette Park. It was a gorgeous French chateau made of white limestone, with columns flanking the entrance and huge windows draped with white curtains. After the doorman announced them, they descended into an open salon at the back of the house. Artful flower arrangements on pedestals were spaced around the perimeter of the room and polished hardwood floors rang under their heels. Chandeliers blazing with dozens of real candles illuminated the room. Floor-to-ceiling windows revealed the distant lights of Angel Island sparkling in the dark expanse of the bay.

"Flying Toads," Val breathed. "So this is how the other half lives."

Zoe smirked at her. "This is how my family always lives. Now do you see why you're not remotely qualified to lecture me on how to use my power?"

Val smirked right back. "If you think living in a snow globe helps you understand the world, you're more out of touch than I thought."

The girl just rolled her eyes and grabbed a glass of champagne from a passing server. "Just stay close, watch my back, and keep your mouth shut. Do you think you can do that?" Without waiting for an answer, she strolled off into the crowd.

The ball was a black-tie affair and Val found herself grateful for the black suit Vasilevski had sent her. Of course, the women wore sleek gowns, not suits, but Val was more than fine with not wearing a gown. For one thing, her job was to protect Zoe, and she couldn't do that in clothing that restricted her movement. Also, she wasn't a gown type of girl. So she was glad to adhere to the masculine side of the dress code. Others dressed in black suits exchanged cool, professional nods when they caught her eye. Apparently, Vasilevski had given her the standard security uniform.

She stayed just behind Zoe's shoulder, trailing her charge through the crowd. Close enough to protect her, but the step back gave the appearance of discretion. And in a crowd like this, appearances were everything.

Val recognized several people from the masquerade ball. She saw an older man dripping Dream into his eyes, his face so pale it looked powdered. She remembered there were a lot of pale faces at the masquerade ball, too. A side effect of the drug?

She thought about Zoe's assertion that Dream was not dangerous. Chen had told her the toxicology report wasn't complete yet. Maybe he'd been jumping to conclusions. She needed to speak to the maker of the drug and find out for herself.

She was watching Zoe chat with a circle of women she didn't recognize when Melinda Pearl's voice in her ear sent shivers down her spine.

"You have something of mine. I want it back."

She shifted on her feet, turning slightly to face the woman while keeping an eye on Zoe. Vasilevski had been right, there were vampires at the ball. Maybe that was the reason for so many pale faces. She glanced around nervously, wondering what other monsters the fancy gowns might be concealing.

The vampire queen was dressed in a black sleeveless gown with onyx earrings and long silk gloves that concealed her arms up to the elbow. Blood-red lipstick and smoky kohl around her eyes were stark against her porcelain skin.

Val raised an eyebrow. "Are you trying to be a walking stereotype, or does it just come naturally?"

Pearl ignored the barb.

"My property, Keri. I want it back."

"I have no idea what you're talking about."

The vampire smiled, showing Val her fangs. "Do not play dumb with me. You were seen leaving with Hillary after the masquerade. You fought four of my minions."

Val kept her expression blank. "I fight a lot of assholes in my line of work. You'll have to be more specific."

Pearl stepped forward until only inches separated them. Val gritted her teeth and held her ground.

"I can feel her presence, Keri. I know she is still within the city."

"Nice to know you're in touch with your feelings. We'll make a Jedi out of you yet."

"If you return her to me within two days, I will overlook your insolence."

"And if I don't?"

"Your friends will begin to die. Starting with that one." Pearl's gaze locked onto Zoe, standing just a few paces away, oblivious to their conversation.

"You stay away from her," Val said, her hands clenching into instinctive fists.

"Give me what I want, and no harm will come to her."

"She's not even my friend. This is a job. I hardly know the girl."

"But you care about her, nonetheless."

Val said nothing and the vampire queen laughed. "This is your weakness, Val Keri. You care about the mortals. You do not realize they are no more than fruit flies. Here today, gone tomorrow. Their lives are but a blink to beings such as us."

"Speak for yourself," Val snarled. "I'm as mortal as the next girl."

The vampire studied Val's face for a long moment.

"You truly believe that, don't you? How do you lack self-knowledge entirely?"

"What the hell are you talking about?"

"I don't think it's my place to share that information. Though I would love to be a fly on the wall the day you find out." Pearl smiled wickedly, her teeth gleaming in the light of the candles. "Until then, remember my words. You have two days."

The vampire strode away before Val could ask any more questions.

"What the hell did she mean by that?" Val fumed.

"I'm sure I don't know." Mister E appeared, perched upon her left shoulder.

She glared at him. "That's funny, because I'm sure you do. And you're going to tell me."

Her companion refused to meet her gaze, keeping his attention fixed on the paw he was cleaning.

"What did she mean, I'm not entirely human? She's just messing with me, right?"

Before she could press him further, Zoe called to her. Val started as she realized the girl had drifted away while she was distracted.

"Hey, bodyguard! If you're done talking to yourself, we're heading outside to enjoy the view." Without waiting for a response, the girl pushed through the double doors and stepped out onto the patio.

Cursing under her breath, Val stomped after her.

24

The view from the patio was magnificent. The city fell away beneath them, an orderly grid of lights unrolling down the hill, only to be swallowed by the dark expanse of the bay. The graceful arches of the Golden Gate bridge were visible off to Val's left, the yellow lights illuminating an enormous fog bank that billowed in the wind. The bay breeze was crisp and cold, and Val crossed her arms over her chest, hugging her jacket tightly around her.

Zoe stood by the iron railing, beckoning. "Keri, come over here. I want to introduce you to my friends."

Val growled under her breath, "I'm not some pony on display."

"*Oh, but you are,*" Mister E laughed. "*Just look at those haunches. You're a thoroughbred, Valora Keri.*"

"And you can piss off."

"Come on, Val. Don't keep me waiting." Zoe smirked at her.

She grudgingly moved closer to the girl. Zoe slipped her arm through Val's and pulled her into the circle.

"Everyone, this is Val Keri. Val, this is Padraig, Shen, and Joumala."

Zoe's friends gave Val an appraising look. There were three of them, a girl and two boys, all around Zoe's age. They were immaculately dressed and looked rich and powerful. Val wondered if she was meeting the next generation of crime lords.

"Is it true you fought an angel?" asked a Chinese boy with a red streak in his hair. He wore a matching red jacket with a high collar buttoned up around his throat. Val decided he must be Shen.

"A seraph, actually," Val admitted.

"What's the difference?" Joumala interjected. She had long brown hair and a soft accent.

Val spread her hands, palms up. "I don't know. I've never met an angel, so maybe there's no such thing."

"Are you saying there's no God?" the other boy, Padraig, asked. He was elegantly dressed in a brown velvet jacket, white shirt, and golden earrings, which set off his red hair and freckles. From his looks and accent, Val gathered he must be from Ireland.

She paused for a moment before answering, judging her audience. The last thing she wanted was to get into a religious debate. But she saw only curiosity in his eyes, not hostility, so she answered honestly.

"If you're talking about the capital-G God, I haven't seen any evidence of their existence personally. But I do know there are plenty of small-g gods running around, and I definitely don't know everything, so I wouldn't rule anything out."

"Very diplomatically put," Zoe mocked. "Not what I expected. You have a reputation for being blunt."

"I'm honest," Val corrected. "If people choose to interpret that as bluntness, that's their problem."

Zoe laughed. "There it is. How delightful."

"Why am I here, really?" Val challenged. "You're surrounded by your friends. I hardly think you need a bodyguard."

"But that is precisely when you need a bodyguard the most," Padraig answered. "When your enemy's guard is down, it's the perfect time to strike. We all have people here watching our backs. My man's over there." He gestured to a lanky man in a black suit standing next to the doors, watching them.

Val cocked her head at the boy. "Who are you, anyway? Are you all having your coming out party tonight?"

Joumala laughed. "It beats getting baptized. There's a lot less crying involved."

"Are you all...?" She left the question hanging, glancing meaning-fully at Zoe.

"They are all heirs to prominent family businesses," Zoe answered smoothly. "Importers and exporters. Construction. Financial services. All kinds of things. Just like my family."

That last bit confirmed Val's suspicions. These were the children of some of the city's most powerful crime families. People she'd prefer to stay well clear of. She silently cursed Vasilevski for getting her involved in this.

"Nice to meet you all. Now, if you'll excuse me, I've got a job to do." She inclined her head and backed off to a spot by the wall where she could keep an eye on them. She didn't want to talk to them any more than she had to. The last thing she needed was more criminals thinking they were her friends.

Zoe allowed her to retreat without protest. Apparently, she'd just wanted to show Val off like a prized pet. Show-and-tell accomplished, she was content to let her guardian drift back into the shadows.

Val scanned the balcony, noting the other bodyguards doing the same. Like her, they were all dressed in black suits. It seemed there was a strict dress code. White for the serving staff, black for the body-guards and security.

As she surveyed the patio, she saw stairs leading down one side. She casually drifted in that direction until she could see they were dark stone steps set into the hillside. They curled around and disappeared into the shadows beneath the patio. Presumably there was another level down there, which made sense. A house on a hill like this could have any number of basements carved out of the bedrock.

She was about to turn back to the party when a familiar face flick-ered in and out of a pool of light at the base of the stairs. There and gone so quickly, Val might have been imagining it.

But she wasn't imagining it, and her pulse quickened as she real-ized who it had been. Baron Blood.

She wasn't surprised to see him at the party—he'd been at the masquerade ball also—but what was he doing skulking around the lower level?

"*Maybe he's stealing snacks from the kitchen,*" Mister E supplied.

"Maybe. Or maybe he's up to something. Don't forget, we're looking for a necromancer. And anyone who calls themselves Baron Blood is at the top of my list of suspects."

She glanced back at the patio. Zoe and her friends were chatting away, oblivious. Did she dare leave her post?

Despite what Padraig had said, Val didn't believe Zoe was in any danger. She was at a private party, surrounded by friends. No one would try to harm her here.

If Zoe noticed Val was gone, she might kick up a stink to Vasilevski, though.

Whatever. When you compelled someone to do a job, you shouldn't be surprised when you got subpar service. Should anyone ask, she'd say she snuck off to smoke a joint or something.

With a final glance around to make sure no one was watching her, Val stepped off the patio and slipped down the stairs.

25

Half a dozen steps down, Val saw light spilling onto the hillside from an open door. Voices drifted on the cool breeze. She tensed and slowed her steps, listening.

"I need more hors d'oeuvres. They're like wild jackals up there."

"It'll be a minute. I can only roll these things so fast."

She relaxed. It sounded like the lower level was the kitchen.

A peek in the doorway when she reached the bottom of the stairs confirmed this. She stood at an intersection: The bustling sounds of a busy kitchen came from the hallway to her right, including the voices of the staff she'd heard. Tile floors and unadorned walls told her this level of the house was purely utilitarian. Ahead of her, the corridor ran in a straight line, passing several doors before it finally curled up into a spiral staircase. But where was Baron Blood?

The corridor to her left was unlit, but she saw a soft glow of light receding around a corner forty feet down. If the Baron was up to something, this direction seemed like her best bet.

"I need your eyes," she whispered as she slipped into the dark hallway.

"*Ask and you shall receive,*" Mister E replied.

It felt like someone had turned on a light as Val's golden eyes flared with the cat's night vision. She crept up and peered around the corner. Thirty feet away, a small light moved down the corridor. Baron Blood was clearly illuminated in the glow.

"Where is he going?" she muttered.

The corridor stretched into the darkness ahead of them. Her feline vision let her see quite a way beyond the small circle of light surrounding the Baron, and the corridor continued for at least another hundred feet without intersections or turns. She quietly followed the light. Soon they'd traversed that distance, and still the passage continued, unswerving.

"We have to be beyond the foundations of the house by now, right?"

"*Undoubtedly,*" Mister E assured her. "*We are now underneath Lafayette Park.*"

"What it is with this town and tunnels lately?"

"*All cities are crisscrossed with underground passageways. Sewers, utility corridors, older construction. I'd wager this is a servant's passage, built so the mansion's staff could travel to the other houses around the square without disturbing the wealthy owners lounging in the park. Judging by its cleanliness, this passage is still used regularly.*"

"The more I learn about class divisions, the more my mind is blown. I thought we left stuff like this behind last century. I had no idea people still lived like this."

"*That is because you are poor. And the poor never know what they are missing.*" Mister E chuckled. "*The rich are careful to keep it that way. People might become upset if they discovered how the other half lives.*"

"You've got that right." Val thought of all the girls at the Alley Cat, dancing for dollars, struggling to keep food in their mouths and a roof over their heads. Upset would be an understatement.

"*What about you?*" Mister E asked, his sly Cheshire Cat grin drifting up the wall. "*Aren't you upset?*"

"Now that you mention it, yes, I am. Those silver-spoon kids upstairs have no idea what real life is like. The whole world is a playroom to them. They think they can buy and sell anyone and anything."

"*Can't they? Isn't that why you're here tonight?*"

Val scowled. "I suppose it is, isn't it?"

The corridor finally started intersecting with others. A few had lights running along them, but most of the corridors they passed were as dark as the one they followed.

"Other mansions?" Val guessed.

"Your powers of deduction are astounding, Sherlock."

After some time, Baron Blood turned down one of these passages. Val stopped at the intersection, frowning at the walls.

"Is something the matter?"

"Just wishing I had something to mark the wall with so I can find my way back. Where's Malcolm's magic backpack when you need it?"

"I've always found that blood works well."

"Very funny."

"Do I sound like I'm joking?"

Val made a face, but realized the idea wasn't without merit. She certainly didn't have anything else to mark the wall.

"Fine."

Drawing her knife, she pricked a finger and squeezed it so the blood welled up. She used the blood to smear a small arrow on the wall.

Closing her eyes, she reached out with her power, just to be sure. Sure enough, the little smear of blood on the wall called to her like a magnet.

She brightened. "Great. That's one less thing I have to worry about."

The Baron's circle of light was now pretty far ahead of her, and she hurried to close the distance. She followed him through a couple more intersections, stopping to make blood arrows each time.

"I'm going to have to start carrying antiseptic and Band-Aids around with me."

Mister E rolled his eyes. Which in his case meant that his entire disembodied floating face rolled over in midair. For a being thousands of years old, he could be rather melodramatic.

"Modern humans are so prissy," he said.

"I mean, it would be pretty embarrassing to die of a staph infection, wouldn't it?"

"Your fear of tiny things you cannot see is ridiculous."

"You're afraid of invisible magical forces. How is that different?"

The cat bared his teeth. *"First of all, I am not afraid of anything. Second, magical forces are a million times stronger than bacteria. If you get an infection, you simply use your magic to burn it out of your blood."*

"I can do that?"

"Sometimes I don't know why I bother. If you'd let me instruct you, you would know these things." Mister E disappeared with a disgusted pop.

Val considered the empty spot where he'd been. She didn't like it, but he had a point. Maybe the time had come for her to allow Mister E to teach her. She'd let him show her some basic things as a child, of course. Otherwise, her power would have overwhelmed her completely. But at the time, she'd been too young to grasp anything more than the most basic concepts, and as she'd gotten older, she'd grown afraid of her power, and shied away from learning real magic.

Paula had showed her a few rituals during her time living at the Emerald City in New York, but that felt different. Ritual magic didn't really tap into the primal power of Mister E. It felt academic. Safer.

Her fingers strayed over her memento mori tattoos. Since day one, her power had caused death and destruction. Because of that, she'd tried to use as little of it as possible, and had resisted Mister E's advanced instruction. Letting him teach her would be admitting that he was an integral part of her life, and that his presence inside her might actually be a good thing. Which would in turn be a kind of tacit acceptance of all the deaths her power had caused.

She shook her head emphatically. No. Those deaths had not been acceptable. Every single one of them could have been avoided. The world would be better off if she'd never found Mister E. Never made the deal that released him from his cage.

For starters, her mother would still be alive.

"What about Stephen? What about Ruby and all the other innocents murdered by monsters?" Mister E whispered. *"Without your power, how could you have avenged them? With proper instruction, you may have even prevented some of their deaths. Blunt force power can only destroy. Well controlled power can protect as well."*

Val cursed. She hated it when Mister E seemed to read her mind. She hated it even more when he made sense.

"I'll think about it," she growled, ending the conversation.

And she would. But right now, she had more pressing things to focus on.

26

V al slowed as she neared the end of the corridor. The room ahead was bright, with light spilling across the floor. She could hear Baron Blood's voice, but other voices as well. The Baron was not alone.

She stopped just beyond the edge of the light and leaned back into the shadows. She could see one point of a pentagram on the floor, inside a painted circle. Both the pentagram and circle looked old, but as she watched the Baron moved around the room, painting over the lines with a fresh coat of something that glistened red. Given his name, Val didn't have to stretch her imagination very far to guess what the substance was.

The Baron lit a few candles and slipped a large gold ring on his middle finger before his voice started to rise and fall in a musical chant. The words were in a language Val didn't recognize, but the hair prickling on her arms told her clearly enough that he was working magic. She couldn't see any more than the edge of the circle from her place in the shadows. If she wanted to see what he was doing, she'd have to risk moving up into the light.

She took a deep breath, weighing the odds. If the Baron was in the middle of some kind of ritual, all his attention should be on the magic.

As long as she didn't make noise or do something to call attention to herself, she could get a better view without being noticed.

Val crept forward, placing one careful foot in front of the other, her body pressed against the cold stone of the corridor wall. The room revealed itself inch by inch, little slices of vision serving themselves up with every step. When the center of the pentagram came into view, she stopped, breath catching in her throat. A naked man was chained to the floor, limbs splayed out. His skin was very pale and his eyes were closed. For a moment, Val feared he was dead, but the slight rise and fall of his chest revealed his slow breathing.

She hovered there, frozen, trying to figure out what was going on. The man didn't appear to be in any pain—not yet, anyway—but the chains told her he probably wasn't there by choice. She could only see about half the room, and the Baron's voice came from the half she couldn't see. The man on the floor was older, perhaps in his sixties, but he seemed to be in good physical shape. His silver hair was neatly parted and combed. She couldn't spot any bruising or signs of violence on his skin.

The tone of the Baron's voice changed, the syllables becoming staccato and harsh. The man chained to the floor tensed, pulling against the chains, his mouth opening in a voiceless scream.

That was enough for Val. Her hands clenched into fists as she prepared to charge into the room and put a stop to the ritual.

"*Wait,*" Mister E hissed. "*Look before you leap.*"

Her vision shifted, and once again she was looking through the cat's eyes. In addition to seeing better in the dark, Mister E's eyes also saw other things that her eyes could not. Chief among these was magic.

The room before her was full of power, colorful clouds of it flowing like coastal fog on the wind.

"Yes, he's doing magic," Val snapped. "I already knew that."

"*Look at the direction of it, foolish child,*" Mister E admonished.

Val paused, studying the eddies and flows. The room was full of magic, swirling in a great whirlwind, following the outline of the circle, stirred by Baron Blood's chant. At first, she didn't understand what Mister E was talking about. Then she saw it. The magical energy wasn't being pulled out of the chained man, as she'd assumed. Instead, she watched a thin tendril of magic branch out of the swirling energy and flow down into the man's chest.

As it touched him, his back arched, every muscle so tense he was practically vibrating. His lips pulled back from his teeth, turning his face into a rictus mask.

What was it doing to him? Turning him into some kind of monster?

Val couldn't tell, and she wasn't going to wait around to find out.

She stepped boldly into the room. "Baron... Blood?"

The words faltered on her lips as the rest of the room came into view. The Baron stood chanting atop a pedestal, conducting the ritual magic like a maestro. The skull ring on his finger shone a deep sunset red.

He wasn't alone. On cushioned chairs behind him sat a dozen elderly men and women who reeked of money. With their perfectly coiffed silver hair, tuxedos, and sheer gowns, they looked for all the world like an audience at the opera. If you ignored the fact that they were all wearing what looked like cheap 3-D glasses.

Val stared at them. They stared back.

Baron Blood didn't stop his chant—he couldn't, or the spell would dissolve—but he did shoot Val a glare. He was definitely not happy to see her.

"What the hell is going on here?" Val wondered.

It was a gaunt woman all in black who answered her. She had a shaved head and wore an elaborate gold neckpiece, with delicate chains draping down over her collarbones. It looked heavy and cere-monial—like something you'd expect to see at a Mayan temple. The woman crossed the room in three quick strides, looking down her nose at Val.

"Ms. Keri, you are late. Please sit down and stop interrupting the demonstration."

"Demonstration?"

"Please, sit." The woman took Val by the elbow and began steering her towards an empty seat.

Val tried to jerk her arm away. "What are you doing to that man?"

"It is a very delicate ritual, and the man has paid a lot of money for it." The woman hissed, tightening her grip, her fingernails sinking into the flesh of Val's bicep. "Sit down and we will explain everything after the ritual is complete."

As the woman pulled her towards the seats, Val was thinking furiously. Judging by the audience, what the woman said was probably true.

But what were they doing to him? And was it something she should be putting a stop to?

She examined the elderly faces behind the ridiculous 3-D glasses. She was surprised to realize that she recognized some of them. The lady in the blue gown was Mrs. Paulson: a wealthy widow, well known as a philanthropist around town. The frail man behind her was John Eggers, a publishing tycoon.

As Val took her seat, the audience's attention returned to the ritual. All these wealthy people were clearly here by choice. But why?

She focused on the man in the circle, the energy flowing around him. As she watched, his skin grew smooth and firm. His hair began to darken, the silver becoming a rich mahogany.

"The ritual is making him younger," Val gasped.

"Yes, but where is the energy coming from?" Mister E wondered.

An excellent question. Magic didn't create energy, it just transferred it from one thing to another, usually transforming it in the process. If Baron Blood's ritual was giving this man new life energy, it had to be coming from somewhere else.

Val studied the fog of energy swirling around the circle. The colorful mist was thick, nearly filling the room. She couldn't tell where it was coming from. It seemed to be rising straight out of the circle itself.

Was it the blood? Had the Baron created a conduit between the circle and someone else using their blood? If so, for every year of life energy the man in the circle was gaining, there would be someone else on the other end of the link losing the same. This unseen person would be aging, skin sprouting wrinkles, hair falling.

No, wait. There it was.

A thin tendril of power curled down from the ceiling like smoke. It was sucked into the vortex, but it continued to trickle down, slowly and steadily. It matched the flow of power moving into the man in the circle. There was also a flight of stone steps running up the wall to her left, and a rusty metal door at the top.

"Up there," Val muttered. "What's above us?"

To her surprise, Mrs. Paulson answered from the chair next to her. "It's the Queen Anne Hotel, dear. A grand piece of San Francisco history."

"The Queen Anne Hotel? A hotel full of people?" Val's eyes almost popped out of her skull as she stared at the tendril of power winding its way down from the ceiling. Was Baron Blood sucking life from people inside the hotel?

She gasped as the realization hit her. Was this how Stephen had died?

Val snarled and sprang from her seat, eyes glowing like hot coals as power roared through her. Her words thundered across the room, shaking dust from the ancient walls.

"This ritual is over!"

She stepped forward and broke the circle with the sole of her boot. The night exploded.

27

To say that all hell broke loose would be an understatement.

Released from the confines of the circle, the energy gathered by the ritual burst outward in a wave, throwing everyone back. The spectators were knocked sprawling, and Baron Blood flew from his pedestal and slammed into the wall. Val had braced for it, but even she was buffeted off her feet. She slid across the floor, the winds of power pushing her like a sailboat in a winter storm.

Then, as quickly as it started, it was over.

Val lay on the floor, ears ringing in the silent aftermath. The elderly spectators moaned and cursed, tangled together like seaweed left by the tide. She hoped none of them were seriously hurt, but there might be a few broken bones due to their age.

It couldn't be helped. If Baron Blood was killing people in the Queen Anne, he had to be stopped.

She stood and turned to face the necromancer, who was struggling to his feet. He strode toward her, shouting, "What have you done? How dare you..."

"How dare I?" Val interrupted. "How dare you! You are siphoning life from people in the Queen Anne. My friend died due to your magic!"

Baron Blood's face crinkled in confusion. "No, I'm only...."

Val got up in his face, shoving him back. "Don't give me that bull-shit. The only way you can give life is to take it from somewhere else. You were sucking life energy down through the ceiling. I know what I saw."

The blood mage raised his hands, palms out, thick skull ring glinting just below his knuckle. The rubies in the eye sockets of the skull shone.

Baron Blood lowered his voice. "There has been a misunder-standing here. I'm not killing anyone. Let me show you."

Val bit back hot words. The necromancer seemed sincere.

"Fine. Show me. But make it fast."

"Thank you. Follow me." He gave her a nervous smile, his gold incisor flashing, then turned and led her up the stairs. He called out to the rest of the room. "My apologies. Ms. Keri thought something shady was happening, and she got carried away. It's all a big misunderstand-ing. I'm going to clear things up with her. Marla, please see to our guests. I'll be right back."

His assistant started untangling the audience while Baron Blood pulled an antique key from his breast pocket and unlocked the metal door at the top of the stairs. He wore a long black coat with a gold-embroidered silk vest underneath. Black pants and a top hat completed his ensemble, and he leaned on a polished mahogany cane with an onyx handle. Dust smudged his coat, and there was a small rip in the fabric where he'd fallen against the wall.

Val refused to feel bad about that. Until she saw something that proved otherwise, he was a murderer in her book. She balled her fists, sinking her nails into her palms. She was thrumming with power, ready to lash out at any moment. She wouldn't be caught unaware if this was some kind of trap.

"This way, Ms. Keri." He held the door open, gesturing her through. She noticed the skull ring was now missing, tucked away in one of his many pockets. That told her the ring was a specific-use item, and not something the mage wanted to keep active at all times. It must have something to do with the ritual.

She followed him up another flight of stairs and out into a carpeted hallway. Dusty trolleys and folding tables were stacked against the walls: They were in the basement level of the Queen Anne.

She followed him the length of the corridor, then down another flight of stairs.

"Flying toads. How many basements does this place have?" she muttered.

"More than you'd expect." She hadn't intended for him to hear, but the Baron answered her anyway. "They used to hide gold down here during the rush."

"That tracks," Val said. "Those forty-niners were like squirrels, stashing their nuggets in every hole they could find. And digging new holes when they couldn't find any that were empty. The whole city is riddled with secret basements and tunnels. A lot of them collapsed during the earthquakes over the years, so who knows how many undiscovered stashes are still lurking underground."

"You know your history. I'm impressed." The Baron gave her a sharp, assessing look.

Val shrugged. "Not really. But my housemate loves this stuff. He's always spouting random historical factoids. I forget most of it as soon as he tells me, but occasionally something sticks in my thick head."

"I'm sure." The Baron's tone told Val he didn't believe her, but he wasn't going to challenge her either.

She scowled but didn't push it. Frankly, she didn't care what he believed. She was here to figure out what the hell he was doing with that ritual. Everything else was wasted chatter.

The hall ended at a wooden armoire with an ornate design carved into the doors. It looked like a reproduction of Rodin's sculpture, The Gates of Hell, full of demons and people in torment.

Val shuddered. "Cheerful subject matter for a creepy basement."

Baron Blood smiled. "This is only art, Valora Keri. I'm sure you've encountered much worse than this."

"That doesn't mean I like to be reminded of it. I prefer my art full of sunshine and kittens. There are too many shadows in the world as it is."

The Baron chuckled and twisted some part of the sculpture, hiding his hands so she couldn't see what he was doing. There was a metallic click, and the front of the armoire pivoted open, exposing a dark crevice in the earth. The blood mage muttered a few words and the handle of his cane gained a pale light. He held it aloft as he stepped through the opening. "Watch your step."

Val wasn't sure if the crevice was manmade or natural, but it was definitely old. The walls were dark grey stone, striated with ribbons of burgundy and white. Gravel crunched underfoot.

A gigantic spider web loomed up to one side, and she shuddered and ducked away. She tried not to imagine the spider that lived in it, but of course her mind did just that, serving up a vision of a hairy-legged monster as big as her head.

Val moved a little more quickly. Spiders. Just perfect.

"Where are you taking me?"

"You wanted to see where I was drawing energy from. This is it."

The Baron stepped out into a small cave, lifting his cane high. The cave was a dozen paces across, with a ceiling that was equally high. On the far side of the cave, a pair of dark crevices led further into the darkness.

Several pairs of shackles were fastened to the wall, the heavy chain links thick with rust. They looked like they might have been down here for a hundred years. Three gaunt, pale people were chained to the wall. They sagged against their shackles and didn't look up at the newcomers.

No, not people.

"Vampires," Mister E hissed.

Val took a step back. "You're pulling life energy from them?"

Baron Blood was experimenting on vampires. Hillary was right.

"Who better? You wouldn't believe how much power they have in them."

"But life energy? Aren't they dead?"

"Undead," he corrected. "Not fully dead, not quite alive. Somewhere in between. It takes a lot of power to maintain that state. And if you can tap that power, turn it toward your own ends..." He raised his eyebrows, leaving the rest to her imagination.

Val swallowed. Her imagination took her to a very dark place.

28

V al's mind had no problem filling in the blanks. These vampires' whole existence was magical. If you could tap into their power, they would be like magical batteries.

"This has to be torture for them."

Baron Blood actually laughed, his warm baritone filling the space.

"Torture? They are vampires, Valora Keri. Do you think any of them would hesitate to tear out your throat?"

One of the starving creatures caught her eye. It bared its fangs and hissed, its dark eyes pits of pain and need. Val shuddered. The mage had a point. These creatures had been driven mad with hunger. If any of them got free, they would kill her in a heartbeat.

"But... it's still wrong," Val said weakly. She knew she should have a better argument, yet the Baron had a point. They were monsters. Killing machines. Would Val shed a tear if she saw any of them burned to dust by the light of the sun?

Sensing her internal conflict, the necromancer said, "Their very existence is a curse. Vampires are a blight on humanity. Isn't it poetic justice? That one of humanity's most deadly predators should be our salvation instead? Vampires live for centuries. Now, so can we."

Val thought of Hillary. She remembered the terror in the young woman's eyes as she told Val her story.

"They might be killing machines, but they're still sentient beings. They still feel pain. Killing them quickly is one thing, but this is monstrous. I can't let you do this."

The Baron looked sad. "I'm sorry you feel that way, Valora Keri. I had hoped we might be friends."

Before Val could reply, a new voice rang out from one of the dark crevices opposite.

"I could have told you she would never play along. Ms. Keri has entirely too high an opinion of her own moral compass."

Melinda Pearl stepped into the light, her dark eyes glinting. Dressed up for the party, she looked out of place in the rough cavern. Val wondered how she didn't twist an ankle on the uneven floor in those heels.

"Ms. Pearl. I wish I could say I'm surprised to see you." Val took another step back, her fingertips tingling as she gathered power.

Melinda Pearl was by far the strongest vampire in the city. There was no way Val could take her in a fair fight.

The last time she'd faced the vampire queen, she'd gotten lucky. They'd been flying over the bay and Val had been able to fend off Pearl while she was in the form of a giant bat. She hadn't known it at the time, but she'd later learned that when a vampire changed shape, it severely limited their power. If Pearl had been in her natural form, Val wouldn't have stood a chance.

And now the vampire queen was allied with a blood mage. If they wanted a fight, Val was in deep trouble.

"What do you want from me?" she asked.

Baron Blood spread his palms wide. "I don't want anything from you. I only want you to leave my business alone. The Fountain of Youth is one of mankind's most cherished myths for a reason. No one wants to die. I may not have found the fountain, but I've found something almost as good. As you can see, my business is not hurting anyone."

"No one except the vampires."

He shrugged. They'd already covered this ground.

She turned her attention to Melinda Pearl.

"What about you? Why let him drain your children like this? What do you get out of this arrangement?"

The vampire queen regarded her coldly.

"What I get out of it is none of your concern, Ms. Keri. Neither is what I do with my children." She took a gliding step forward. Val took a step back. "Speaking of my children, you have stolen one of them from me. You will give her back."

"I didn't steal anything. When people ask me for help, I help them. That's all."

"Hillary is not free to make such choices. She is a child, and I am her parent. You will tell me where she is."

"I can't do that."

The vampire's eyes were chips of ice. "Can't? Or won't?"

"They're the same thing." Every muscle was tense, her fingernails digging into the palms of her hands. She might not be able to win this showdown, but if Pearl wanted to push it, Val would make sure the vampire queen knew she'd been in a fight.

Strong hands seized her upper arms. Something sharp pressed against her neck. Val froze, hardly daring to breathe. She moved her eyes to the side just enough to see bony white hands holding her in place. One of Pearl's minions had crept up on her from behind. The vampire's fangs pressed against the soft flesh of her neck. A touch more pressure and they'd break the skin.

Val couldn't suppress her shudder. Getting bitten by a vampire was one of her oldest fears.

"You will return my child to me, Ms. Keri. Or I will make you into one of my children and compel your obedience. Decide." Pearl's voice was as flat and cold as her eyes.

Desperate options ran through Val's mind. Could she blast the vampire holding her before it had a chance to bite her? Unlikely. Vampires were faster than humans, and this one's fangs were only a hair away from breaking the skin. The instant it felt her magic, it would bite.

Could she push it away once it had bitten her? Again, unlikely. Vampire saliva was a powerful sedative. If the fangs broke the surface, she'd be a ragdoll in seconds. Even if she did manage to push it away, the damage would be done.

Still, she had to try.

Whenever she ran out of options, Val always chose the thing that would give her the most satisfaction, even if it wasn't necessarily the winning play. And blasting vampires would be very satisfying. She took a slow breath, trying not to let it show as she gathered her power for one big release. If she could replicate the explosion that had ripped through the ritual room when she'd broken Baron Blood's circle, maybe she'd have a chance. One big boom to blow everyone off their feet and give her a few seconds head start. The vampires would still probably catch her, but at least she'd go down swinging.

Val sucked in power, careful to give no outward sign, swelling with it until her skin felt full to bursting. She set her jaw and clenched her fists. This was it. She prepared to let it all go.

Zoe's voice rang out behind her.

"Did anyone ever tell you that you're a really bad bodyguard, Val?" The sound of guns cocking filled the cave.

Her captor wrenched Val around to face the newcomers.

Zoe and her three friends stood in the entrance, guns leveled. Zoe's tiny hands held a gun almost as big as she was. Joumala, Shen, and Padraig looked as comfortable cradling submachine guns as they had holding cocktail glasses. At the party, they'd seemed like carefree, rich teenagers. Now, they looked like what they were: the heirs to some of the most powerful crime families in the city.

Zoe Vasilevski leveled her gun at Melinda Pearl.

"Val Keri is working for me. Let her go."

29

F or several seconds, nobody moved.

Then Melinda Pearl laughed.

"You are making a mistake, children. Walk away and I'll forget this ever happened."

Zoe's doll-like face could have been carved from porcelain.

"I don't think so. Release Val and we'll let you live."

The two women locked eyes, the tension so thick between them you could cut it with a chainsaw.

"*Oh, this is getting good,*" Mister E purred. He floated above the action, blowing smoke rings with his candy cigarette. "*Where's the popcorn when you need it?*"

Val ignored him, her eyes flicking back and forth between the two antagonists. A second ago, this had been her play. Now she found herself little more than a shiny prize the contestants were vying to win.

"Don't try it, vampire," Padraig said suddenly. "You know I'm as fast as you are, and these bullets are even faster."

Val raised an eyebrow at that. Padraig was as fast as a vampire? If that was true, Padraig must be more than human. That was definitely something she'd need to look into further.

Assuming she made it out of this cave alive, that is. Despite the standoff, the vampire holding her still had fangs pressed to Val's throat.

Pearl sneered. "Bullets. You know bullets won't stop me."

"No," Padraig acknowledged, "but a hole in your face can be damned inconvenient. And why would you assume these are regular bullets?"

"They still won't kill me," the vampire queen spat. "And is that a war you really want to start? I can make things very difficult for your business interests."

"Which is why you're going to give us Val and we'll all stay friends," Zoe said in a reasonable tone. The barrel of her enormous gun looked a lot less reasonable than her words.

"Also, your associate doesn't look as bulletproof as you are," Joumala added, centering Baron Blood between the crosshairs of her own gun. "Is he an acceptable casualty?"

The Baron raised his hands, sweat beading on his high forehead.

"Let's just slow down now," he said. "Nobody has to get hurt."

"Nobody else, you mean," Val corrected. She glanced meaningfully at the chained vampires. "They've already gotten hurt."

Zoe's forehead wrinkled. "I feel like I've missed something. Are those vampires friends of yours, Val?"

"No. But even vampires don't deserve to be tortured."

"Okaaaay. I've definitely missed something. Do we need to rescue them, too?"

Pearl narrowed her eyes. "Do not overstep, little girl. What happens within my family is none of your concern."

"Val?" Zoe quirked an eyebrow, waiting.

Val considered the question. She did want to free the vampires, and Pearl was already pissed off at her, so making the queen mad wasn't a concern. She studied the emaciated creatures straining at their chains. Their eyes were empty of all thought, their consciousness submerged beneath their primal hunger. There would be no controlling them if they were set free. No reasoning with them. The vampires would be after them like rabid hounds.

Val sighed. "No, we can't. They're starving and they'll attack us as soon as we take the shackles off. There's no way to reach them in that state."

"Makes sense." Zoe nodded and shifted her attention back to Pearl. "We'll just be taking Val then."

The vampire queen and the Russian doll locked eyes, the air crackling between them. Behind Pearl, Val could see the whites of Baron Blood's eyes.

"Let's all take it easy," the Baron said, holding up his hands, palms out. "They can take Val Keri, and in exchange, Val Keri will promise to stay out of our business. Everybody can win."

Pearl's eyes flicked toward him, then back to Val.

"That would be peachy. And part of staying out of our business would be giving me back my child. But we all know Ms. Keri is too much of a do-gooder to make that promise. Isn't that right, Val?"

Val licked her lips. She could end this right now. Everyone could walk away in one piece. All she had to do was allow Pearl and the Baron to continue with their unholy business. And betray Hillary's trust.

She sighed. "You know I can't do that, Pearl."

The vampire queen's smile didn't reach her eyes. "Proving once again that you are a fool."

Many things happened at once, almost too fast for Val to follow.

Pearl shot toward the wall, and Padraig fired, followed a moment later by Zoe, Joumala, and Shen. It was impossible to tell if any of the bullets hit the vampire queen, but if they did, they didn't slow her down at all.

Baron Blood lifted his cane in front of him and began to chant. A translucent red shield shimmered in the air before him, centered on the tip of the cane.

The fangs of the vampire holding Val punctured the skin of her neck. She released the power she'd been holding, sending the creature tumbling across the room. She staggered back, putting her fingers to her neck. They came away red. She cursed and summoned more power, hoping the fangs hadn't had time to deliver their sedative.

Pearl reached the shackled vampires. With her bare hands, she snapped the chains holding the starving vampires to the wall. The trio of hunger-crazed monsters immediately charged the humans.

Shen was closest to the wall, and he calmly put six shots into the first of the freed vampires. The thing didn't even break stride before barreling into him, taking the boy to the ground.

Val chopped her arm sharply across her body. A low wave of energy scythed across the cave, catching the other two vampires charging at them just below the knees. The razor edge of power met flesh and bone and parted it easily. Both vampires went down, their legs cut neatly in two.

"Not bad," Mister E commented.

Val gaped. "That's not what I meant to do. I didn't even know I could do that. I was trying to knock them off their feet."

"Well, in that case, mission accomplished. Quite literally. You could use more finesse, though." He flicked his golden eyes toward Joumala.

She followed his glance and was horrified to see the girl lying on the ground, clutching one bleeding leg. Val put a hand to her mouth.

"Shit, I only meant to hit the vampires."

"And this is why you need to let me teach you. I know you have a thick skull, but this is getting ridiculous, don't you think?"

Val bit back a hot reply. She didn't like it, but he was right. If she was inadvertently hurting her allies, she needed to work on her control.

"Fine. Let's get out of this alive first, then we can talk about it."

She felt Mister E's satisfied smile as she turned...

... and the walls of the cave went soft around her. The sounds of battle receded into the distance.

She shook her head to clear it and found herself sitting on the rocky floor.

"Toad spit," she slurred. "The vampire's fangs..."

The world slid away into darkness.

30

S ilk sheets slid beneath her fingertips, cool and smooth to the touch. Val pressed her face into the pillowcase, relishing the softness against her cheek. Curled against her side, she could feel a cat purring. She sighed. She'd been having a delicious dream. Something about a vampire...

Val jerked awake. She was lying beneath a cream-colored canopy in an enormous bed. A down comforter was snugged up beneath her chin and soft light filtered through the stained-glass lamp on the bedside table, painting the canopy with little blobs of color. The sheets smelled like vanilla fabric softener. A calico cat blinked up at her, annoyed at her movement. The cat sneezed her disapproval.

How had she gotten here? And where was here? The last thing she remembered, they'd been fighting off those vampires...

A musical voice interrupted her thoughts: "Decided to rejoin the living, have ye?"

She turned her head to find Padraig sitting in a chair beside the bed, a thick hardback book open on his lap.

"Padraig?"

"Last time I checked," he replied, his face relaxing into a smile.

Though he didn't look any older than she was, little smile lines crinkled the corners of his mouth and eyes, telling her he smiled often. His hazel eyes sparkled with secret laughter. Without meaning to, Val found herself smiling back.

"What are you doing here?"

"Just brushing up on my fairy tales," he said, lifting the book so she could see the title on the cover: *Forgotten Tales of Faerie*.

"No, I mean, what am I doing here? Where is here? How did I get here?"

Padraig laughed, a sound as pure as morning bells at sunrise. Val noticed that he had beautifully curved lips, and her eyes followed his jawline up to his soft russet curls. Her half-asleep mind wondered what those curls would feel like slipping between her fingers.

Her face grew warm at the direction of her thoughts, and she fought the urge to dive back beneath the covers.

"Slow down, that's a lot of questions. Give me a chance to answer before you swamp me with new ones," Padraig said, seeming oblivious to her discomfort. "What you are doing here is sleeping off that vampire bite you got. Those fangs put you on your ass faster than a bottle of whiskey and four pints of stout. As to where we are, we're on the upper floor of the manse, in one of the guest bedrooms."

"This is a guest bedroom? What kind of guests are they expecting? Royalty?"

Padraig laughed again. "In the old days, yes. Plenty of royalty hung their hats here. These days, you're the most royal thing I've seen inside these walls in a long time."

Val's blush deepened, then his words hit her.

"Wait. Is this your mansion?"

"Well, it technically belongs to my Da, but he doesn't stay here much. Mostly it's just me and the cats." As if aware it was being discussed, the calico butted her head under his hand. Padraig smiled and scratched her behind the ears.

Val tried to digest this information. She'd known Padraig was one of Zoe's friends, and the heir to some criminal enterprise. But if his family owned this mansion, and presumably others like it... she revised her estimation of the size of their operation several orders of magnitude upward.

"What exactly does your family do?" she asked carefully.

"Antiques, mostly," he answered without missing a beat. "There are still plenty of people around who pay good money for really old stuff."

Val raised a dubious eyebrow.

"Antiques? All of this is from antiques?"

"Well, mostly. I mean, ye've got to diversify in this day and age. We dabble in other things as well. But mostly antiques."

"And are these antiques legal?"

He laughed again. "Anything's legal if you can get away with it."

"I'll take that as a no."

"Let's just say there's a lot of gray area. I mean, who can really say they own something that's been buried in the ground for thousands of years?"

Val acknowledged the point with a nod. Then her eyes widened.

"Have you sold a ring lately? A gold skull with rubies for eyes?"

Padraig shot her a sideways look. "That's oddly specific."

"Baron Blood was wearing a ring like that. It seemed like it might be important."

He pursed his lips. "Can't say that it rings any bells. But that doesn't mean we didn't help move it. I can ask around, if you like."

"That would be great, thank you."

He sat back in his chair, steepling his fingers in front of his lips.

"What's the origin of the ring? More details would be helpful."

"I don't know, I only saw it in passing. It was pretty striking though. You'd remember it if you saw it. I can draw a picture of it for you."

"That would be grand." He fished around in the bedside table drawer, coming up with a pad of paper and a gold pen.

Val read the name embossed on both, her tongue tripping over the unfamiliar name. "O' Ceallaigh Importers."

He laughed. "It's pronounced 'Kelly'. They used a lot of extra letters back in the day."

"Ah, right. O'Kelly."

She put pen to paper and drew a quick sketch of the ring she'd seen on Baron Blood's finger, then handed the pad back to Padraig.

He whistled. "That's a good sketch. You've got some artistic talent in there."

Val shrugged. "Product of a lonely childhood. I spent a lot of time amusing myself. Drawing was a good way to escape."

He bent his head over the paper, examining the ring. "That's a very distinctive piece. I'd definitely remember it if I'd seen it. But the sketch will come in handy. I'll ask around, see if anyone knows anything about it."

"Thank you." She cocked her head, narrowing her eyes suspiciously. "Why are you helping me?"

"When a beautiful woman makes a request in the bedroom, I always aim to please."

Val snorted, though her face felt like it was on fire. "Funny. I'm serious. You hardly know me."

"Is chivalry so dead that a man can't help a woman out of the goodness of his heart?"

She fixed him with a flat stare. "Yes, it is. What's in it for you?"

"You wound me, madam." He put his hand over his heart, gasping in mock outrage. Then he got a wicked gleam in his eye and wiggled his eyebrows. "Maybe I'm just trying to get into your good graces."

Val kept her expression stony, ignoring the fact that her face must look like a tomato. What was it about Padraig that put her so off balance? She worked in a strip club, for fuck's sake. People propositioned her every day of her life. She did her best to imagine he was a customer at the bar.

"If by 'good graces' you mean my pants, let me save you a lot of trouble and tell you right now that's never going to happen."

He didn't miss a beat. "Consider it a favor, then. Favors performed for favors owed."

Something in his words sounded alarm bells in Val's head. Favors could be dangerous in the magical world.

Padraig's words from the showdown with the vampires surfaced in her mind. Hadn't he said something about being as fast as Melinda Pearl?

Apparently, Mister E agreed because he appeared on the bed beside her, curled in the warm spot recently vacated by the calico. *"I don't trust this one. He's more than he seems. Be careful."*

The calico's eyes locked onto him. Her fur puffed up and she hissed.

Val was astonished. Could the cat actually see Mister E?

Padraig ran his fingers lightly over the calico's back.

"What's got ye worked up there?" He followed her gaze, narrowing his eyes as if he was trying to make out something in the distance.

Val held her breath. If Padraig could see Mister E, that would confirm her suspicions about him.

But after a few seconds, he chuckled and shrugged, turning his smile back to her. "Cats. Always jumping at ghosts."

"You said something last night about being just as fast as the vampires." She said carefully. "What did you mean by that?"

He looked sheepish. "You remember that, do you?"

"It's a pretty bold statement. Kind of hard to forget."

"Fair point." He scratched the back of the cat for a moment, his face pensive. He sighed. "I don't mean to offend you, but I don't think I know you well enough to be sharing all my secrets just yet. My apologies."

"I understand. We all have secrets."

"I appreciate your understanding." He tilted his head at her, a gleam lighting his eyes. "Perhaps if we got to know each other a little better first. What would you say to dinner, Ms. Keri?"

Val looked away, her flush deepening.

"I don't know if that's appropriate."

"Appropriate? What are these, the Middle Ages? It's just dinner. You don't have to be accompanied by a chaperone." He was laughing again.

Val scowled in return. She had enough criminals in her life already with the Vasilevskis. She didn't need to add the Irish-whatever to the list.

"You may be accustomed to getting everything you want, but I can assure you that I am not for sale. I'm not your friend and I don't want to be."

She threw back the covers and swung her legs out of bed, intending to storm out. It was only then that she realized that her feet were bare and she was wearing a pale yellow silk nightshirt that barely reached her knees.

She ground her teeth over a fresh wave of embarrassment.

"Where are my clothes?"

"They're hanging in the closet." Padraig pointed across the room. "I had the maid wash them for you. I hope you don't mind."

His smirk told her he was waiting for her to ask who had taken her clothes off and put her to bed. She refused to give him the satisfaction.

"Thank you. Now if you'll excuse me, I'd like to get dressed and get out of your hair."

"Of course." Padraig rose and smoothly crossed the room, the purring calico cradled in his arms. He turned at the door, eyes sparkling with suppressed laughter. "I'll see you around, Valora Keri."

With a wink and a smile, he stepped through the door and was gone.

31

P adraig's driver took her home. The old Victorian houses looked insubstantial and haunted in the early morning fog, like faded images from a daguerreotype. She couldn't believe she'd spent the whole night in the O' Ceallaigh mansion. That vampire venom had really knocked her for a loop. Padraig had mentioned that Zoe was disappointed in her bodyguard services, and that she'd expect Val to make it up to her in the future.

"Wonderful." Val sighed. "Just what I need, more favors owed to the Vasilevskis."

As they drove past the Queen Anne, Val eyed the old hotel. Baron Blood's rituals were one possible explanation for Stephen's death, but the Baron seemed certain he was only draining energy from the vampires chained up in the basement. Which meant the real cause of Stephen's death was still unknown.

Perhaps there was something about the hotel itself? Old San Francisco buildings always had secrets, and the Queen Anne had been rumored to be haunted forever. Maybe it was time to go digging.

Malcolm was awake when she got home and readily agreed to help her look into the Queen Anne's history. After a quick shower and change of clothes, they grabbed a pair of lattes from Zombie Coffee and headed out.

The barista gave Val another frowny face on her foam.

"What's that about?" Malcom asked.

She grimaced. "Sandra."

"Ah. Well, you kind of deserve that."

"Don't start."

"I'm just saying, you can be hard on people. If roommates were pants, all of yours would have holes in the knees."

"What about you?"

"I'm more the kind who gets holes in the ass."

Val snorted.

"If I'm such a bitch, why are you still around?"

"Because I'm the alpha queen bitch. I see your bitchiness and raise you a capital B. Rawr." He made finger claws at her, then his expression turned serious. "We do need to find a new roommate though. Again."

"I know." Val sighed. "I'll deal with it when I can. There are quite a few things on my list more important than that right now."

"Well, just so you know, Sandra's room is empty."

"Already?"

"She moved in with her girlfriend. Just boxed up all her stuff and disappeared. Poof. I think you set a new record for the shortest time anyone has lived with us."

Val grimaced. "I'm sorry. She caught me at the wrong time and I just snapped. I intended to apologize, but..." She waggled her fingers vaguely at the city. "You know. Everything."

"If that doesn't perfectly capture life, I don't know what does." Malcolm raised his latte in a toast. "Here's to best intentions and... everything."

"I'll drink to that."

The Library sat on a small hill overlooking the Market Street chasm. The columned building, known as the Granite Lady, had been built in 1874 and functioned as the San Francisco Mint until 1937. Like many buildings, it had been abandoned and fallen into disrepair during the turbulence. Nowadays, its walls guarded a far more valuable treasure.

The Library was one of the greatest caches of human knowledge remaining on the planet. The Collapse had proven how fragile electronic storage systems could be, with enormous databases lost in the blink of an eye. Paper books, which had been sliding toward extinction for years, suddenly became valuable again.

As far as Val knew, the library now contained the largest trove of magical books in North America.

Twin gryphon statues watched Val and Malcolm climb the steps to the entrance. The gryphons were magical guardians, ready to spring from their pedestals and attack anyone approaching the library with the intent to do it harm. Val had no idea how the guardians knew what someone's intentions were. That type of magic wasn't in her repertoire.

Stepping through the doors, she took a deep breath as the old book smell washed over her. Real paper books. Shelves and shelves of them, stretching as far as the eye could see.

At an unassuming desk sat the organizing force behind it all.

The Librarian's glasses drooped to the end of her nose. Her hair was loosely gathered in an untidy bun. She wore two sweaters, and the elbows of her mustard-yellow cardigan sprouted holes. In short, the Librarian looked like what she was: a mousy, disheveled woman who spent most of her time in the company of books. There was no hint that she was responsible for one the greatest treasures on the planet.

Until she looked up.

Her eyes were a deep violet, like the gloaming sky between sunset and full dark. They glimmered with the cold light of a thousand stars. Mister E flattened himself against Val's shoulder and pressed his face to the back of her neck, trying to escape that all-knowing gaze.

Then the Librarian blinked and smiled, and became just an ordinary woman once again.

"How may I help you today?" she asked.

"We're looking for information on the Queen Anne Hotel."

The Librarian nodded and began jotting notes on a small card.

"Oh yes, there are many books about the Queen Anne. These are a good place to start. Check their bibliographies for more books if you don't find what you're looking for."

"Thank you." Val took the card and started to leave, then stopped and turned back. "Would you happen to have a book that could tell us about this?" She made a quick sketch of Baron Blood's skull ring and pushed it across the desk.

"Hmmm, that could be a number of different things." The Librarian frowned at the sketch before pulling another card and making more notes. "These books on enchanted items should get you started."

"Excellent. Thanks again."

The Librarian waved distractedly, her violet gaze already a million miles away. Not for the first time, Val wondered what the Librarian really was. A witch? A fairy? A goddess? Definitely much more than the mousy little woman she appeared to be.

Val and Malcolm each took a card and split up to gather books. A half hour later, they had two big stacks arrayed before them on one of the upstairs reading tables.

They set to work researching, surfacing from time to time to share facts or interesting stories, but mostly working independently. After a couple of hours, Val called a halt. She stood to stretch, her spine popping and cracking from so much time hunched over reading.

"What have you got?" she asked.

"Well, the consensus seems to be that the Queen Anne is definitely haunted." Malcolm's eyes shone; he was clearly delighted by this information. "Most people think the ghost is Miss Mary Lake, the headmistress of the original girls' school."

"Girls' school?"

"The building was built in 1890 and was originally a girls' school. Mary Lake was the headmistress."

"Why do people think she's haunting it?"

"Well, the exact reasons are unclear. Some people say the school was Miss Mary's life's work and she couldn't bear to leave it, so she's still shepherding her girls' spirits in death. Some think Mary Lake died of a broken heart because the school only lasted for six years and had to close in 1896 due to a lack of funding. Personally, I think they may be right about the broken heart, but I think they are wrong about the reason." Malcolm's enthusiasm had grown as he lectured her, his hands painting pictures in the air as he spoke. "The school was funded by Senator James Graham Fair. He was divorced, and his two daughters attended the school. There were rumors he and Miss Mary were having an affair. They both denied it of course, but I think that was just because of the times they were living in. The lines on what was proper and what was not were very strict in that era, and an affair with an unmarried headmistress would definitely not be socially acceptable. Also, Mary's students were the daughters of wealthy aristocrats, and she had a public image to maintain. Having an affair with a senator? There is no way Mary could ever admit that in public. So the poor thing pined away, and her heart was broken when Senator Fair died. Her school being forced to close was just the icing on the cake." He finished with a flourish, obviously pleased with his story.

Val jotted some quick notes.

"OK, so the ghost of Mary Lake is one possibility. Anything else?"

Malcolm made a disgusted sound with his lips.

"That's all you've got to say after all that? Sometimes I don't know why I even bother telling you stories. I could send you a telegraph and you'd have the same reaction. QUEEN ANNE HOTEL HAUNTED STOP GHOST OF MARY LAKE STOP DIED OF BROKEN HEART STOP."

Val endured his sarcasm stoically.

"Are you finished? Are you going to answer the question?"

Malcolm huffed.

"There is speculation about other people, too. Girls who attended the school. People who've died in the building over the years. But none of them are as exciting as Miss Mary's story." His enthusiasm had been eaten by his annoyance at Val's lack of excitement.

"OK. Can you make a list for me? If I'm going ghost hunting, I'd like to be as prepared as possible. Ghosts are self-absorbed, and they can get annoyed if you don't know their names."

"Fine." He stuck out his tongue at her. "What did you find?"

Val waggled her head. "Eh, nothing for certain. I found a few skull rings in the books, but none of the descriptions match what I think Baron Blood was using it for. So it's probably not any of them. Unless he was using it to do something other than what I think he was, in which case it could be one of these, after all."

"In other words, you've got no clue."

"Yup. Pretty much." Val started gathering up the books. "But that's all the time I have for research today. I have to be at work in an hour, and if I don't eat something first, I'm going to be Queen Bitch behind the bar tonight."

"You say that like it's a bad thing."

That got a wry smile out of her.

"Come on, I'll buy you a crepe on the way home."

Malcolm sprang out of his chair. "Oh, hell yes. You can buy my assistance with crepes any day."

32

Belly full of crepe and arms full of books, Malcolm sighed contentedly as he unlocked the apartment door. He thought it had been an excellent afternoon. While the library guarded their magical book collection jealously, it turned out they did allow people to borrow books that were not about magic, so Malcolm had a whole stack on the Queen Anne and San Francisco history.

He stepped inside, flicked the living room light on... and screamed, dropping the books all over the floor.

A young woman with a bob cut and black-rimmed glasses sat in the armchair, watching him.

"Oh my god, girl. You almost gave me a heart attack." He bent to gather the books. "What are you doing sitting here in the dark? Are you Sandra's friend? Did she forget some stuff?"

The woman didn't answer. She just stared at Malcolm with dark eyes. Her skin was bone-white, her lips ruby red. She was disturbingly thin, her skin stretched too tight over her cheekbones.

"OK, this is getting creepy. Can you talk? Do you have a name?"

"My name is Hillary," she said quietly. Her expression never changed, her eyes never moved from his face. She reminded him of an overly serious child—all big, staring eyes. Like one of those spooky Margaret Keane paintings.

Malcolm forced a smile.

"Hi, I'm Malcolm. I'd shake your hand, but... you know." He stood up, arms full of books again.

Hillary said nothing. She just watched him with those hungry eyes as he set his treasures on the table.

"Would you like some coffee? Tea? Snacks?" He knew he was babbling, switching into host mode to cover his discomfort.

"No."

"Well, I'm going to have some, so it's no trouble. I'll go put the kettle on."

As he flicked on the kitchen light, it struck him that the rest of the flat was dark. Which meant nobody else was home. Living with house-mates, you developed a pretty high tolerance for random strangers wandering through the house. People brought home friends and lovers all the time. But leaving a friend alone in the flat when you weren't home was bad etiquette. And something about this girl felt different.

For one, she was creepy as all hell. And now he'd discovered that she was here alone. Sitting in the dark. The hairs rose up the back of his neck.

"Where is Sandra, anyway?" he called out, trying to make the question sound casual.

"How would I know?" Her quiet voice came from right behind him, and he yelped, doing a little jump-turn to find her there in the kitchen.

"Girl, you are determined to kill me, aren't you?" He sidled away, keeping one eye on her as he groped after a box of green tea in the cupboard.

"Oh, I wouldn't go that far." Hillary smiled, the first expression he'd seen her make. Her teeth were long and too white. Her smile did not put him at ease.

His discomfort made no sense, really. She was so thin a strong wind would blow her away, and her chunky glasses made her look quiet and nerdy. Girls that looked like her generally wouldn't hurt a fly. So why was she making his alarm bells ring?

He cleared his throat. "Well, I mean you're Sandra's friend, right? That's how you got in?"

Hillary shook her head ever so slightly.

"No, I've never met Sandra."

Malcolm's unease turned to ice in his stomach.

"How did you get in then?"

"Val invited me to stay here."

This statement conjured mixed emotions. Part of him relaxed. She knew Val. Of course, that explained everything.

Another part of him kicked into an even higher level of alert. Val didn't have many friends. She'd never once brought a lover home the entire time they'd been living together. And this girl wanted him to believe that Val had given her a key to the flat?

No. Something was definitely not adding up here.

"Are you hungry?" he blurted. "I make the best chocolate pancakes you ever tasted."

"That sounds wonderful. But no, I can't eat pancakes."

"You can't eat pancakes? Whatever diet you're on, we need to get you off that thing immediately. A life without pancakes is no life at all."

"You're right. It's not much of a life. In fact, you could accurately say it's no life at all." Her smile was melancholy.

"OK, no pancakes. Can I get you something else? Let's see, I've got some crackers, hummus, an apple..."

"I just need a little blood," she whispered. The words were so soft he almost didn't hear them.

"I'm sorry, what?" Malcolm laughed. "I know you goth kids are into some weird shit, but seriously, that stuff's not safe. You can catch all kinds of diseases from blood."

"Just a little. You won't feel a thing."

Hillary's big eyes caught his, and Malcolm sank into their depths. He felt sleepy and warm. Her request didn't sound outrageous anymore. She wanted a little blood. So what? He had plenty, didn't he? What would it hurt?

She had to break eye contact as she leaned in toward his neck. Her breath was cold against his skin.

Malcolm jumped back. "Whoa, slow down there. I did not consent to this. This is not OK." He grabbed a frying pan and held it like a shield in front of him.

Hillary shrank away.

"I'm sorry," she whispered. "I didn't mean to do that. Instinct kind of took over. I'm just so hungry."

Malcolm stared at her. The white skin, the long teeth. It all made sense now.

But she looked so small and hopeless. And she was clearly starving. He was confused. Weren't vampires supposed to be powerful?

"Are you really a... you know?"

She gave a small nod.

"OK. Sit down and let's talk about this." Malcolm's mind was racing. Part of his brain was screaming at him to run. But another part of him wanted to help. That part of Malcolm always wanted to make people pancakes and coffee and let them share their troubles. And this girl looked as miserable as a kitten dropped in a cold bath. She needed a friend in the worst way. Vampire or not, he wanted to help her if he could.

He poured hot water over his tea and sat down across from her at the little kitchen table. The girl was gnawing on her nails, which had already been bitten down to ragged nubs. Outrage filled Malcolm's heart. Nails should not be treated like that. He started to say something about it... but no. One thing at a time.

"Are you really a friend of Val's?" he asked.

She nodded, not meeting his eyes.

Malcolm sighed and took a sip of his green tea. He grimaced—it needed to steep longer.

"And you're in some kind of trouble?"

Her eyes flicked up, narrowing suspiciously. He raised a placating hand.

"No judgment. That's just what Val does. It's a miracle this flat isn't overflowing with lost puppies and stray goldfish."

Hillary's lips quirked.

"Stray goldfish?"

"Hey, with Val anything is possible. Is a stray goldfish any more improbable than a vampire sitting at my kitchen table?"

She acknowledged the point with a small tilt of her head. Malcolm sipped his tea again—better now—and studied her over the rim of the mug.

"What's your story? Let me guess, you're hiding from someone?"

She gave a small nod, her fingernail back between her teeth.

"Is that why you're so thin? Because you're in hiding? And you can't go out and do your"—he waved his hand vaguely—"thing?"

Another nod.

"And no pancakes either? How can you stand to live without real food?"

"Oh, I can eat food. Just not pancakes."

"Explain."

"I can't have gluten."

"Ah." That was oddly reassuring. He knew lots of people that didn't eat gluten. He could relate to gluten-free.

Malcolm sighed. She didn't look like a monster. And he really did want to help her.

"I wouldn't have to become a vampire, would I? Because I am not giving up my morning yoga in the park."

Hillary looked up at him, slow hope dawning on her face.

"You would do that?"

"Not if it'll turn me into a vampire. If that shit is catching, we'll have to figure something else out. Maybe I can get you some blood bags or something."

Hillary shook her head regretfully. "It doesn't work like that. I can't drink blood bags. Fresh blood only. And you don't need to worry, it's not catching. I mean, it can be, but it takes a lot more than one feeding. It also takes intention. You can't catch it on accident."

"Have you made many vampires?"

"No. I haven't made any. I'm pretty new myself."

That was reassuring.

Malcolm studied her. Was he really going to do this? This was much more personal than making someone pancakes.

"How do you do it?"

Hillary didn't meet his eyes. "Most people do it pretty much the way you see in the movies. Our saliva has a healing enzyme in it, so the wound disappears in a few hours."

"Does it hurt?"

"No. Our saliva is a pretty powerful numbing agent as well."

Malcolm swallowed. "Would you need to bite my neck?"

"No, your wrist would work just as well. I'm a little unusual because I used to be a nurse, so I prefer to do a blood draw with a needle, the same way you would do if you were getting a blood test. But, if you like, I can lick the area to numb it first." She looked up and met his eyes. "Why would you help me? You don't even know me."

"Val is helping you, and I trust her judgment. Besides, you clearly need help. You're as pathetic as a street urchin in a Charlie Chaplin movie."

"You would"—her words were hesitant, as if she couldn't believe she was actually saying them—"let me feed on you?"

"Why does it sound sexual when you say it that way? Not that I think it is," he reassured her. "Don't worry. Even if I was into girls, biting and blood are definitely not my thing."

He thrust his arm forward before he could second-guess himself.

"Go ahead, do it. Lick me." He covered his eyes with his other hand. He definitely did not want to watch.

Hillary gently took his hand in hers and pushed back his sleeve, exposing the veins in his forearm. Malcolm whimpered as she pulled a long needle from a brown leather kit.

"Don't worry," she said softly. He could hear her barely suppressed hunger. "You won't feel a thing."

33

The Ural hummed as Val threaded her way through the darkened streets. She'd just finished her shift at the Alley Cat and the city was deserted. That was one good thing about getting off work at four a.m., anyway. No traffic.

She was thinking about the Queen Anne, and how she might determine who, exactly, was haunting the hotel. And if that ghost was the entity that had killed Stephen.

She remembered the presence she'd discovered during her ritual in the police station. The overwhelming blackness that had trapped Stephen's shade. The glacial cold when she'd gone inside of it, followed by soothing warmth and colored lights. Being inside the presence had felt timeless, as if she could let everything go and be safe there forever. It was a powerful temptation, and if it weren't for Mister E, she'd probably still be there.

Was that presence a ghost? If so, it was more powerful than any ghost she'd ever encountered before.

She crossed the Market Street chasm on the Van Ness Bridge and was just turning onto a side street when the Ural died. Cursing, she coasted to the curb. She tried to start it a few times, but nothing happened. The engine wouldn't even turn over. The bike was as dead as a slab of granite.

"Well, that's annoying." She sighed and put her helmet in the lock-box. At least she wasn't far from home. Her feet hurt from standing behind the bar all night, but she could still walk.

Out of the corner of her eye, she saw a shadow standing on the sidewalk.

"Is it as annoying as being stood up on the top of Twin Peaks?"

Val whipped her head up to find Anastasia looking back at her.

"Because that..." Maria appeared on her other side.

"... was very annoying." Olga finished right behind Val.

Val eyed them warily. She couldn't keep all three of them in sight, so she had to keep turning her head to check the one in her blind spot. It was nerve-wracking, which was almost certainly the reason the sisters did it.

"Look, I can explain. It wasn't my fault."

"Is it ever your fault, Valora?" Paula stepped into the bright circle cast by a streetlight. She wore a dark blue cloak with a deep hood pulled up over her head, her face in shadow.

"Hello, Paula. How's the fellowship of the ring going? Have you found a way into Mordor yet?"

"I see time hasn't dulled your sense of humor. Did you find murdering Amber and Sylvio funny as well?"

Val's jaw clenched. "You know I didn't."

"I know nothing of the kind. You ran from the scene of the crime. I have no idea what your feelings were. Or your intentions."

"I didn't have any intentions. It was an accident."

That horrible night flashed in her memory. Walking in on Sylvio and Amber, naked in bed. The pain of betrayal. The humiliation. The anger. The black cloud of grief and power that had risen in a cyclone, obliterating everything.

Her whole life, her powers had been connected to her emotions. When she got upset, they spun out of control. Destroying things. Hurting people.

Amber and Sylvio had been her friends. More than that, Amber had been her best friend. She'd broken Val out of a facility for troubled teens in upstate New York and brought her down to the city. She'd introduced her to other mages, and for the first time in her life Val had felt like she belonged.

They'd lived in an abandoned warehouse in Brooklyn, which they'd dubbed the Emerald City. The Three Sisters and Paula had lived there too. They called their little magical family the Coven.

Sylvio had shown her around the neighborhood and taught her how to dumpster dive. He was funny and cute and played the guitar. He eventually became her lover, which was another first. For a short time, Val was deliriously happy.

Until the night she walked in on Amber and Sylvio together.

Until the night she killed them.

Until the night she ran.

"Why did you come all the way out here? Is this about revenge? An eye for an eye?" Val spread her arms wide. "I killed my two best friends that night. That guilt gnaws at me every day. If you want to kill me, fine. I deserve it. Just give me a few days to finish what I'm doing first, OK? People are counting on me, and I can't let them down. Give me a week to help them. After that, you can do whatever you want. I won't fight you."

She meant every word. As far as she was concerned, her soul had been lost a long time ago. She'd caused so much pain. So many deaths. She'd never be able to balance the ledger.

But Stephen deserved justice, too. Malcolm deserved closure. Hillary needed her help.

"One week, that's all I ask. Then you can do with me what you will."

The witches regarded her silently, the only sound the faint hum of the street light overhead. The fog was thick and wet, the world swaddled in cotton. Somewhere, a dog barked.

Finally, Paula spoke. "Why should we believe you? You've run before. What's stopping you from running again?"

Val laughed bitterly.

"I'm too tired to run anymore. I spent years moving from place to place, running from disaster after disaster. My life was always in splinters. It was exhausting. For the first time since New York, I've found somewhere I belong. I've built a home here. I'm trying to do right. To, in some small way, make up for all the bad shit I've done. I know I'll never be able to balance the scales. I know that. I've hurt too many people. But I'm done running. San Francisco is my home. If you need to find me, I'll be here."

Paula considered Val's words. She nodded grudgingly.

"All right. One week from tonight you will surrender yourself for judgement. Midnight at the top of Twin Peaks."

"What if I need to get in touch with you before then?" Val asked, remembering the way her night in jail had messed things up last time.

"Leave us a message at the Harvey Milk statue."

Val bowed her head in acceptance. Strangely, she felt lighter, knowing her judgment was at hand. She'd carried the weight of her guilt for so long. It was an anchor in her gut. A rusty anchor, slowly poisoning her. Her whole life had been a struggle. She'd caused pain and death wherever she'd gone. Knowing she only had a week left was a relief. Soon her struggle would be at an end. She could put the burden down.

In one week, she would be free.

34

Val met Malcolm across the breakfast table the next morning. She studied him over her coffee, through the wafting steam framing his face. He seemed a little pale, and quieter than usual.

"Is something wrong?"

He looked startled. "No. Nothing. Why would you say that?"

"You seem tired. Did you stay up too late with your books?"

"Oh. Yeah. I was reading about the history of the Queen Anne." He fidgeted with his spoon, clinking it around the inside of his mug.

"Did you learn anything interesting?"

"Lots of things. There was a fire that killed several people in the 1920s. A pair of girls went missing during the time when it was a school. And there was a murder-suicide just a few decades ago. All terrible stories, but none of them jumps up and screams, 'I'm a ghost.'" He continued to stare into his mug, not meeting her eyes.

"That's it? You're not going to tell me all the gory details?" She narrowed her eyes at him. "What's going on, Malcolm? I've never seen you this quiet. What's on your mind?"

He sighed and sipped his coffee. Ran his finger around the rim of the cup. Sighed again.

"I might have done something really stupid."

"Might have?"

"Well, it seemed like a good idea at the time."

"All the best stories start with that sentence." The corner of Val's mouth quirked up. When he didn't elaborate, she said, "Come on, out with it. You know you can't start with that and leave me hanging."

Malcolm sighed and sipped his coffee again. He still wouldn't meet her eyes.

Finally, he said, "You know your friend, Hillary?"

Val went still, all traces of her smile wiped away in an instant.

"How do you know Hillary?"

"When I came home last night, she was sitting in the living room, and..."

"She was what?" Val sprang to her feet, looming over the table. Her power thrummed. "What happened? Did she hurt you?"

Malcolm leaned away from her, his eyes wide.

"Take it easy, Val. She didn't hurt me. I think."

"You think? What the fuck does that mean?" Then it was her turn to widen her eyes. "Did she feed on you?"

Malcolm winced. "Well, yes, but..."

"How dare she?" Val was trembling with rage, fists clenched at her sides. "She asks for my help and then attacks my friend? I should have known better than to trust a vampire. I'll kill her."

She lurched toward the door. Malcolm grabbed her arm.

"Val, wait. It wasn't like that."

She stared at him. "It wasn't like that? What was it like then?"

He cringed before her intensity but didn't release her.

"I kind of volunteered."

"You volunteered? This isn't a bake sale, Malcolm. You don't just volunteer to be fed on by a vampire." She shook her head. "No. Vampires are crafty. You might not realize it, but she must have done something to you. Compelled you."

Malcolm stood his ground, his voice growing firmer. "No, Val, she didn't. I volunteered. I mean, yes, she tried to compel me at first, but then she caught herself and apologized. I offered to help her of my own free will." He held her gaze for the first time all morning. "She needed help, and I helped her. That's what happened."

Val's rage cooled a little in the face of his sincerity. Malcolm was compassionate. He always wanted to help, to take care of others. If anyone would volunteer to let a vampire feed off them out of the goodness of their heart, it was him.

Val scrubbed her hands over her face and sighed. She paced across the kitchen.

"OK. Tell me what happened."

He told her everything. From the moment he entered the apartment and found Hillary sitting in the armchair until she finished feeding on him and released his arm, courteously pressing a napkin to his wound.

"It hardly bled at all," he said.

Val leaned back against the stove, thinking.

"That was a really stupid thing to do, Malcolm. Brave, but stupid."

"You must be rubbing off on me," he said, venturing a small smile. "Brave but stupid is kind of your brand."

"God help us if that's true. I should not be anyone's role model." Val snorted and pushed herself upright. "I'll go down to the basement and talk to her. You may have volunteered, but this is still not OK."

"Ummm. About that."

"About what?"

"Hillary's not in the basement."

Val narrowed her eyes.

"Where is she?"

"I might have told her it was OK to sleep in Sandra's room."

"You what? She's still in the apartment?"

"Well, there aren't any windows in Sandra's room, and Sandra's already moved out, so the room is just sitting empty. It seemed wrong to send Hillary back to the basement when we've got a perfectly good bedroom available."

Val wasn't listening anymore. She charged down the hallway and yanked open the door to Sandra's room. The bedroom was in the middle of the flat, and barely big enough to hold a mattress. It was so tiny Val suspected it might have been a storage closet or a bathroom when the flat was initially built. As Malcolm said, it didn't have any windows, and it took Val's eyes a second to adjust to the darkness inside.

Hillary lay wrapped in an orange blanket on the carpet, her head resting on one of the couch cushions. She didn't move, seeming dead to the world.

Val didn't let that stop her. Contrary to popular myth, she knew that vampires could be woken up during the day. They were just very heavy sleepers, and it took a determined effort.

No problem there. Val was determined.

"Wake up," she barked.

She nudged Hillary with her foot. When the vampire didn't react, she nudged her harder. An ungenerous person might have even called it a kick.

"Val, stop." Malcolm grabbed her arm.

She shook him off.

"I said, wake up!" She kicked Hillary again.

This time, the vampire's eyes cracked open. As Val wound up for another kick, Hillary moved, scooting until her back was pressed into the corner, her knees drawn up to her chest. She eyed Val grumpily.

"What the hell, Keri?"

"I want you out of here," Val growled. "I want you gone."

Hurt flitted across Hillary's face, then her eyes narrowed as her expression hardened.

"I knew you were all talk. You never really wanted to help me."

"You crossed the line," Val shot back. "You fed on my roommate."

"He asked me to. Was I supposed to say no? If someone offered you a meal when you were starving, would you turn it down?"

"That's not the point. You were in my apartment. I told you to stay in the basement."

"Stay in the basement and starve, you mean? It's been days, Val. I told you I was hungry. You said I had to go find food myself. So I did."

"This is not what I meant."

"You'd rather I preyed on a stranger? Took someone's blood against their will?"

"Yes. No. I don't know." Val ground her teeth. "Stop twisting this all around."

"I'm not twisting anything. I'm just laying out the facts. The realities of my existence are messy. Believe me, I don't like any more than you do. My choices are feed or die. That's it. There's no third option. If you wanted me to die, you never should have helped me in the first place."

Val was panting like she'd just run up five flights of stairs.

"I want you gone at sundown. You'd better not be here when I get home."

Hillary's mouth was a sullen slash.

"Fine. Can I go back to sleep now?"

Val shot her one more glare then turned away.

"Sundown," she said, slamming the door behind her.

Malcolm was standing in the hall, wringing his hands.

"Val..." he began.

"Save it, Malcolm. I don't want to hear it."

She grabbed her jacket and stormed out, slamming the front door as well.

35

V al rode the Ural up and down San Francisco's hills, her thoughts whirling. She didn't know where she was going; she only knew she had to get away. She needed the wind and the motion.

What the hell was Malcolm thinking? Letting a vampire stay in their home?

And Hillary was way out of line. Val wanted to help the young woman, but entering her apartment? Feeding on her flat mate? In what world was that acceptable behavior?

"He did offer," Mister E said. He sat in the sidecar, wearing a ridiculous pair of motorcycle goggles. *"Maybe you should trust your friend to make his own decisions."*

"He doesn't understand what he's choosing. Malcolm doesn't know anything about vampires. Letting him make that choice would be like letting a six-year-old girl decide if she wants to free a cat-demon in exchange for magical powers."

"How droll. And also an inaccurate analogy. Just because you feel you weren't ready to make the choice you were given does not mean that Malcolm is not ready to make his own choices. Stop projecting your own feelings onto him. He is a grown adult. And I am not a demon."

"Until you decide to tell me what you actually are, I'm sticking with demon," Val shot back. "And I'm not projecting."

If she was being honest, Val knew she really was projecting. She had in no way been ready for the choice that was presented to her at six years old, and she'd been paying for it ever since. Her entire life hinged on that one moment. What might she have been if she'd said no? If she'd refused the power and left Mister E trapped beneath that ancient temple? Would her mother still be alive today?

She knew one thing: She wouldn't be dealing with vampires, that was for sure.

Val parked the Ural at Land's End and grabbed a latte from the coffee cart at the top of the cliff. The cart didn't have butterscotch, so she had to settle for vanilla. She climbed down to the beach and sat on a rock, watching the waves crash against the shore.

The wind coming in off the Pacific was icy, as always, and she gathered her knees up against her chest and snugged her leather jacket under her chin, cupping her hands around the paper cup for warmth. Her eyes moved over the beach, past the scorch mark left by the frequent bonfires, down to a spot by the water's edge. The last time she'd been out here, a young woman had died, right there.

She had been a seal shifter named Shanna. She'd been helping Val track down the person who'd killed Ruby. Shanna had been cute, with big brown eyes and a ready smile. And she'd gotten killed for her trouble. Murdered by the same asshole who'd killed Ruby.

If Val had rejected Mister E's offer, would any of that have happened? Would Shanna still be alive? Would Ruby?

"Do I make bad things happen?" she whispered.

"That's ridiculous," Mister E answered. *"You no more make bad things happen than you make the tide. Bad things would happen with or without your presence. The only difference is that you would not be there to fight against them."*

"Maybe. Or maybe I stir them up somehow. Maybe I'm a trouble magnet. I never prevent anything from happening. All I do is run around trying to pick up the pieces after everything falls apart. I think the Coven is right. The world will be a better place after I'm gone."

"If you truly believe that, why not fill your pockets with stones and walk into the sea right now? Why wait for the Coven's judgment?"

"Maybe I will." But she didn't move.

Mister E smirked. "No, you won't. Because you know you make a difference. You know you still have seven days to do good, and you will use every hour to do just that. You're a fighter, Val Keri, and you always have been. That's why I came to you on that mountaintop. Not because you were small and weak. Because you were strong. You were ready to fight back in the face of overwhelming odds, even knowing that you would lose. That's what drew me to you. That is what makes you unique. Anyone can have power, but fighting spirit cannot be taught. That's what makes you special."

Val's eyes were moist. Stupid wind.

Mister E jumped down off the rock and noisily hacked up a hairball.

"Now, if you're done feeling sorry for yourself, can we get off this godforsaken beach? I believe you still have a killer to find. And you're running out of time."

Wiping her eyes with the back of her hand, Val unfolded from the rock and got to her feet, ignoring the protests of her stiff joints. Downing the last of her coffee, she headed back to the Ural. Mister E was right. She only had a few days left to make a difference.

And she was going to need every second.

36

Her first stop was the Library. If she wanted to free Stephen's spirit, she needed to figure out how to fight the black presence on its home turf. The Librarian pointed her towards a couple of books on astral projection and she sat down to read.

"If only you had someone you could turn to with questions about magic." Mister E lounged on the dark wood of the table, blowing smoke rings with his candy cigarette. *"Some kind of wise, ancient being who could be your mentor."*

"If you have something useful to say, feel free to say it. No one's forcing you to lay there making snarky comments."

"Snarky? Moi? You wound me, Val. I am the very picture of sincerity."

She didn't look up from her book. "Uh-huh. I'm still waiting to hear something useful."

He turned up his nose and started cleaning himself. *"Well, I'm not an expert on astral projection, per se. It's not really something that comes up when you don't have a body to project out of."*

"You're all talk. What a surprise."

"Now who's being snarky? You know there are lots of things I could teach you, just not in this particular type of magic. I'm not omniscient; I can't know everything."

Val ignored him. She was reading about a ritual supposed to get you into the astral plane at full strength. Apparently, one of the biggest obstacles to astral traveling was that when people's spirits left their bodies, they also left most of their power behind. Their astral projections were little more than ghosts themselves, which rendered them vulnerable. This was the reason Val hadn't been able to resist the pull of the dark presence. She'd only had a tiny fraction of her power.

The ritual she'd found sounded promising. Supposedly it sent the traveler through with all the strength their physical body contained.

The only catch was that it required several mages to perform the ritual. The mage going on the journey was the object of the ritual, not a participant. Which meant Val would need other magic users to conduct the ritual for her. It also meant she would be entirely at their mercy while they did.

Even if she knew enough witches in San Francisco to perform the ritual for her, being helpless before them did not sound appealing. But the point was moot because she didn't really know any of the other witches in town. She knew a few by reputation, but their paths had never crossed, and Val wasn't the type to make a social call simply to introduce herself. She was a lone wolf here. She didn't have a community to fall back on like she'd had in the Emerald City.

That thought gave her pause. The Emerald City Coven was in San Francisco now. Of course, they were here to pass judgment on her, so she doubted they'd help her even if she asked.

And she was far from sure she wanted to ask. Putting herself at their mercy did not seem like a wise thing to do.

On the other hand, wasn't that exactly what she'd agreed to do anyway? Meet them on Twin Peaks and put herself at their mercy? How was asking them for help with a ritual any worse than that?

"Do you think the Coven witches would help me if I asked?"

Mister E was so surprised he choked on his candy smoke and started to cough.

"Help you?" he sputtered. *"Would that be before or after they kill you?"*

"Before, obviously."

"And why would they want to help you?"

"I can think of two reasons. First, the sooner I conclude my business, the sooner they can have their way with me."

"Have their way with you?" Mister E smirked. *"This is a judgment, not an orgy."*

Val ignored him.

"And second, I know those ladies are basically good people. At least Paula is. The three sisters are a little scary, but I think they'll follow Paula's lead. Anyway, if the purpose of the ritual is benign, they might agree to it. And I think freeing a trapped soul definitely counts as benign. It certainly can't hurt to ask."

"Can't it? What if they decide they're tired of waiting and they'd rather judge you on the spot? Or what if they decide that having you tied up inside a ritual is the perfect way to ensure they'll be able to pass their judgment without any interference from you?"

"That's a chance I'll have to take, isn't it? If I want their help, I'll have to trust them."

"Well, I think it's a monumentally foolish idea." Mister E rolled onto his back and blew smoke rings at the ceiling. *"But you've never taken my advice before. I don't know why you would start now."*

Val grinned at him. "You're right about that. But I'm not going to jump into it on the spur of the moment just to spite you. I'll keep looking and see if any better ideas come along before I make my final decision."

Three hours later, she sat up and groaned as the vertebrae of her spine popped. Her eyes were dry and gritty from reading, and her left leg had fallen asleep some time before. Val winced and hissed at the pins and needles as she massaged some circulation back into it.

"I swear, body parts falling asleep is proof there is no capital-G god," she grumbled. "Why would an omnipotent creator make such a poor design?"

"Maybe the Big G is focused on the big ideas and not the small details," Mister E offered. He'd been napping on the table for some time, and now reluctantly cracked one golden eye open.

"You're saying God threw together the human prototype and said, 'Hot damn! It works!', then strode off into the sunset? So we're still in beta testing? That would explain a lot."

"It certainly would. And not just about humans." He yawned and stretched, arching his back as his claws dug into the wooden surface. *"Did you discover anything useful?"*

Val grimaced. "Not really. I think that group ritual might be the best bet."

"Oh, goody. I can't wait to see how this turns out. 'Hey Paula, I know you hate me and you've traveled all the way across the country to execute me, but would you mind doing me a tiny favor first?'"

Val stood up and pulled on her leather jacket, shaking her still-tingling leg irritably.

"All we can do is try, right?"

37

Val couldn't simply call Paula on the phone, so she had to leave a message at the Harvey Milk statue the Coven witches had told her to use if she needed to get in touch with them. She had to hope they got the message in time. And that they'd be willing to talk when they did.

In the meantime, mundane realities required her attention. She had to go to work.

She stopped back at the apartment to change. As soon as she stepped in the door, she knew something was off.

There wasn't anything immediately apparent, just a feeling. The hairs on the back of her neck rose. Her breath came short and fast. Her muscles tensed.

She put her hand on the hilt of her knife as she peered into the kitchen... and found Malcolm and Hillary sitting at the kitchen table.

"What is she doing here?" Val growled.

To his credit, Malcolm didn't flinch. He simply got up and poured her a cup of coffee.

"Stay calm, Val. Sit down. We're going to talk about this like adults."

She took the mug from him but remained standing.

"Why is she still here?"

"Well"—Malcolm licked his lips nervously—"I was thinking about it, and I don't really understand where this prejudice is coming from."

"Prejudice? She's a vampire. She literally eats humans."

"That's not true," Hillary objected softly. "I've never eaten anyone. I've never even killed anyone."

Val glared at her. "That's not the point."

"Actually, it kind of is." Seeing that Val wasn't going to sit down, Malcolm leaned against the stove next to her. "You're judging Hillary based on some vampire stereotype in your mind. You're not seeing her as an individual."

"I don't believe we're having this conversation. She drank your blood, Malcolm. In what universe is that OK?"

"In the universe where I gave her my consent first. Come on Val, you work in a strip club. I know you understand consent."

Val scowled and slurped her coffee. This conversation was not going the way it was supposed to. She tried to get it back on track.

"This is all beside the point. Why is she still here?"

Malcolm and Hillary exchanged a look. Malcolm took a deep breath.

"Well, Sandra just moved out. We need a new roommate."

Val stared at him. "Are you insane? No. Absolutely not."

"Why not? Give me some logical reasons that aren't based in your prejudice."

"Because she's... she's..." Val sputtered. She threw up her hands. "Why is it so hard for you to understand that living with a monster who might eat you in your sleep is a bad idea?"

"We've already addressed this. She doesn't eat people."

"No, she just drinks them like they're a juice box."

Malcolm shrugged. "And you cast spells and I have OCD and roll my toothpaste tube from the bottom. This is San Francisco. We've all got our quirks, Val."

"Quirks. Vampirism is not a quirk. It's like... I don't know... bringing in a roommate who has a big smelly dog."

Hillary sniffed. "I am not a big smelly dog."

"Fine, bad example." Val glared at her before turning back to Malcolm. "But you know what I mean. This is something that affects our entire living space. This isn't some personal quirk that'll be kept out of sight in her bedroom."

Malcolm sipped his coffee, regarding her thoughtfully over the rim.

"Let me ask you a question: If you hate vampires so much, why did you offer to help her in the first place?"

"I don't hate vampires." Malcolm raised an eyebrow at that, and Val insisted, "I don't. And I offered to help her because she needed it. Melinda Pearl is an evil bitch, and no one should have to put up with that on a daily basis." A tiny laugh squeaked out of Hillary, and Val caught herself almost smiling in return. She quickly smoothed her features. "But there's a big gap between helping someone and letting them into your home. Let alone living with them. I offered to help Hillary get to a safe place. Somewhere Melinda Pearl couldn't reach her. That place isn't here."

"Isn't it?" Malcolm challenged. "I thought you were the toughest witch in San Francisco. Do you mean to tell me Melinda Pearl could walk right into your home and abduct your roommate? Because if that's the case, I may need to start looking for another apartment myself."

"Of course she couldn't. Don't be ridiculous," Val snapped. She may not know much about traditional magic, but she knew how to ward her own home. No monsters could cross the threshold without her permission.

Which was another reason it was so vexing that Hillary had gotten inside. Val knew it meant that as far as her magic was concerned, she had invited the young woman into her home when she offered to let her stay in the basement. Which meant that on a purely technical level, she'd already lost this debate.

She glanced at the clock and sighed.

"Look, much as I'd love to sit her and argue with you all night, I've got to get to work. I suppose Hillary can stay in the empty bedroom for tonight. But we are not done talking about this."

Hillary's face brightened. Val stomped out of the kitchen and down the hall. Flaming Toads. Taking a vampire in as a roommate. If that wasn't the worst idea ever, she didn't know what was.

Val did her best to push away the memory of Hillary's relief at the temporary reprieve. And the way her own protective instincts flared with satisfaction at the sight.

38

Val finished tapping a new keg and glanced at the clock over the bar. Five minutes to midnight. The Alley Cat had been pretty quiet so far, which was the opposite of how she wanted it to be. It gave her too much time to think. Too much time to worry about Hillary, and the Coven, and the black void that had trapped Stephen's ghost. When the club was busy, she could lose herself in the flow, in the task at hand. There was no time to worry about anything else.

Being busy made the time go faster, too. You'd get caught in a rush and the next time you looked up, two hours had gone by. When it was slow, time dragged along like a ship dredging out the deep channel of the bay.

Val wondered if the Coven had gotten her message. She wondered if they would agree to help her if they had.

She hated having to ask for help, but she hadn't been able to find a better path forward. She needed to be able to challenge the black spirit on its home turf. And the only way to do that was to have the Coven witches send her through to the astral plane, using the ritual she'd unearthed.

She scowled and went back into the kitchen for a rack of clean glasses.

When she came back out, she swore. Vasilevski and his crew had arrived and were settling in at their usual table.

Val sighed and poured a round of vodka shots. On a slow night like this, there was no way to pretend she hadn't seen them.

She was halfway to their table when gunfire barked from the doorway. Mandy screamed and scampered off the stage. Val hit the deck, her tray forgotten, shot glasses skittering across the floor like spilled ice cubes. She crawled behind a chair and watched in horror as the Alley Cat became a war zone.

Vasilevski and his men leapt out of their seats and flipped the table onto its side, crouching as they drew their own weapons and returned fire.

But the Russians only had pistols, and their attacker held a submachine gun. Bullets chewed up their cover like a buzz saw. At least one of the gangsters was hit. The person in the doorway laid down a steady stream of fire, the bark of the gun impossibly loud in the enclosed space. Val could feel the sound in her bones, like all the thunderstorms in the world rolled into one.

Malina joined the Russians in returning fire from the DJ booth up the stairs, her Glock barking at the intruder. From behind the stage, a rifle boomed as Mandy jumped into the fray. Val cursed. She was letting her side down. She needed to move.

But before she could gather her wits enough to do anything, the submachine gun fell silent as abruptly as the onslaught had begun. Her ears rang in the sudden quiet. Smoke filled the air.

Val staggered to her feet, taking stock of the situation. At least two of the Russians were lying on the floor, bleeding. Malina and Mandy had both come through unscathed. She peered toward the doorway. Had the attacker fled? Or were they just reloading?

Her blood ran cold as she saw a pair of familiar boots sticking out beneath the curtain that covered the entryway.

"Oh no."

Junior had been guarding the door.

She stumbled over and yanked back the curtain. The big bouncer lay on the floor, a nasty gash on his temple.

Val knelt beside him, her heart in her throat as she pressed her fingertips to his pulse. Relief flooded through her. He was alive, just unconscious.

Hard on its heels came rage. Someone had shot up her bar. Someone had hurt her friend.

Val burst out onto the street in time to see the gunner dive into the passenger seat of a black BMW.

"Oh, no, you don't," she growled.

The car peeled out as she sprinted towards it. Val flung a gust of wind, but it did little against the weight of the car. The BMW quickly started to pull away from her, accelerating down the dark street.

She reached deep and pulled the wind to her, funneling it down between the buildings, concentrating it into a narrow stream. It roared around her, and she twisted it so that it was beneath her feet, lifting her.

Val flew.

She hadn't flown since the night she'd chased the Scepter of Sutro across the city. The night she fought off a vampire queen and defeated a seraph.

It wasn't exactly like riding a bicycle.

Val yelped as she dipped and dove, the wind pushing her first to one side of the street, then the other. She narrowly avoided a brick building, then almost ate the rearview mirror of a parked truck. Frantically, she worked to get a little more height, to at least get up above the parked cars.

That accomplished, she looked up and caught a glimpse of the BMW skidding around a corner two blocks ahead.

Val accelerated, wind roaring in her ears, shooting down the street like a meteor.

She bounced off a building as she took the corner—turning at speed was tricky—then she nearly fell from the sky as the gunman leaned out the window and opened fire on her.

Flaming toads. Val was many things, but bulletproof was not one of them. Would it be better to go high or go low in this situation? She didn't know, she'd never had to dodge bullets while flying before. She'd just have to pick one and find out.

She swooped low, veering toward the opposite side of the street, trying to put the bulk of the BMW between her body and the gunman. It seemed to work. The shooter couldn't lean out far enough to angle the gun over the roof of the car for a clean shot.

Of course, now she had to dodge parked cars again, but that seemed better than dodging bullets.

She was less than half a block behind the car, whizzing along only five feet above the asphalt. Her low altitude gave her a perfect view of the car's license plate number. All she had to do was memorize it and she'd be able to track down the assassins, even if they managed to get away.

At least, that's how things would have gone if the car had a license plate.

Instead, only an empty rectangle of metal stared at her from where a license plate should have hung. So much for that idea.

She was trying to figure out her next move when the gunman shot out the back window of the BMW from the inside. Glass exploded all over the street, bouncing and sparkling in the light. Her low height gave her a perfect view of the muzzle flash as bullets came towards her once again.

Val panicked and did what she'd done the last time. She dove. Unfortunately, she was only five feet up this time around, and ended faceplanting right into the street.

She got her arms up in time to avoid literally eating concrete, but skidded and rolled, finally coming to rest against the back wheel of a parked delivery van. She lay there for a minute, stunned, her whole body ringing like a bell from the impact.

"Well done," Mister E laughed. *"Maybe the baby bird wasn't ready to leave the nest after all."*

Val ignored him and sat up slowly, taking stock of her injuries. Her palms were a bleeding mess, her jeans were shredded, and a lot of things hurt, but she was relieved to not discover the sharp, stabbing pain that would indicate a broken bone.

The BMW was long gone.

Wincing, she gingerly got to her feet and began a slow, limping walk back to the Alley Cat.

39

F lashing lights washed the street blue and red in front of the Alley Cat. Police cars were parked across the intersections at both ends of the block, with an ambulance sitting right outside the club. A crowd had gathered on the sidewalk, held back by yellow police tape, and Val had to push her way to the front. The young policewoman on crowd duty confronted her when she ducked under the tape, but the familiar voice of Detective Chen cut her protest short.

"It's all right. Let her through."

Chen looked tired, the lines around his mouth and eyes more pronounced. He stuck his hands in the pockets of his jacket as he looked her up and down.

"Rough night?"

"You could say that." Val tried to walk past him, but Chen stopped her with an outstretched hand.

"Forensics is working in there. We need to stay out here so they can do their job."

Val glared at him, then sighed and nodded. She leaned against the hood of a parked car, happy to take the weight off her aching legs.

"What happened to you?" Chen asked.

"I tried to catch the gunman."

"From the looks of you, I'm guessing it didn't go well."

"No." Scowling, Val picked bits of gravel out of her palm.

"Did you get a good look at them?"

"No."

"Anything useful you can tell me?"

She sighed and shifted her attention to her other palm.

"They were driving a black BMW. No license plate. The gunman wore black leather and a black mask. The gun was a submachine gun. An Uzi? AR-15? I don't really know anything about those things."

Chen nodded, taking notes in his notebook.

"Were you here when the attack happened?"

"Yeah."

"You want to tell me what happened?" he prodded.

Val told him, and the detective continued to nod and take notes. As she was wrapping up her statement, a gurney was wheeled out with a human form on it, covered by a white sheet.

"Shit," Val breathed. "Is that a body? Did somebody die?"

Chen turned to watch the gurney, the lines around his mouth getting deeper as he scowled.

"I'm not at liberty to discuss the details of the case."

"That's bullshit," Val snapped. "That could be a friend of mine under there. Tell me what's happening."

Chen met her eyes, his gaze as cool as the bay. Val refused to look away. After a minute, he sighed and stepped close to her, lowering his voice.

"You're right. You deserve to know what's happened. You didn't hear it from me, though. Understand?" He glanced around, then whispered, "Vasilevski's dead."

"Holy shit." Val felt her knees go weak as the world tilted on its axis. She wouldn't have called Vasilevski a friend, but the imperturbable gangster had been a big presence in her life. "Anyone else?"

Chen shook his head. "A couple of his goons were shot, but they'll probably pull through. None of the other people in the club were wounded."

Val nodded numbly. "Thank goodness for small miracles."

They stood in silence for a minute, watching the paramedics load the body into the ambulance, the lights strobing red.

"What happens now?" Val asked.

"Now we do our jobs. Investigate the crime scene. Try to find the perps."

"No, I mean," she gestured toward the ambulance containing Vasilevski's body. "Is this going to create some kind of power vacuum? Is this the start of a gang war?"

Chen shrugged. "I doubt there's a power vacuum. I'm sure someone else will step up inside the Vasilevski family."

Val's mind went to Zoe. Had she been close with her uncle? Would she be upset? Should Val reach out to offer her condolences? She had no idea how these things worked.

Chen continued, "As far as a gang war goes, we'll see. Obviously, there will be some retaliation against whoever carried out this hit. Hopefully that won't escalate into a full-blown war. God help us all if it does."

"What about the Alley Cat?"

"It'll be closed for the foreseeable future. It's a crime scene now, and we're going to need it undisturbed for at least a few days. After that, the owner's going to need to have some repairs done before the place is ready for business again." He gave her a grim smile. "Looks like you've got some unexpected vacation time coming."

"Yeah." Val had a million questions, but just then she caught sight of Junior and Malina standing off to one side, so all she said was, "Thank you, detective. Excuse me, I need to go check on my friends."

Junior was wrapped in a blanket, with a square bandage taped to his head. Malina stood beside him in a fluorescent yellow jacket, looking furious.

"Are you both OK?" Val asked.

Junior nodded. "Nothing to worry about, Val. That *pendejo* pistol-whipped me, but they don't think I have a concussion. Nothing damaged but my pride."

Malina cut in, waving her hands angrily. "Those fuckers shot up the club. Cops say we might be closed for weeks! What the hell am I supposed to do for weeks with no work? I've got bills to pay!"

Val had no answer for that, so she kept quiet. Thanks to the money she'd earned from the extracurricular jobs Vasilevski forced her to do, she'd actually be able to survive a few weeks with no work. But it would be tactless to tell Malina and Junior that. Val knew they came from big families, and they had a lot of people relying on their income. The Alley Cat closing would be a blow.

"I'll let you know if I hear of any work," she offered weakly.

Malina and Junior nodded, but they all knew the chances of that happening were slim. Jobs were hard to come by.

Val let the paramedics clean and bandage her hands before she left. She flexed them as she climbed on the Ural. They looked like boxer's hands, taped up and ready for a fight. Which was fitting, since she definitely felt like hitting someone.

She kicked the motorcycle into gear and roared off into the night.

40

The witches were waiting for her. Just after she crossed the Van Ness bridge, the Ural coughed and cut out, forcing her to drift over to the curb.

As she pulled off her helmet, Val was unsurprised to see the Three Sisters standing on the sidewalk.

"I take it you got my message," she said.

"We did." Paula stepped out of the shadows, making her dramatic entrance. Val rolled her eyes. "What did you wish to speak to us about?"

"I need your help."

The older witch raised an eyebrow. "Our help? Have you forgotten that we are here to judge you for your past actions?"

"Yeah, that completely slipped my mind," Val said dryly.

Paula frowned at her. "You've made us chase you all the way across the continent, and you have the gall to ask for our help?"

"First of all, I didn't make you do anything. You chose to chase me across the continent. That's on you. But since you've come all this way, you may as well make yourselves useful. It seems like an awfully long trip just to remove my head from my shoulders. I thought you might, like, to do some actual good while you're at it."

Paula's face could have been sculpted from ice.

"You have a strange way of asking for help."

Val sighed. "Look, I'm not good at this. And I'm especially not good at asking for help from people who want to kill me. Let's try this again." She flexed her bandaged hands and took a deep breath. "My roommate's friend was killed and his spirit was trapped by... something. I'm not sure what it is. Some kind of dark presence in the astral plane. All I know is that it's really strong. Too strong to confront alone."

"You want us to fight this spirit for you?" Paula asked.

"No. I found a ritual that will send my full spirit to the astral plane. Not just the fraction that normally travels. Using this ritual will allow me to confront the presence with the same strength I would have in the material plane."

Paula frowned. "You would be committing your soul entirely to the astral plane. If you were to be killed while you were there, your death would be real. There is a reason we only send a small part of ourselves when we walk the planes."

"That's a risk I'm willing to take."

The older witch eyed her for a long moment.

"You would risk your life to save the soul of another. You've grown up, Valora Keri."

Val held Paula's gaze, her golden eyes flashing.

"I have a lot to atone for. I'm trying to balance the scales as best I can."

Paula weighed her words and finally nodded. "What do you ask of us?"

"I can't perform the ritual myself. It requires at least three witches to cast. Also, I will be the focus of the ritual, so I can't be one of the casters myself."

The Sisters spoke up, their words traveling from mouth to mouth.

"You would put yourself..."

"... in our power?"

"That seems..."

"... awfully trusting of you."

"What is to stop..."

"... us from simply..."

"... judging you?"

Val turned to face the one who had spoken first. She thought it was Olga.

"As you say, I will be completely in your power. There will be nothing at all stopping you from judging me. I'm relying on your honor."

"Honor?" The Sisters laughed.

"What a concept."

"You are truly..."

"... a woman out of time..."

"... Valora Keri."

Paula held up a hand to silence them.

"When would you want to do this?"

"As soon as possible. Tomorrow night?"

Paula thought for a moment then nodded, her crystals and pendants swaying.

"We will help you. But you will be judged immediately upon completion of the ritual."

Val didn't blink. "Fine. Meet me tomorrow night in front of the Queen Anne Hotel."

The head of the Coven inclined her head and turned to go.

"Oh, you might want this too," Val called after her. She retrieved her notebook from her saddle bag and tore out a couple of pages, handing them to Paula. "These are my notes on the ritual. So you have time to prepare."

"You don't need them?"

"Like I said, I'll be the focus of the ritual, not one of the casters. All I have to do is show up."

Paula took the pages. "Until tomorrow."

"Until tomorrow," Val echoed.

She stood staring into the darkness long after the women had disappeared.

"I don't trust those witches." Mister E appeared on her shoulder, his tail lashing in agitation. *"You do not have to go through with this."*

Val sighed. "You're wrong. I do. It's the only way to free Stephen."

"You don't know that. You're just hoping you'll have enough power to

defeat that black thing. Take some more time. Do some more research. Find another way that doesn't require you to put yourself in their power."

"I'm going to be putting myself in their power when I surrender for judgment, anyway. I might as well get something useful out of them first."

"I still don't like it."

She swung her leg back over the Ural. "That's because you've got your cranky pants on."

"I am not wearing pants."

"Which is actually worse, if you think about it. It's cold out here. Don't your little kitty balls get chilly?"

"I don't have balls either."

"Well, maybe that's your problem right there. Grow a pair, dude."

Mister E hissed at her. *"Please don't call me 'dude'. It demeans us both."*

"Come on, 'dude' is completely gender neutral. It's the perfect form of address, if you think about it. Especially for someone in your situation."

Mister E glared at her and disappeared with a huff.

Val laughed as she pulled away from the curb. It was odd, but the closer to the final confrontation with the Coven she got, the lighter she felt. She'd been running from them for too long. Carrying the guilt of Sylvio and Amber's deaths for too many years.

Soon she'd put herself in the witches' power, and they could do with her what they would. They'd probably execute her. The knowledge was strangely freeing.

Perhaps the secret to happiness was simply letting go of the reigns.

Or perhaps it was finally facing up to her sins. Accepting what she'd done, and not running from the consequences.

Whatever it was, Val felt more relaxed than she had in years. Almost at peace. She breathed in the chill night air and turned the Ural towards home.

41

The third floor of The Queen Anne hadn't changed since Val's last visit. Yellow police tape still stretched across the doorway to Stephen's room. Val pushed it aside and she and her witch entourage tromped into the dark room. At least this time, she hadn't had to sneak past the desk clerk. The Sister's magic had simply made the man look the other way as they all filed across the lobby floor.

It was dark inside the room, thick gloom hanging in the corners like moss. Dim yellow light filtered in from the street outside, slanting across the carpet in a sickly slash.

They pushed the bed to the side of the room, and the Sisters chalked out a circle with sure strokes while Paula and Val lit the candles.

"Are you sure about this?" Mister E floated above the bed, his eyes narrowed. *"I don't trust these witches."*

"That makes two of us," Val muttered. "But I don't see any better options. Sometimes you have to work with what you have."

"Even if what you have is a steaming pile of garbage?"

Val sighed. "Especially then."

"If you're done talking to yourself, the ritual is prepared," Paula interrupted testily. "Time is wasting."

Val shot her a dark look. "What is it with you and your obsession with time?"

"Magic ebbs and flows like the tides. For a working like this, we need as much magical energy at our disposal as we can get. The timing is crucial."

"And midnight is what? High tide?"

"One of them. There's a reason people call it the witching hour. Now, if you're done wasting time, I'd like to get on with this. Step into the circle, please."

Val chewed her lip. This was it, her last chance to back out. Once she stepped inside the circle, she'd be putting herself completely into the power of the Coven. At that point, they'd be able to do anything to her they liked, and she'd be powerless to resist them.

She sighed. Who was she kidding? She was already committed. In for a penny...

"Remember, we have a deal." She caught Paula's eyes. "An innocent soul is at stake."

The head of the Coven looked offended. "Yes, yes. A bargain has been struck. We will hold up our end."

Val nodded, took a deep breath, and stepped into the circle.

Nothing happened, of course.

She sat down in the center, crossing her legs. Her throat constricted as the four witches took their positions around the chalked perimeter. She tried to focus on her breathing, tried to keep the flow even, in and out, but her breath sounded ragged, as if it were catching and tearing on something deep in her chest.

Paula started to chant, her voice resonant and steady, filling the small room. One by one, the Sisters joined in, though they did not all chant in unison. Rather, the witches seemed to be chanting the same words with a slight delay between each speaker, the words blending and overlapping as if they were singing a song in rounds. The candles flared and Val felt the pressure change, all the hairs on her body standing on end as the circle closed.

There was no escape now. She was sealed inside.

A frantic, animal part of her brain jumped up and started scream-ing, gibbering in terror. She clenched her teeth, fighting the urge to hurl herself to the edge and pound her fists against the magical barrier.

This had been her idea. It was what she'd wanted. What she'd agreed to.

Now, if only her stomach would get the memo.

She swallowed bile and focused on her breathing, air hissing between her teeth as the spell gained power. She heard Stephen's name in the chant, and she focused on that. On Stephen. On where she wanted to go. Her skin tingled with electricity. The candle flames flared, bright as spotlights, making her squint. The air inside the circle congealed, growing heavy as honey on her tongue as she struggled to draw it into her lungs.

Her head swam. Candle smoke made her eyes sting. She struggled to keep her eyes open, to focus...

The world gave a lurch, and the hotel room was gone.

Val sat up with a jolt.

Soft moss coated the ground beneath her, curling gently downward. She was sitting on top of a small hill facing a dark forest. Fog drifted between white trunks, which punctuated the undergrowth like upright bones. At the foot of the hill, the midnight mouth of a cave beckoned.

As she approached, she could see nothing inside the dark maw. But she could feel Stephen's soul in there. Trapped, just as before. But this time, she wasn't merely astral projecting. Now her entire spirit was present in this place. Now she could do battle with the darkness on even terms.

She hoped it would be enough.

Val took a deep breath and stepped through the opening.

Icy cold gripped her as before, stealing her breath in an instant. She couldn't see a thing, not the wall of the cave, not her hand held up before her—nothing. But she could feel Stephen's spirit somewhere before her, a gentle tugging onward.

"I need your eyes."

The darkness became tinged with gold as Mister E gave her his sight. But she still couldn't see anything. Even her hands were invisible until she brought them close enough to touch her nose.

"Not very useful," she groused.

"Better than your eyes," he shot back. He sounded sulky, though, as if he were as unhappy at his ineffectiveness as she was.

Val clenched her teeth and stepped deeper into the darkness, hands held out before her, feet feeling carefully along so she wouldn't walk into anything or trip over a rock. She couldn't tell how long she walked like that. It might have been an hour; it might have been a minute. Time was slippery in the dark.

Finally, she felt Stephen's spirit drawing near.

Two steps later, the darkness was washed away by a golden light.

42

V al squinted and shied away from the sudden glare. She heard laughter and the happy chattering of a stream. When her eyes finally adjusted, she found herself standing in a sunlit glade. Green tree limbs spread against the blue sky, swaying in the breeze. Puffy clouds drifted above.

In the center of the glade, children splashed in a sparkling stream. A handful of adults sat on blankets along the banks, picnic baskets and plates scattered about. They were chattering happily, smiling and watching the children play.

Val frowned. This certainly didn't look like a group of people being held prisoner.

A little girl stepped into her path, skinny arms crossed over her chest.

"You can't have them." The girl eyed Val suspiciously, mouth set in a thin line. She was maybe ten years old and wore an old-fashioned red summer dress, her feet bare upon the grass. Her black hair was braided into rows, her skin almost as dark as the interior of the cave had been.

"Can't have who?" Val asked, trying on a friendly smile.

The girl did not return the smile. "My friends."

Val tried another tack. "Hi, my name's Val. What's yours?"

"They call me Macy."

"Nice to meet you, Macy. Where are we, anyway?"

Macy's face did not soften. "You just got here. You tell me."

"I'm looking for my friend, Stephen. I think he might be over there. Can I go talk to him?"

Distrust swirled over the girl's face, but she finally nodded and stepped aside. Val felt Macy's eyes on her back as she crossed the glade.

The people looked up from their picnic as her shadow fell across the blanket.

"Stephen?"

A man with a neat brown beard smiled at her hesitantly.

"That's me." He scrutinized her face, his brows drawing down over his nose. "Do I know you?"

"I'm a friend of Malcolm's. My name is Val."

"Oh! You're Malcolm's roommate. He's told me all about you." His smile grew puzzled. "Is Malcolm here?"

"No, he's not."

"Where is he?"

"That's complicated." Val squatted onto her haunches so she was eye to eye with him. "I'm afraid I have some bad news, Stephen. There's no easy way to say this, so I'm just going to say it. You died a few nights ago."

Stephen laughed. "Don't be absurd. I'm having a picnic."

"Think about it, Stephen. How did you get here? Where are we?"

"We're..." He faltered and gave a little nervous laugh. "Give me a minute. I'm sure it'll come back to me."

"What's the last thing you remember?" she asked gently. "Do you remember the Queen Anne hotel?"

"Of course I do. Such a charming old Victorian."

"Think back to the Queen Anne. Tell me what you remember."

"Well, Malcolm came to meet me at the Queen Anne. He showed me around town — well, we went barhopping, to be honest. I was pretty tipsy when he dropped me off back at the hotel. I went up to my room and passed out." He shrugged. "That's all I remember."

"You don't remember anything strange happening before you went to sleep?"

"Strange? How do you mean?"

"I don't know. You tell me."

Stephen put a finger to his lips. "Now that you mention it, there was something. I remember hearing a voice. Some kind of chanting. And there were colored lights dancing around like I was at a club." He frowned. "Something was pulling at me. It hurt. I tried to open my eyes, but I couldn't. The room started spinning, and it sucked me down and... then I woke up here."

His face went pale, and Stephen stared up at her through frightened eyes. "What does that mean? What happened?"

"It means you died, Stephen. I think that sensation is what killed you. Something pulled your soul right out of your body and trapped you here. But don't worry, I'm going to get you out."

"You can't have him." Macy spoke right behind Val, her voice tight with fury.

Val turned to face the girl.

"It was you, wasn't it? You killed him. You brought him here. Did you kill all these people?"

"I didn't kill anybody. This is a safe place. They're here so I can protect them."

"Protect them from what?"

"From the bad people." Macy glared at her. "People like you."

Power swelled within Val as her anger rose.

"I may not be a good person, but I'm not the one holding these souls prisoner. They don't belong here. Let them go."

Macy's hands balled into fists. "I ain't letting anyone go. This is my place. I make the rules. You need to go." She stepped forward and shoved Val with both hands.

Val flew across the clearing, air exploding from her lungs as she slammed into the trunk of a tree. She winced as she got back to her feet, pain shooting through her ribs with every breath. She felt like she'd been kicked by an industrial-sized mule. Something was probably cracked in there.

"Get out." Macy was standing in front of her again, fists balled at her side, red dress whipping in the wind.

Val met her glare, golden eyes blazing. She felt Mister E smile.

"No."

She lashed out, and it was Macy's turn to go flying across the clearing. Val had a moment of satisfaction, but it lasted no longer than that. Macy bounced up and came right back at her, screaming like a banshee.

Val stepped forward to meet her, and the battle was truly joined.

Macy was incredibly strong. Whatever she was, she wasn't just a girl, no matter what she looked like. Maybe she had been, once. But not anymore. Her blows hammered Val like mule kicks. If Val had been astral-projecting like the last time she'd come here, she wouldn't have stood a chance. Especially here, in Macy's place of power.

But Val wasn't astral-projecting. This time she'd brought her full soul here, her full power. And Val at full power was no pushover.

They went back and forth, dealing and absorbing damage. Val knocked Macy down again and again, but each time the girl popped back up, unhurt.

Val, on the other hand, was definitely feeling it. Her cracked ribs stabbed through her with every breath. Her shoulder ached, her leg hurt, and her jaw felt like she'd been hit with a frying pan.

Even worse, while the girl's energy seemed inexhaustible, Val was getting tired. Her throat burned as she gasped for air. Her muscles were thick and heavy. She was a beat slow at blocking, and Macy caught her with an uppercut that lifted her clean off the ground. She hit the earth with a jarring thud, and lay still, ears ringing, the clearing swimming in and out of focus around her.

Macy's blurry figure stood over her.

"This is my place. You are not welcome."

Suffocating pressure bore down on Val. Blackness closed in. Just like the last time she'd come here, Macy was too strong. Only this time, Val wasn't only astral-projecting. This time, her whole soul was here.

If she died, there would be no waking up from it.

Her strength ebbed as she failed to find breath. Colored lights flashed in the darkness. Val struggled to push Macy's power off, struggled to breathe.

It was no use. The girl was too strong.

"Quit fighting nice," Mister E hissed. "You're letting her set the terms. You've got to fight dirty."

Fight dirty.

The words rolled through her mind, but she couldn't process them. She couldn't think of anything beyond the burning need in her lungs.

Dirty...

All she wanted was air.

Dirty.

She seized on the word, channeling every bit of wind she could gather directly into the ground at Macy's feet.

It scraped a bare circle in the earth, shearing dirt and rocks from the surface, spinning them up into a whirlwind. Macy screamed as rocks pelted her face, dirt filling her eyes and nose.

The girl's concentration broke. The pressure released.

Val sucked in air, coughed, then sucked in some more, cool oxygen quenching the fire in her lungs. Air had never tasted sweeter.

When her coughing finally subsided, Val turned her attention to Macy.

The girl had created a shield around herself, a little bubble of force to hold the swirling grit at bay. She cursed and spat, eyes watering as she wiped the dirt from her lids.

Val's eyes fell on the bare circle of earth the wind had scraped around the girl. That gave her an idea.

She focused the force of the wind downward, using all its strength to gouge the earth more, to dig like the coastal winds hollowing out the face of a cliff. Macy stumbled and went down as the earth was ripped out from under her feet.

Val kept digging. Excavating as if her magic were some kind of demented, industrial strength sandblaster. Macy could only huddle inside her protective bubble as the hole got deeper and deeper around her. The swirling wind became black and heavy with earth.

Then, when the girl's head was just barely above ground level, Val put all the dirt back.

She filled in the dirt around Macy, trapping her body beneath the ground, packing the earth tighter and tighter until the girl could not move. When she finally released her wind, only Macy's head was visible, sticking out of a raw patch of earth.

"Not exactly what I meant," Mister E said. *"But that works too."*

To Val's surprise, Macy was crying.

"Please," she sobbed. "Don't take them. I have to keep them safe. I can't let the bad people get them."

Val limped over to the raw patch of earth. Everything hurt. She had to keep her breathing shallow to minimize the sharp pains in her ribs.

Carefully, she knelt beside Macy, keeping firm pressure upon the earth, in case the girl tried to escape.

But all Macy did was cry. Fat tears carved clean streaks through the dirt caking her cheeks. The fight had gone out of her.

"What bad people?" Val asked gently. "Show me."

Macy showed her.

43

Val found herself standing in a Victorian drawing room. Beautiful patterned wallpaper had blue fleur de lis running in vertical rows over cream. A Persian rug covered the hardwood floor. Men in jackets sat smoking in sumptuously cushioned armchairs, while girls in corseted gowns served them drinks on silver trays.

It took her a minute to realize she was in the Queen Anne. A glance through the doors told her they were in a side room just off the main lobby.

She examined the scene, trying to figure out why Macy had brought her here. Everything seemed normal. The men were a bit boisterous, waving their cigars about while they talked and laughed, but their attire marked them as gentlemen of the era. The girls serving them were teenagers, with their hair pinned up in elaborate folds. There was no sign of Macy.

None of the people reacted to Val as she cautiously circled the room. Apparently, she was just an observer in this vision.

A woman entered the room and announced, "Please take your seats gentlemen, and turn your attention to the front of the room. This is the moment you've all been waiting for."

The men hooted and cheered while those who had been standing took their seats. They turned their chairs to face a small raised platform at one end of the room.

The heels of the woman's boots clicked as she stepped onto the platform. She was a strong, matronly woman, with ruddy cheeks and lively curls. She was full of confidence, and her sly smile gave the impression she had a secret to share.

"Thank you for coming, gentlemen. I needn't tell you that this is a one-of-a-kind opportunity, and the invitations you all received are highly valuable. I also needn't tell you that this event is very exclusive. If you're here, it's because you are a highly valued customer, and a man whose discretion can be relied upon. As the Admiral would say, loose lips sink ships." Her eyes settled on an older man with a distinguished silver mustache as she said this, and an appreciative chuckle ran through the men. "But much as I enjoy it, I know you didn't come here to listen to me talk. So, without further ado, let me introduce our first girl."

A girl in a yellow dress shyly mounted the platform. She was young, perhaps no more than ten, with the hint of breasts just starting to push out beneath her corset. Freckles covered her nose, and her tightly curled hair was frizzy and full of energy. She kept her eyes on the toes of her shoes.

"Our first young lady is a lovely specimen. As you can tell from her demeanor, Lucy is meek and pliable. She can play the harpsichord and polishes boots better than any navy man. She's healthy and fit and works from sunup till sundown without a peep of complaint. If you're looking for a young lady who can feed your children, massage your feet, and still have enough energy to entertain you at night"—the woman winked broadly at this, eliciting another chuckle—"this is the girl for you. Who will start the bidding? Do I hear five?"

One of the men held up an auction paddle, then another. Val's eyes grew wide with horror as she realized the girl was being sold. The spirited bidding went on for several minutes, finally won by a long-faced man in a brown coat. He smugly accepted the congratulations of his fellows.

Then a girl in a green dress was brought out, and another girl after that. They were all around the same age: little more than children. All were introduced like show ponies at the market. All were bought quickly.

Finally, it was Macy's turn.

The girl on the stage looked just like the one Val had fought in the glade. She didn't look down like the other girls. Her dark eyes contrasted with the lively color of her red dress, and she regarded the men solemnly, as if she were memorizing their faces. It made the men uncomfortable, and the bidding was noticeably slower than it had been for the other girls. Nevertheless, someone did eventually buy her, though the set of the presenter's mouth told Val she was not happy with the price.

The room dissolved into smoke around Val, replaced by another scene. Macy was in a kitchen now, her hair tied in a blue kerchief. She was bent over a washing tub, scrubbing laundry. The man who had bought her came up behind her, possessively grabbing her bottom. Macy squealed in surprise and shrank away from him, but he simply pressed forward, trapping her against the cabinets. The girl held herself very still as his hands moved over her, jaw clenched and unshed tears glistening in her eyes. Val recognized that look. She'd seen it on her own face. Banked rage and a silent promise of revenge.

Other scenes followed, a montage of years of abuse. Val wanted to look away, but she couldn't. Tears glistened in her own eyes now.

Finally, the scene changed to show Macy back at the Queen Anne. Her eyes were wild, her clothing ragged. She held a knife covered in blood. Val hoped the blood belonged to the man who had bought her.

Macy burst into the ballroom, interrupting another auction in progress. She flung herself at the woman on the stage, her knife rising. Men burst from their chairs to seize her, and both women disappeared beneath a crowd of struggling bodies.

When the men finally stepped back, Macy was lying still and broken.

The scene dissolved, and Val was back in the glade. Macy's tear-streaked face stared up at her.

"You see? The bad people are still out there. I have to protect them."

Val knelt in front of her.

"That was a long time ago," she said gently. "The bad people are gone."

Macy shook her head. "No. They're not. There are more bad people."

"Look, I know this is hard to hear. But you killed Stephen. Maybe you were trying to protect him, but..."

"I didn't kill him! I saved him!"

"I don't understand."

Macy showed her again.

Val's eyes widened. Something else had killed Stephen. Macy had pulled his spirit into her realm to protect him.

She summoned a cyclone to dig into the earth, freeing Macy in seconds. She offered the young woman her hand.

"I'm sorry. I didn't know. I'll stop the bad people, I promise."

Macy let Val pull her out of the earth. The young woman brushed off her skirt, giving Val a radiant smile.

"Thank you. Please, take this with you." She stretched out her palm. On it lay a single red rose.

Val sensed magic as she took the bloom between her fingers.

"It's a port key," Mister E supplied. *"The rose connected to this realm."*

"Call me with this blossom. Let me know when you've stopped the bad people."

Val nodded once, her gaze firm.

"I will."

44

Val opened her eyes with a gasp. Around her, the witches were still chanting. Candlelight flickered across the ceiling.

"Stop," she shouted. Or tried to shout, anyway. Her mouth was too dry, and she only managed to produce a dry sound. She swallowed and tried again. "Stop!"

At a signal from Paula, the chanting grew quieter, but did not stop entirely, keeping Val trapped inside the circle.

Paula raised her voice and intoned solemnly, "Valora Keri, now is your hour of judgment."

Val struggled to her feet. "No, wait. It wasn't the ghost. There's something worse."

Paula regarded her skeptically. "You are not talking your way out of this."

"No, I'm not trying to. Just listen for a minute."

Paula folded her arms, her mouth pressed into a thin line. "One minute."

"The dark presence I felt is the ghost of a girl. She died here a long time ago. They sold her into slavery, her and a lot of other girls. I'll spare you the details, but as you can imagine, it was horrible. Anyway, she's the one who trapped Stephen's spirit, but she's not the one who killed him. Or maybe she did kind of kill him while trying to protect him. That part's a little unclear. But that's not the point." Paula was looking impatient, so Val hurried on. "A necromancer named Baron Blood has been using a gold skull ring with ruby eyes to siphon life out of vampires and transfer it to wealthy customers, extending their lives. I saw the ritual. I saw an old man grow young again, and I saw the vampires chained up in a cavern down below this hotel. The Baron claims the ring is the new fountain of youth or something."

The witches' chant had fallen to a whisper while Val spoke. They watched her now with curiosity.

"But Baron Blood didn't tell me the whole story. He left out one very important element to his ritual. The ring lets him transfer life from the vampires, true. But it requires more than just their life. It requires a blood price. A life for a life." The Sisters looked puzzled, but understanding dawned in Paula's eyes. "That's why he's performing the ceremony below the Queen Anne. His ritual magic is killing people inside the hotel. For every rich asshole who gets their life extended, an innocent person in the hotel dies. That's what happened to Stephen. Baron Blood's ritual magic caught and killed him. Then the Queen Anne's ghost girl stepped in and caught Stephen's soul before the necromancer could take that too. She's trying to protect him, and all the other souls who have died here. The way she couldn't protect the other girls while she was alive."

"This necromancer is taking people's lives and giving those years to his customers," Paula said. She held up her hand to the others, and the chanting stopped. Val felt the pressure in her ears change as the magic dissipated.

"Exactly. We have to stop him."

"We?" the Sisters chimed in.

"Who is..."

"... this we?"

"You are the do-gooder..."

"... Valora Keri."

"You are the one..."

"... who fights monsters..."

"... to soothe your guilty conscience."

"There is..."

"... no 'we'..."

"... in this equation."

Val glared at them.

"A necromancer is killing people for money. Working with vampires. And you don't care?" She shook her head in disgust. "And you think you have the moral superiority to pass judgment on me? You're pathetic."

One of the Sisters opened her mouth to answer, but Paula held up a hand.

"She's right. We cannot ignore this evil." She pursed her lips, considering Val. "What do you need us to..." Her eyes widened, her face contorting in pain. Paula crumpled to the floor with a low moan.

One of the Sisters went to her, while another hissed at Val, "What have you done?"

"I didn't do anything." She cocked her head at Paula, murmuring to Mister E, "Give me your sight."

Her eyes shone as the world shifted. She could see a fog of magical energy swirling in the room, the remnants of the ritual magic slowly dissipating. But there was something else. A thread of dark magic had latched onto Paula, sucking her energy down through the floor of the room.

Val cursed. "It's got to be the ring. Baron Blood is performing the ritual right now, and it has targeted Paula."

The Sisters turned on her.

"This is..."

"... your doing."

"Release her..."

"... at once!"

"It's not me," Val growled, her hands clenching into fists.

"I do not..."

"... believe you."

The Sisters started to chant again. Val saw the magical fog start to thicken. The circle was powering up. In seconds she would be trapped again.

She dove out of the circle just as the spell snapped into place. Pain shot through her as the barrier sheared through the trailing toe of her boot, sharp as any razor.

But Val didn't have time for pain.

She whirled and drove her fist into the stomach of the nearest Sister. Olga folded around her fist like a paper crane, collapsing with a groan.

The other two Sisters raised their hands and voices, starting a new spell. But this was close fighting, and that kind of magic was best used at a distance. Val didn't give them time to complete the incantation.

She kicked one of them in the ribs and hit the other with a straight jab to the face. Val dashed for the exit, turning back in the doorway.

"The only way to save Paula is to stop the ritual. If you want to help, follow me."

"Oh, we will follow you..."

"... Valora Keri."

"We will follow you..."

"... to your grave."

The Sisters hurled a bolt of entropy at the doorway, but Val was already gone, sprinting away down the hall. A chunk of the doorframe rotted away to dust behind her.

Val didn't have time to convince them. She had to get down to the cavern. Had to stop the ritual before it was too late.

If she didn't, Paula would be Baron Blood's next victim.

45

Val sprinted down the hallway of the Queen Anne. She hoped the Sisters were following her; she could use their help confronting Baron Blood. But she didn't have time to wait and see. She didn't know how quickly the ring worked. All she knew was that every second she delayed was a second closer to death for Paula.

The hotel had been remodeled extensively over the years. Rooms had been torn out and replaced. Whole wings rebuilt on different plans. She had no idea where the basement was, or how to get down into the caverns below. But she knew it was possible. She'd seen it with her own eyes. She just had to keep heading in a vague downward direction and hope for the best.

She pounded down a flight of stairs and scanned the hallway for the next flight. She growled in frustration as she found it at the end of the hall, to her right. Who built a multi-floor building and didn't stack the stairs on top of each other?

Any doubt as to whether the Sisters were following her evaporated when she reached for the handrail, only to have it crumble to dust beneath her grip. She shuddered. That entropy spell was nasty. She didn't want to think about what it would do if it hit her.

The Sisters' voices followed her down the stairs.

"Give up..."

"... Valora Keri."

"You cannot run..."

"... from fate."

"Shows how little they know," Mister E chimed in. *"You've been running from fate your whole life."*

"That's not the compliment you think it is," Val huffed.

As the stairs dumped her out into the lobby, she skidded to a halt. The night clerk at the front desk didn't even glance up to acknowledge her, his nose buried deep in a book.

"This is not where I wanted to end up."

Val cast about frantically for another set of stairs that would take her to the basement housekeeping level. Nothing looked promising. There was the main entrance that let out to the street, the stairway she'd just climbed down, an open archway that led to the dining area, a small doorway behind the desk, and an ancient elevator closed off by a metal latticework door so warped and rusted it hardly counted as a door at all.

"Well, the elevator is out. There's no way I'm trusting my life to that deathtrap." She swept her eyes across the lobby again, hoping she'd missed something. No such luck. Maybe the small door behind the desk? "Or the dining area might have a service entrance..."

"Die, Valora Keri!"

Val leapt to the side a second before the floor crumbled where she'd been standing.

"Goddammit! Don't you witches have any other spells?"

The Sisters didn't answer, they simply continued chanting, preparing to cast the entropy spell yet again.

Val rolled her eyes. "One-note villains are so boring."

She sprinted for the dining area, praying that her hunch about a service entrance was correct. If it wasn't, she'd be trapping herself, and any hope she had of reasoning with the Sisters was gone. The three witches were in a full-blown rage. Nothing she said was going to reach them.

She wove her way across a sea of dining tables towards a set of swinging doors. Pushing through the doors, she found herself in an industrial kitchen, with stainless-steel counters and pots hanging on hooks, and a stove with so many burners you could park a car on it.

"Holy hand grenades. Are they cooking for an army? I didn't think this hotel was that popular."

"It's not. This is no doubt a remnant from the Queen Anne's heyday. Fattening girls up to sell takes a lot of food, after all," Mister E said.

"Very funny. Do you see a set of stairs anywhere?"

"No, but there's another door at the far end of the kitchen."

"Let's hope it doesn't lead to a pantry or we're screwed." Val dashed off in that direction.

She heard the doors swing open again behind her. She gestured irritably with her hand and three of the pots flew in that direction.

She allowed herself a small grin as the Sisters' curses told her she'd hit at least one of them.

Val pushed through the door and skidded to a halt. She was in an enormous pantry.

"Flaming toads, this is bigger than my living room." She cast about wildly for another exit. All she saw was shelves full of food. "I guess I know where to head when the next apocalypse hits."

"Over here, behind the stack of soup cans," Mister E said, helpfully materializing in mid-air and pointing the way with his tail.

She found a small doorway hiding behind the stacked soup. Through it, a narrow stairway descended into darkness.

"Thank the almighty Bob."

Her moment of relief was interrupted by soup cans crumbling to dust beside her head. With this support gone, the entire stack came crashing down on top of her.

Val lashed out, reflexively knocking the cans away. They flew in every direction, noisily clanging off the stainless-steel surfaces. Another curse from the Sisters told her at least one soup can had connected with a softer target.

She didn't wait around to see if it slowed the witches down.

Val dove into the narrow staircase, the old wooden steps creaking and groaning beneath her pounding feet. The stairs turned to the left at the first landing, and she looked down into darkness.

"Shit, I forgot..."

"To turn on the light; yes, I noticed." Mister E smirked. *"Don't worry, I've got you covered."*

The darkness lit up as the cat loaned her his night vision.

After a couple more turnings, the stairs let out into a hallway. A ratty strip of carpet ran down the center, and the walls were cluttered with stacks of old furniture and serving carts.

"Finally, the service level," she breathed.

"I find your relief disturbing. You do know there are vampires down here, don't you?"

"One problem at a time. First, we have to find them."

She peered up the corridor, one way and then the other. Both directions looked dim, dingy, and disused. She saw no clue as to which way she should go.

Val groaned. "Bat's balls. Where do we go now?"

"They both look the same to me. I'd say pick a direction and start running. And do it quickly, before the Sisters get here." The rumble of feet clattering down the stairs underlined the urgency of his statement.

With a sigh, Val did just that.

46

F or a change, Val's luck seemed to be in. Sort of.

The hallway took her directly to a crevice in the wall. She followed the well-worn path into the old smugglers' tunnel and quickly found herself in the cavern where she'd confronted Baron Blood and Melinda Pearl. Three starving vampires were still chained to the wall, though Val thought the ones she'd seen previously had been replaced by a fresh set of victims. They snarled and strained at their chains, driven wild by the scent of warm blood.

That was the good news.

The bad news was that Baron Blood was not in this cavern.

"The necromancer is no doubt down in the ritual space we found him in before," Mister E said, floating lazily on his back at eye-level.

"Ya think?" Val spat.

She paced the cavern, thinking furiously. Was there some way to interrupt the ritual from here? It didn't seem likely.

"What if I freed the vampires?" she muttered.

"Removing the power source might stop the ritual," Mister E confirmed. *"Or it could cause the spell to shift focus and siphon more energy from the hotel guests. We know the magic is already bleeding over onto the humans. Taking the vampires out of the equation may accelerate that process."*

"I'm open to other suggestions," Val growled. "But you'd better make them fast. The Sisters will be here any second."

The cat-demon spread his paws in an all-too-human gesture.

"On the other hand, freeing the vampires could disrupt the ritual completely. I simply don't have enough information to make an accurate prediction."

"Thanks for nothing." She cocked her head as the Sisters' chanting drifted through the crevice. It sounded like they'd emerge into the cavern any second. She scowled and raised her right arm over her head. "I think our time's up."

A gale sprang up inside the cavern, gathering dust as it howled down the crevice back toward the hotel. She smiled grimly at the Sisters' muffled curses and poured more energy into the spell. She needed time to think, and she couldn't do that with the Sisters throwing entropy spells at her.

Val examined the rest of the cavern. There was only one other entrance, the crevice from which Melinda Pearl had emerged during their previous showdown. She peered down the dark crack. It turned sharply to the right after only a dozen paces. She had no idea where it led after that.

Perhaps it would take her down to the ritual space by an alternate route.

Or perhaps it would take her straight into a nest of vampires.

"Not that I have much choice at this point." She sighed. Out of the frying pan and into the fire would be the words engraved on her tombstone.

Then the time for thinking was over.

The Sisters came into the cavern, leaning forward into her gale, pushing an umbrella of force before them. Val's wind bent around the shield, leaving the witches untouched.

"You are out of time..."

"... Val Keri."

"This little chase..."

"... ends now."

The Sister on the left—Maria?—drew glowing symbols in the air for what Val was sure would be another entropy spell.

"I guess we're at the try-it-and-find-out stage," she muttered.

Val focused a tendril of wind, amplifying the speed exponentially as she funneled it down to a handsbreadth. The stream of air hit the wall like a sandblaster, shearing away the surface of the rock where the chain holding the vampire closest to the Sisters was anchored. The shackle exploded from the wall.

The witches' eyes barely had time to widen before the starving vampire was upon them.

Val hesitated, caught by a horrified fascination at what she'd done. She knew she should flee. That was the whole point of her little distraction. She didn't think the vampire would occupy the Sisters' attention for long.

Nor did she want it to, really. She wasn't trying to harm the Sisters, just slow them down long enough to escape. That was the reason she'd freed only one vampire, not all three of them. She thought the witches would be able to handle one of the creatures.

But the speed and ferocity of the vampire took her off guard. Starved as it was, she expected it to be weak and slow, but its desperate hunger had the opposite effect.

The vampire moved so fast her eyes could barely track the movement. In the space between breaths, it had crossed the cavern and leapt into the air.

Val felt a moment of shock, followed by swift guilt. What had she done? She remembered her own vampire attack in this cavern, how quickly a single bite had overcome her defenses. There was no way the Sisters could react in time to save themselves. Had she just condemned them all?

But the Sisters surprised her.

In a blink, they angled their umbrella of force to intercept the airborne vampire. The creature collided with the invisible bubble and bounced off to the side.

It landed on its feet, catlike, already moving towards them again.

The witches were prepared. This time, they loosed the entropy spell they had prepared for Val. It caught the vampire in full stride as it blurred toward them, fangs bared.

Between one step and the next, the creature dissolved into dust.

Val's mouth hung open. That was what the Sisters were trying to do to her. If they got their way, there would be no trial. Just a merciless execution.

The three witches turned their attention back to her, their chant already starting again.

So much for taking it easy on them.

Val blasted the shackles for the remaining vampires free as well.

The Sisters snarled and angled their shield umbrella back toward this new threat.

But only one of the freed creatures was heading toward the Sisters.

The other one was coming straight for Val.

Val yelped and aimed her funnel of focused air at the vampire's chest. It hit with the force of a train, sending the creature sprawling, tumbling across the cavern.

But like its brethren before, it was back up in an instant, moving toward her with hideous speed.

Val tried to hit it again, but the vampire had caught on to what she was doing. It didn't move toward her in a straight line, instead bobbing and weaving, zigzagging across the cavern. She tried to follow, but the creature was too fast, easily staying ahead of her all-too-human reflexes.

The vampire would be on her in seconds. If it got too close, she was in trouble. One bite and the sedative in its saliva would ensure that it was all over.

In desperation, Val retreated into the tunnel from which Melinda Pearl had previously emerged. She widened her funnel and put every ounce of power she could scrape into it, doing her best to maintain the same force while covering a larger area.

Dust exploded from the walls as she blasted the entire mouth of the tunnel, sending a thick cloud boiling out into the cavern, engulfing the vampire, the Sisters, everything. She didn't stop there, though. As she continued to back down the tunnel, she focused on the roof, tearing out huge chunks of rock, sending them tumbling along with the thickening dust.

Finally, a massive cracking sound split the air, so loud it shook her bones. With a roar, the entire mouth of the tunnel collapsed behind her.

Val didn't wait to see what would happen next. She turned and fled into the darkness.

47

V al found herself creeping down a labyrinth of tunnels, some natural, some man-made, which took her even deeper into the darkness. It was impossible to tell which path Melinda Pearl had followed to get to the ritual cavern, or even which path was the main trail. After the fourth intersection, every branch looked the same. She kept one ear cocked for sounds of pursuit behind her, but so far she'd heard nothing.

"Hopefully that means the cave-in sealed the entrance," Val muttered. "Although even if they do get into the tunnel, with all these intersections the Sisters should have a hard time tracking us. Also, our odds of stumbling into a vampire's lair get lower with every turn."

"Matched by a correlated rise in the odds of us getting lost and never finding our way out again," Mister E added cheerily. *"We certainly can't go back the way we came."*

He drifted along beside her, floating on his back, appearing unperturbed by the prospect.

"Thanks. You're a real ray of sunshine."

"One does what one can."

Her glare bounced off him without effect.

At the next fork, she bent low, examining the ground. If she could find tracks or scuff marks, they'd at least tell her that other people had come this way before.

Unfortunately, clean rock had risen to the surface here, leaving almost no dirt or sand to hold impressions.

"Instead of algebra, I wish school had actually taught me useful things. Like how to navigate an underground cave system while running from witches."

Mister E tutted. *"The failures of the modern education system."*

She was about to pick a direction at random when something caught her attention. At roughly eye level, three vertical lines the length of her little finger had been carved into the stone of the right-hand passage. They were thin slashes, each no more than the width of a blade.

"They look like the kind of marks you'd carve into the wall of a jail cell to count the days," Val said, running her finger over them.

"Perhaps someone was lost and wandering in circles. This is the number of times they passed through this particular intersection."

"Let's hope it was something a bit more useful. Like an exit-this-way sign."

"It could also be a warning," Mister E said mildly. *"Danger ahead. Abandon all hope ye who enter here."*

Val sighed. "Remind me again why I keep you around?"

"It must be my winning smile." He demonstrated by baring his teeth in a crescent moon smile bigger than his head.

Val snorted.

"Yeah, that must be it."

The right-hand tunnel seemed more natural than manmade, with the roof of the crevice cleaving straight above her head into a dark cut that continued far beyond the limits of her sight. The floor was remarkably level beneath her feet, though, and the walls remained just wider than her shoulders.

"If we were on the surface, I'd call this a slot canyon," Val mused, running her fingers along a set of wavy striations.

"What would you call it now?"

"Fuck if I know. Geology is another subject they should teach instead of algebra."

The maybe-a-slot-canyon led them on for nearly ten minutes without any other intersections.

"If I'd known we were going spelunking, I would have brought some snacks. Or at least a water bottle." Val stopped to wipe the sweat from her forehead. "Is it just me, or is it getting hotter down here?"

"Anything is possible."

"I'm starting to suspect this isn't going to lead us to the ritual chamber," she said as she resumed walking. "I hope it leads somewhere soon. I'm starting to get hungry."

"We passed through a whole kitchen back in the Queen Anne. We could always head back there."

Val considered the idea. In the right light, she supposed it might not be terrible.

"I guess that would depend on two things," she finally said. "One, can we even find our way back the way we came?"

Mister E made a rude noise. *"Please. I could take us back there blindfolded."*

"And two," Val continued, "did my little cave-in completely seal the entrance? If it didn't, it would also be good to know who won the fight between the Sisters and the vampires."

"If those witches couldn't defend themselves against a couple of half-starved vampires, they're not very good witches." Mister E scoffed.

"Yeah, that's what I figure, too. Especially after seeing how easily they took out the first one. I wouldn't have sicced the vampires on them if I thought they would seriously hurt them. I just needed to slow them down long enough for us to get away." She tapped her fingers against her thumb, thinking. "But would they have given up the pursuit afterwards? Or will we run into them on the way back?"

"Well, we have passed through several intersections. Even if they did manage to get into the tunnel, what are the chances they chose the same branches we did?"

"Slim if they're choosing randomly. Much higher if they've got some kind of tracking spell."

"And do they?"

"I have no idea," Val admitted. She sighed. "Anyway, that's really beside the point. The important thing is we need to stop the ritual before it kills Paula."

"Assuming it hasn't already."

"Right."

After a few more intersections, Mister E's ears perked up.

"Do you hear that?"

Val paused, listening. All she heard was a deep underground silence.

"No, what is it?" she whispered.

"Chanting." He swiveled his ears, then turned his face toward the tunnel on their right. *"That way."*

"Is it Baron Blood?"

"If it isn't, there are an unreasonable amount of crazy spell casters in this town."

Val rolled her eyes and crept down the tunnel. After a minute, she heard the chanting too, a faint whispering in the distance. It grew steadily louder as she progressed, stepping as quietly as she could.

Finally, she saw light at the end of the tunnel. Creeping closer, she crouched and peered at the ritual chamber through the doorway. Candles again blazed around the circle on the floor. Baron Blood stood on his platform on the far side of the room. There was no gallery of spectators this time, and an old woman was chained in the center of the circle. The woman had the same pale skin as the man who'd been chained there the last time. As Val watched, her grey hair began to take on blond highlights.

"Do the people not know where the life energy is coming from?" Val mused. "Do they not realize they are killing other people to sustain their own lives? Or do they just not care?"

She got to her feet, her face grim. "Either way, we're going to put a stop to it."

A voice spoke from the darkness behind her.

"I'm afraid I can't let you do that."

48

Val turned to find herself facing Rodrigo. Melinda Pearl's top lieutenant was as polished as ever, black hair slicked back from his widow's peak, white dress shirt casually rolled up to the elbows. An expensive-looking black vest with silver buttons matched his sharply creased trousers. His polished shoes shone. He looked like he belonged in an art gallery or a fundraising dinner.

"Rodrigo. Aren't you a bit overdressed?" Val said, masking her surprise behind the sarcasm. "Or is there a five-star restaurant lurking down here I don't know about?"

"Don't change the subject, Keri. How did you get here?" The vampire stepped closer, trying to intimidate her by crowding her space. The effect was somewhat ruined by the fact that Val was taller than he was.

Which is not to say that she wasn't intimidated. She absolutely was. Rodrigo wasn't someone you wanted to find yourself alone with in a dark cave. But she did her best not to show it.

"Well, it was a such a lovely night, I figured I'd take a stroll and see some of the famous sights. You know, the Golden Gate Bridge, Coit Tower, the underground ritual room. That kind of thing."

Rodrigo's lips pulled back, baring his fangs in a thin smile.

"You're not fooling anyone, Keri. I can hear your heart racing. I know you're scared."

"Well, that's just rude. Don't you know it isn't polite to comment on the speed of a girl's heart? I mean, I didn't say anything about your bad breath, did I?" Sweat trickled down her temple.

She might not be fooling Rodrigo, but her brave front was as much for her own benefit as it was for his. It was like an affirmation. Tell yourself you are brave, and you will become brave. At least she hoped it worked that way.

Also, she wanted to keep him talking. Fighting off a half-starved vampire who has been chained to a wall for weeks is one thing. Fending off the second most powerful vampire in the city was quite another.

Especially at such close quarters. If Rodrigo decided to go for her throat, Val doubted she'd even register the movement before he sank his fangs into her.

Still, she had her power gathered and ready, just in case. She thrummed like a battery, barely keeping the magic in check. If Rodrigo made a move, she'd do her best to make him regret it.

But she was far from sure of her ability to do that. Better to keep him talking.

"What are you and Baron Blood really up to here? I know you don't care about extending the lives of rich assholes. What's in it for you?"

He smirked. "You haven't figured it out yet? I thought you were supposed to be good at solving things."

"Pretend I'm a little slow. Enlighten me."

"Let's examine the clues, shall we?" He began ticking things off on his fingers. "Clue number one, the ritual makes the recipients younger. Clue two, their skin grows pale in the process. Clue three, the energy being transferred to them comes from vampires." He stopped and cocked an eyebrow at her. "Ringing any bells yet?"

Val's jaw dropped. Laid out like that, it was obvious.

"You're turning them into vampires?" She looked back at the woman chained to the floor. Her hair was now almost completely blond, the wrinkles on her face smoothed away. "Do they know that?"

"We may have neglected to put that little detail in the brochure." He chuckled. "By the time they figure it out, it doesn't matter. They're hooked. They'll do anything to stay young."

Val's hands clenched into fists. "How many people have you turned? How many innocents have you killed in the Queen Anne to do it?"

"This isn't twenty questions."

"That's good. Because if it was, you'd be really bad at it."

"How did you get here?" Rodrigo growled, his expression darkening to match hers.

Val could feel his breath on her face. Which was just gross. Nobody wants to be breathed on by a vampire.

She bit back another sarcastic retort. She'd probably pushed him as far as she could. One more flippant response and he'd probably rip out her throat.

"I found this room by accident. I was lost in the tunnels, and I heard chanting. I followed the sound."

"Bullshit." Rodrigo shot forward, his hand clamping around her throat. The tips of his nails dug into her skin. He lifted her off her feet and pinned her against the wall.

Val gave a mental sigh. She'd tried to be honest, and look where it got her.

Fine. They'd do this the hard way.

Val kicked him in the balls.

She wasn't sure if it would work—Did vampires' balls still hurt if you kicked them?—and she was ready to follow it with a spell if Rodrigo simply took the kick and laughed at her.

She needn't have worried. Undead or not, Rodrigo groaned and folded up just like every other male on the planet would.

"Huh. Good to know."

She kicked him in the face for good measure, and the vampire curled into a whimpering fetal position on the floor of the tunnel.

Val squared her shoulders and turned toward the chamber. She had a necromancer to stop.

49

"Baron Blood!" Val roared, stepping into the chamber. "This ends now!"

She didn't wait to see what the necromancer's response would be, unleashing a rush of wind that extinguished every candle in the chamber, plunging the room into darkness.

"Whoops. Maybe I didn't think that all the way through," she muttered. "Eyes?"

Mister E laughed and gave her his vision again.

The first thing she noticed was that the ritual spell was still active. Bright power swirled around the chamber, green and black and gold, fed by a thick tendril of energy coming through the ceiling. It spiraled down into the woman chained to the floor, who arched her back and pulled against the restraints, teeth bared in a grimace. The woman might have volunteered for this, but the procedure looked far from painless. Also, candles were apparently not an essential part of the ritual once the transfer was in full swing. Val hadn't done anything to stop the spell.

Baron Blood continued chanting, though his gaze was now searching her end of the room. She was glad the darkness kept her hidden, because the murder in his eyes would have burned her to a crisp.

The other thing she noticed, now that she was fully inside the room, was that she had been mistaken about the lack of an audience. There were other observers watching the ritual. Though it would be a mistake to call them mere observers.

Nearly a dozen figures were spaced about the chamber, their backs to the wall. Their eyes gleamed with reflected power. Their skin was pale, and they all stood as rigid as statues.

All their eyes were fixed on Val.

"Vampires," she breathed. "Shit."

Two of them stood flanking the doorway she'd just come through. They were almost close enough to touch her.

Val stepped forward, intending to scuff the line of the circle with her toe and interrupt the ritual the same way she had before.

But the vampires were too fast. The one to her left grabbed her by the arm, spinning her around and slamming her into the stone wall.

She groaned and returned the favor, sending the vampire tumbling with a focused punch of wind. Another came at her, and she sent it flying too.

They were all moving toward her now, cutting her off from the circle. There were too many to fight, and she couldn't get past them.

Cursing, Val called up a whirlwind, using it as a defensive wall. It roared and shrieked around her, picking up dust until all she could see was a whirling mass of red and brown.

A pale hand emerged from the storm, groping blindly toward her face. Val focused the wind on that spot, accelerating it until the tiny bits of gravel and sand cut like a buzz saw.

Shreds of cloth fluttered as the sleeve around the arm was torn away. Then bits of skin joined them.

Still the vampire refused to pull away.

Val watched in horror as the wind stripped flesh from bone in seconds, then ground through the bone itself. The hand and half of the arm it was attached to were severed completely, flopping to the ground at her feet.

"Gross." She kicked the thing back into the swirling wind.

"At least there's no blood. That's one good thing about dismembering the undead," Mister E said lazily.

Val kept the winds at buzz-saw speed, but no more groping hands followed that one. There was only the tiny storm swirling around her.

"I guess they must have learned their lesson."

"Well, if their objective was to keep you from interrupting the ritual, it seems to me you've done an excellent job of cutting yourself off. As long as you stay inside this little storm, you're doing their job for them."

Val scowled, but he had a point. She couldn't see or hear anything beyond the whirlwind, but she was sure Baron Blood was still out there, chanting. But if she dropped her shield, the vampires would overwhelm her.

On the other hand, if she did nothing Paula would die. If the witch wasn't dead already.

Fuck it. All she had to do was break his concentration. Stop the ritual. Whatever happened after that happened.

She gathered the wind, narrowing the funnel over her head until it looked like she stood at the bottom of an inverted tornado.

"Here goes nothing."

She lifted the base of the storm over her head, trying to figure out where the Baron was. In the process, she got an excellent view of four very surprised vampires, standing just outside the perimeter marked out by her storm. They blinked at her, unsure if her barrier was still there or not.

She ignored them and searched for the Baron. There. His platform was over to her left.

Val bent the tip of the storm funnel across the ceiling, reaching toward the Baron. It elongated slowly, a worm groping through the air. She couldn't move it too quickly or it would lose its force and become no more than a directional breeze. Which might annoy the Baron, but it probably wouldn't be enough to stop the ritual.

No, she needed to hit him with the full force of her little tornado. There was no way he could stand against that.

Unfortunately, maneuvering the storm was taking too long. One of the vampires finally plucked up its courage and reached out a tentative arm towards her. Finding no resistance, it bared its teeth and took a step forward.

Val took a step back. She needed to stay out of reach long enough to get the funnel to the Baron. After that—well, she'd worry about that after.

Another vampire followed the first one's lead. Then another. They circled her, still wary, but growing bolder by the second. Val shuffled away as best she could, keeping her back to the wall, trying to keep them all in her peripheral vision as she kept her attention on the funnel, bending toward Baron Blood. Almost there. A few more seconds and the tip would reach the necromancer's platform.

Val ran out of time as the vampires attacked.

50

As a bony hand closed around her throat, Val gave a desperate push, flinging her mini tornado at the platform where Baron Blood stood. She never saw if it got there. Air whooshed out of her as the vampire slammed her against the wall. Fangs filled her vision.

She kicked out, trying to drop the creature the same way she had Rodrigo. The kick connected, but it was only after the vampire did not crumple that she realized this one was a woman.

"Flying toads," she croaked.

As the vampire leaned towards her neck, Val yanked her knife free and jabbed up into the creature's jaw.

That did the trick. The vampire's grip slackened as it stumbled back, clutching at the wound. Val kicked it in the chest for good measure, knocking it back, then crouched in a defensive stance. Half a dozen vampires surrounded her in a loose semi-circle.

She couldn't tell if her funnel had reached Baron Blood—there hadn't been a massive explosion of energy like when she'd broken the circle. And there wouldn't be. If she'd broken the Baron's concentration, the spell would just quietly dissipate.

Regardless, she didn't have any attention to spare for it. She had done her best to stop the ritual, and she'd either succeeded or failed.

She would have to be content with that. Now she was fighting for her life.

She ducked a swipe as another vampire tried to rake her with its claws. There might be a lot of them, but these clearly weren't the most powerful vampires. They were clumsy and slow—which meant they probably hadn't been vampires for very long.

Val grimaced. More evidence that the vampires were aggressively expanding their ranks. Not good.

Claws slashed her cheek, and she cursed as she spun away from the attack. Saying they were clumsy and slow was relative, of course. Even clumsy and slow vampires were faster than most humans.

Several feet to her left, the mouth of a tunnel yawned. She thought it might be the tunnel she'd come down the last time she was here, when she'd followed Baron Blood from the party at Padraig's house. She couldn't be sure, but it offered her a slim ray of hope. She started shuffling in that direction, slashing at any vampires that got too close. If she was really, really lucky, maybe she could make a run for it.

She started to raise another whirlwind around herself. The vampires realized what she was doing and came at her in a frenzy, trying to get to her before the wind barrier became too strong to cross again. Her world became a furious rush of motion. Vampires lunging and biting. Slashing with their claws. Trying to grab her and drag her down with sheer numbers.

Val became a dervish. Dodging and darting. Parrying and lashing out with vicious counterattacks. Spinning almost as quickly as the winds she controlled.

It wasn't pretty. Blood ran down her face from a number of cuts. Some of it dripped into her eye, burning and half-blinding her. Her leather jacket was getting shredded. But step by painful step, she managed to inch the melee closer to the mouth of the tunnel.

In her peripheral vision, she noticed the spell energy in the cavern was dissipating. The tendril of energy coming down through the ceiling had disappeared. Val allowed herself a grim smile. It seemed her funnel cloud might have reached Baron Blood after all.

Finally, the mouth of the tunnel was two long steps away. Only a single vampire stood between Val and a dash for freedom. To get past it, she'd have to give that vampire her full attention, attack it with everything she had. That would mean turning her back on the others. If she didn't get free, they would be on her in seconds. It was all or nothing.

Taking a deep breath, she gathered herself, turned, and lunged straight at the creature, slashing at its face.

Surprise almost got her past it. The vampire hadn't expected her sudden pivot, and it reacted slowly, stumbling back a step. Then another.

Val's jabbing knuckles scraped teeth, then she hit it with her shoulder, bulling past it. Claws tore at her skin, but she didn't slow, putting everything she had into her desperate bid for freedom.

Then she was past, ducking into the mouth of the tunnel.

She ran for all she was worth, pounding through the darkness, her lungs burning. She filled the tunnel behind her with wind, pushing at her back, accelerating her steps, sending her flying down the passage like a kite. She couldn't hear the vampires' pursuit. Her ears were full of the rushing of the wind. She didn't dare slow.

The tunnel turned suddenly, too sharp for her to change directions. She bounced off the wall and stumbled, scraping her palms on the stone.

She scrambled back to her feet, but as she ran on, the tunnel started to list to the side. Her vision was growing fuzzy.

Val stumbled again, and this time she did fall, getting a faceful of dust. It was difficult to pick herself back up. Her body was heavy. Exhausted. She just wanted to lie down and sleep.

Somehow she managed to stand, but now the best she could do was a lurching stumble, bouncing off the walls as she veered drunkenly forward.

"Wha... what's wrong with me?" she slurred.

"*It's vampire venom,*" Mister E hissed. "*You must have gotten bit in the fight.*"

Val bounced off another wall, stumbling and sliding down it until she lay in the dirt once again. She could hardly see anything now, the world obscured behind a thick black curtain.

"*Keep moving. You're almost there.*"

She didn't know if that was the truth, or if Mister E was just trying to keep her going. Either way, she appreciated the encouragement.

Walking was impossible, but she managed to lever herself up to a crawl.

Val didn't know how long she crawled. It felt like ages. She could see nothing at all now, and kept her shoulder brushing along the wall as a guide.

As the last of her strength was about to give out, she smelled it.

Cold air. Fresh air. Outside.

Gritting her teeth, she forced her limbs into motion again.

The breeze on her skin grew stronger. The air was cold and moist.

At last, she could go no further. Her body was numb and unresponsive. Her cheek rested on cold stone. Her eyes fluttered closed, but it didn't matter. It was just as black with them open.

With a sigh, Val slid senseless into the San Francisco night.

51

F or the second time in a week, Val awoke in a strange bed. Only this time, it wasn't so strange.

"Padraig?"

She pushed herself up on her elbows, the silk sheets cool beneath her fingers. Her hands were bandaged and wrapped in gauze. The calico cat curled against her side gave a soft questioning sound as it raised its head.

"Oh, hello again." She stroked the cat's cheek and felt its body vibrating against her ribs. "I never did get your name last time."

"That is Fiona," Padraig said, stepping in. The aroma of eggs and tea rose from a silver tray he carried. He carefully placed it over her lap, unfolding little legs on each side so that it straddled her.

Val's stomach growled like a wild thing. She blushed.

Padraig laughed. "It sounds like I arrived just in time."

"Again," Val amended. She held up her bandaged hands. "This is getting to be a habit. How embarrassing."

"Oh, I don't know. Beautiful women collapsing at my feet. Having to nurse them back to health. A man could get used to this sort of thing." He grinned and Val ducked her head as she felt her blush deepen.

"Is that what happened then? I collapsed at your feet?"

"More or less. In truth, it was the gardener's feet. You collapsed on the path below the terrace."

She nodded. That made sense. The last thing she remembered was cool air on her skin. She must have followed the tunnels all the way back to Padraig's yard.

Padraig removed the cover from the tray and settled into the chair beside the bed.

"Eat. You can tell me how you came to be lying in my garden after you've sated that beast in your belly."

Val saw no reason to refuse. She shoveled some eggs into her mouth and took a sip of tea. She sighed. Heavenly.

"Did you make this?"

Padraig laughed. "No. Definitely not. The chef would chase me out with a frying pan if I tried to set foot in the kitchen. She rules her realm with an iron hand."

"Smart woman." Val ate some more and sighed. "And talented. I didn't know eggs could get this fluffy."

"It's definitely witchcraft," Padraig agreed. "I think she sacrifices a chicken every new moon to replenish her dark magic."

Val laughed, her mood rising as the food filled her stomach.

Padraig smiled back, but his hazel eyes were concerned. He cleared his throat delicately.

"If you don't mind me asking. How did you end up in my garden again?"

Val sighed. "The same way I did last time."

"You've been tangling with vampires? That would explain the state of your hands."

"You should see the other guy," she joked weakly.

Padraig quirked an eyebrow. And, little by little, around mouthfuls of food, she told him the story. When she was finished, Padraig sat lost in thought, a crease of concentration between his eyebrows.

Finally, he said, "I looked into that ring, as you asked. It turns out it did come from my family, at least indirectly."

"How so?"

"Our records show that we imported it several years ago. It was part of a shipment of items that disappeared en route."

"Stolen?"

He nodded. "So it would seem."

"Does that kind of thing happen often?"

"No. Which is why I was able to track it down so easily. Stolen items tend to stick in people's memory."

"Where did it come from?"

"We bought it from an auction house in Rome. The item itself was found somewhere in South America."

"Did you know what it could do?"

"No. We knew it was magical, obviously, but we hadn't had a chance to test it. The shipment was stolen before it got to us."

Val tapped her lips. "Baron Blood must have already known what it could do. Otherwise, why bother stealing it?"

"You're assuming he was the one who stole it. Our thief may have turned around and sold the Baron the item. He may be blameless in this."

"He's a necromancer, and he's using the ring to turn people into vampires. He's hardly blameless."

"Touché." Padraig inclined his head. His face grew serious. "Regardless of whether the Baron was the thief or not, I'd like to get that ring back. Even if he isn't the thief, he can tell us who sold it to him, and we can trace the trail back that way. My family doesn't take kindly to people stealing from us. We need to send a message."

Val's hand stilled on Fiona's back.

"What are you saying?"

He turned and held her eyes with his own.

"I'm suggesting we work together. You want to avenge this Stephen's death so his spirit can sleep easy. I want to retrieve my family's property. I say we join forces."

Val pursed her lips. The offer was tempting. Padraig clearly had resources and manpower that she did not. And it looked like she'd have to take on both the vampires and the Baron if she wanted to stop the murders. She couldn't do that alone.

On the other hand, she didn't like the idea of letting Padraig have the ring either. No matter whose hands it was in, the ring was dangerous. It needed to be destroyed.

Val had a choice. She could accept Padraig's help and allow him to take the ring in exchange. Or she could not let him take the ring, in which case he probably wouldn't help her, but might instead go after the ring on his own. Or she could simply reject his help and go it alone. Which hadn't been working out great so far.

She sighed. She needed his help. But Padraig had saved her ass twice now. She also owed him the truth.

"I think that working together to stop the Baron might be a good idea," she said carefully.

"I sense some reservations."

She nodded. "Yes. The ring has to be destroyed. It's too dangerous to have in the city. What's to stop someone else from picking up where Baron Blood left off?"

Padraig's lips thinned. "My family paid good money for that ring. It belongs to us."

"Yes, and I'm sure you've already collected the insurance money for the theft. So you wouldn't be losing anything on the deal. Am I wrong?"

"No, you're not wrong. But it's not about the money. It's the principle."

"And you'll still get to track your thief and satisfy your family's honor by punishing them accordingly." She let her mind gloss over that part. She didn't want to imagine what that punishment might entail. It wasn't her business. If bad people came to bad ends, it was no more than they deserved. Probably.

He snorted. "You'd make a great lawyer, Val Keri. Here's my counterproposal: We agree to work together to take down the Baron and recover the ring. If we succeed, then we can decide what happens to the ring after that."

Val sighed. Translation: Whoever got their hands on the ring first would probably end up keeping it. Either that, or they'd end up fighting amongst themselves.

Still, the main thing was to get the ring away from Baron Blood and the vampires. They were actively using it to kill people right now. Vague considerations of what might happen to the ring in the future paled compared to that.

She met his gaze.

"You've got a deal."

52

"Jesus, Val. You don't do anything the easy way, do you?"

Malcolm eyed her across the rim of his coffee mug. A pink sunset streaked the sky through the bay windows, the last rays falling over his legs as he sat folded on the couch. Val leaned over her knees in the battered armchair across the living room, her own coffee cupped between both hands.

"Is there an easy way?" she reflected quietly. "Because if there is, I'd love to hear it."

"An easy way to defeat a necromancer and a cabal of vampires in order to retrieve a magic ring and free Stephen's soul?" He sighed and readjusted the blanket over his feet. "Probably not. And let's not forget the three witches who are trying to kill you."

"Four, if Paula's still alive."

"Maybe four," he acknowledged.

"That's a separate issue, though." Val sipped her coffee, her eyes still fixed on the battered carpet between her feet. "One crisis at a time."

"You count all that as one?" Malcolm laughed. "I count at least three crises in there. Maybe four if you include the impending showdown with Padraig over the ring."

"Assuming we manage to retrieve it."

"Well, sure. All plans have to assume success. They wouldn't be plans otherwise."

"Not true. That's what contingency plans are for."

"Yes, but then you're assuming the success of the contingency plan. My point stands. One for me." He licked his finger and made an imaginary tally mark in the air.

Val couldn't entirely suppress her smile. She took a sip of coffee to cover it as she leaned back in her chair. She flexed her bandaged hands. Her wounds were healing quickly, the process accelerated by the magic running through her veins. By tomorrow, she'd be as good as new.

"Is this a private conversation, or can anyone join?" Hillary's soft voice came from the doorway.

The vampire wore pink pajamas with cats on them, and her dark hair was mussed from sleep. Fuzzy white slippers covered her feet. She looked soft and vulnerable.

Nevertheless, Val's every muscle tensed at the sight of her, and she had to bite her tongue to keep from snapping at the young woman.

"Good morning," Malcolm said cheerily, doing his best to break the tension. "Sleep well?"

"Like the dead."

From the back of Val's chair, Mister E laughed.

"At least she's got a sense of humor about it."

"Is vampirism really a laughing matter?" Val muttered.

Her words were meant for Mister E, but Hillary's sharp ears picked them up.

"What, you're allowed to make undead jokes, but I can't? If you can't laugh at yourself, what can you laugh at?" she replied calmly.

Val sighed. "I'm sorry. I'm having a hard time adjusting to the idea that I have a vampire as a roommate."

"It's official then?" Malcolm asked hopefully.

"No. It is not official," Val growled. "Hillary can stay here for a few days while I get this other mess sorted out. After that, we'll see."

Rather than be put off by her tone, Malcolm beamed.

"Excellent. Hill, you are now our official probationary roommate."

The vampire scrunched her eyebrows.

"Did you just call me Hill?"

Malcolm looked mortified. "I'm sorry. That was inappropriate. I should know better than to change someone's name without asking. It won't happen again."

Hillary grinned. "I'm just messing with you. You can call me Hill if you want to."

She disappeared for a moment, then reappeared with a mug of her own and the coffee pot in her hand. "Anyone need more coffee?"

They both accepted a refill—Val took hers begrudgingly—then Hillary joined them, sinking onto the other end of the couch.

"What are we talking about?" she asked.

"Nothing," Val said shortly.

Malcolm gave her a look, then turned to Hillary.

"We were talking about Val's vampire problem."

Hillary raised as eyebrow. "You mean other than me?"

Malcolm looked at Val. "Do you want to tell her, or should I?"

"Or we could not tell her at all," Val suggested.

"Come on, Val. She might be able to help. It's her... ah... friends that are being used, after all. Besides, where could you get better inside information on the cabal?"

Val threw her hands up. "Fine. Tell her if you want."

Malcolm grinned and happily filled Hillary in on the details. The vampire listened, chewing her lip.

When he was done, she said, "Baron Blood must have killed Lila."

"It certainly looks like that way," Val agreed.

Hillary blinked her tears. She took a deep breath and set her jaw.

"There's one thing I don't understand. If they're using the ring to make more vampires, and the ritual is pulling its power from people in the Queen Anne, why the chained-up vampires?"

They were silent for a moment as they thought about it.

Finally, Malcolm said, "Flavoring?"

Val almost spit her coffee. "Flavoring? Vampires aren't butterscotch syrup, Malcolm."

"Obviously," he said archly, drawing the word out. "What I mean is, they're using the ritual to create vampires, right? Maybe all the ring really does is transfer life energy. And in order to create new vampires, some of that energy has to be vampiric in nature."

"Otherwise they'd just be transferring life energy from human to human," Val mused. "That's not a bad theory."

"But why doesn't Pearl simply turn them the old-fashioned way?" Hillary wondered. "Why the big production? Why kill her own children?"

"Because the subjects don't know they're becoming vampires," Val said. "It's a bait and switch."

"Right!" Malcolm exclaimed. "And by the time they realize they've become vampires, they're hooked on the renewed health and youth, and they wouldn't want to turn back."

"The first taste is always free," Hillary agreed.

Val frowned over her coffee.

"What?" Malcolm asked. "Don't you like our theory? It makes perfect sense."

"No, it does. That's what bothers me."

Malcolm and Hillary exchanged a look.

"Care to elaborate?"

Val sighed. "If you're right, it means the ring isn't the evil item I thought it was. A ring that turns people into vampires is pretty cut and dried. I'd definitely have to destroy it. But if the vampiric part is only due to the way Baron Blood and Miss Pearl have chosen to use it... I don't know. That makes me wonder if I should let Padraig's family have it back after all."

"Well," Hillary mused. "Even if it doesn't turn people into vampires, the ring itself is still kind of a vampire. You could argue that anything that sucks life energy out of one person and transfers it to another is inherently evil."

"How ironic, coming from a vampire."

Hillary narrowed her eyes.

Malcolm held up his hands in a placating motion.

"Let's not get personal, ladies. We're all on the same side here."

"Are we, though?" Val asked.

"Hey, I'm the one who clued you in about Baron Blood in the first place," Hillary snapped. "My friend Lila was killed. I want to see this ended just as much as you do."

"Whatever."

"In fact," Hillary continued, "I want to go with you when you confront them."

"No. Out of the question."

"If you're going to confront Baron Blood and Miss Pearl, you're going to need all the help you can get."

"That's what Padraig's men are for."

"Do you know how many of them there are? Do you know how effective they are against vampires? I can help."

Val considered Hillary for a long minute. The young vampire didn't look away.

Finally, she said, "I thought the whole point of bringing you here was to get you away from the vampires."

"It was. It is. But I still care about some of them. My friends are being hurt. Lila was killed. Probably others too. I should help."

"Can you fight?"

Hillary nodded. "Better than you think. I took a self-defense class a few years ago and really liked it. After that I started doing Tae Kwan Do twice a week. I've almost got my black belt."

"Almost? You still go?"

"Sure, why not?"

"Because you're a vampire."

"So what? Does that mean I'm only allowed to hang out in goth clubs now? I'm still the same person I was before I was turned. I still enjoy the same things."

"Fine. You don't have to bite my head off." Val held up her hands in surrender. She took a sip of coffee while she thought. Finally, she nodded. "All right. You can come."

"I want to come too," Malcolm chimed in.

Val glared at him.

"Absolutely not."

"Stephen being murdered was the thing that started this whole mess. I've got more reason to go than anyone."

"Just because you have a reason, doesn't mean you should do it. This is dangerous, Malcolm."

"So was breaking into a police station."

"This is not remotely the same thing."

"You broke into a police station?" Hillary asked, eyes wide.

Val stopped her with an outstretched palm. "Not now."

"You didn't want me to go then, either," Malcolm continued. "And I was helpful. Admit it. You were glad I was there."

Val pinched the bridge of her nose between her fingers. She could feel a headache building.

"Getting arrested and getting attacked by vampires is not even close to the same threat level."

"I don't care. I want to help."

"You've already helped. You helped me research the Queen Anne at the Library."

He made a face. "Anyone could have done that."

"Not true. I couldn't. Doing research is a real skill. That's why I needed you."

"True." He looked mollified. "I still want to go."

"Gah!" Val turned to Hillary. "Tell him he can't come."

"I don't see why not." Hilary shrugged. "It's his life, and his score to settle. If he wants to come, I don't think it's my place to tell him he can't."

Val looked from Malcolm to Hillary and back again. Finally, she threw up her hands.

"Fine. If you want to put yourself in danger, I can't stop you. But we're going to do everything we can to keep you safe. We might need to put some new tricks in that backpack of yours. Things that will protect you from vampires. Hillary, I need you to tell us everything you know about vampire's weaknesses. Malcolm, listen close."

"Way ahead of you," he said, grabbing a pen and paper from the coffee table.

Hillary didn't look happy, but she nodded her assent.

As dusk deepened into night outside the windows, they began to plan.

53

"I hate this plan," Val said, for perhaps the hundredth time.

"It's not ideal," Padraig agreed. "I'm open to better suggestions."

They were sitting in the immense drawing room of Padraig's mansion. Through the windows, the orange fog lights of the Golden Gate Bridge could be seen in the distance. The furniture that had been removed for the party had all been brought back in: an antique living room set made of richly polished wood and upholstered in gold velvet, which included a chaise longue, a couch, and a set of four matching armchairs. Val and Padraig sat in the chairs, while Hillary perched on the edge of the couch, silent and tense. Malcolm had claimed the chaise longue and sprawled upon it like a Hollywood starlet of the silent-film era. They all looked very rock-n-roll, with black leather collars around their necks to protect against fangs and claws. Hillary's collar even had spikes.

"What?" the vampire had said when Val raised an eyebrow at the spikes. "It's both defense and offense."

A dozen of Padraig's men stood guard around the house, hard-faced men with flat eyes that took in everything. Val knew the type. Professional killers. It would be good to have the men by their side when they faced the vampires, but they still made her nervous. Men like that followed orders, and they'd put a bullet in her back without blinking if Padraig ordered them to. Which made her uncomfortable and forced her to question her reliance on Padraig for this operation. She hardly knew the man, after all. He'd nursed her back to health twice, but how much could she trust him? How would he react if she tried to destroy the ring? Would his men try to take it by force?

Still, she didn't see what choice she had. There was no way she, Hillary, and Malcolm could confront Baron Blood and the vampires on their own. They needed Padraig and his killers.

"The enemy of my enemy," she told herself.

Padraig's men had spent two days scouting out all the entrances and exits to the ritual room. Unfortunately, they hadn't discovered anything that Val didn't already know. There were only three ways into the room: the door leading up into the basement of the Queen Anne, the tunnel leading to the caverns, and the passage leading beneath the park that eventually ended up back here, in Padraig's mansion.

Now that Val had interrupted the ritual twice, Baron Blood would be on high alert, and the entrances would be guarded. There was no quiet way to stop him. They had to come in with guns blazing.

"A full frontal assault is just so..." She waved her hand in vague disgust.

"Yeah, going full frontal isn't ideal," Padraig said with a grin.

Malcolm laughed. "I disagree. Sometimes full frontal is exactly what the doctor ordered."

Val rolled her eyes. "Are we sure they're going to be there tonight?"

"As sure as we can be," Padraig said. "I'm pretty well connected with the old money crowd. I know several people who've gotten the Baron's treatment: They're calling it the Fountain of Youth."

"They're not going to be thrilled when we put the Baron out of business."

"Not so much, no. We'll be making powerful enemies tonight."

Val sighed. "So what else is new."

"At least you don't have to rub elbows with them on a regular basis. I predict a lot of smiles to my face and knives in my back in the near future."

"Isn't that how things always are in the spheres of the rich and powerful?" Malcolm asked. "It's like living in Los Angeles. A bunch of bright smiles with 'fuck you' hiding between the teeth."

Padraig chuckled. "That about sums it up, yes. But I think the 'fuck you' might not be so hidden if we pull this job off."

Val got up and paced over to the window, too full of nervous energy to sit still. A neat grid of city lights fell away down the hill, swallowed by the dark expanse of the bay. Pale fog streamed in through the Golden Gate.

"Let's go over our assets again," she said.

"Right. Well, we've got a dozen men with crossbows, which you said should serve just as well as the traditional wooden stakes. Is that correct, Hillary?" Padraig asked.

Hillary nodded unhappily. "Yeah. The reasons stakes work is that they keep the wound open and prevent our bodies from healing. There's no reason it has to be a wooden stake. Anything that creates a wound and keeps it open will work just as well. Crossbow bolts should do the trick."

"Unless the bolts go all the way through," Val said.

"Unless they go all the way through," Hillary agreed. "As soon as the object is removed, our bodies will close the wound."

Padraig rubbed his chin. "It's a little late for this round, but in the future, I wonder if we can find a way to prevent the bolts from going through. Something that wraps around the base of the shaft and acts as a plug to stop the bolt and keep it inside the vampire's flesh."

"Why do they have to be through the heart?" Malcolm asked.

Hillary gave him the side-eye. "The same reason any wound has to be through the heart. It's a vital organ."

"Headshots would work just as well?" Padraig asked.

"Theoretically, yes. But heads are harder to hit than torsos."

"Sure, but the heart is a very small part of the torso. If we're talking about a kill-shot, the head is actually a larger target than the heart."

Instead of replying, Hillary leaned forward and put her face in her hands.

"Are you all right?" Val asked.

"No, I'm not all right. I hate this. We're talking about the best way to kill people I know. People who very recently were my friends and family. I'm not all right."

Val exchanged concerned looks with Malcolm.

"You know you don't have to come with us, right?"

"I know. And I don't want to, believe me." Hillary sighed and straightened up. "But I can't sit back and let other people do the dirty work. I've chosen my side and I'm going to fight for it."

"Sticking to your principles is admirable," Padraig said carefully. "But have you ever killed anyone? Have you even tried to kill someone? It's not as easy as it looks in the movies."

In an instant, Hillary was across the room, her hand around Padraig's throat. She bared her fangs.

"I'm a killing machine," she snarled.

The three guards in the room leveled their weapons as Padraig raised his hands.

"OK, you've made your point. You're a bad-ass bitch. I'm sorry I questioned your credentials."

Hillary glared at him for a moment longer before releasing him. She crossed the room and joined Val by the window.

Val looked at her with concern, but Hillary shook her off.

"I'm fine."

She obviously wasn't fine, but there was no point pressing her on it. Val was an expert at pretending to be fine herself. Hillary needed affirmation right now, not questioning. Val gave her a nod and resumed staring out the window.

"All right. That covers the crossbows," Padraig said. "How effective can we expect the sunlight bulbs to be?"

"Depends on how bright they are," Hillary said quietly. "Unlike what you may have read, sunlight does not cause us to immediately burst into flames. It hurts, and direct sunlight will blister our skin. Prolonged exposure would definitely kill us, but it'd be a slow death. Like poisoning. A vampire stranded in direct sunlight would die a very prolonged, very painful death."

"Will the sunlight bulbs even slow them down?" Padraig wondered. "They're nowhere near as powerful as direct sunlight. If the sun itself takes time to kill them, will sunlight bulbs do anything at all?"

"They will. Especially if you shine the light in their eyes. You know the way your eyes burn if you get hot pepper in them? That's how sunlight feels to a vampire. It'll make their eyes water and sting, temporarily blinding them."

Padraig nodded. "Right. Anything else?"

"I brought a big bag of garlic," Malcolm said. Hillary glared at him. "Just kidding. I know you said the garlic thing was just a myth. It's kind of a weird belief, though. Why did people think vampires were repelled by garlic?"

Hillary shrugged. "Maybe there really was a vampire once who was allergic to garlic. Word got out and people assumed all vampires hated garlic. You know how rumors spread."

"True." He shifted nervously in his seat. "That's it then? Crossbows and sunlight bulbs? That's all we've got? What happened to holy water?"

"Another myth, as far as I know," Hillary said. "I've never heard of holy water doing anything more than making someone wet."

"Not that making someone wet is a bad thing," Malcolm added.

Val rolled her eyes again. "Really, Malcolm?"

"I'm sorry. I make inappropriate jokes when I get nervous."

"Just remember that vampires are not invulnerable. They can be hurt, just like anyone else. They're insanely fast and strong and they heal fast, but they still feel pain. If you stab them, they bleed. If you leave something in the wound, it prevents them from healing. The plan is to blind them and stab them. Any questions?"

Malcolm and Hillary shook their heads.

Padraig said, "What about the necromancer?"

"Leave him to me." Val glanced at the clock. "It's almost go time. Check your gear. If you've got to pee, do it now. The only thing worse than fighting vampires is fighting vampires in pants you've pissed. We leave in five minutes."

54

Half of Padraig's men took point, sweeping down the hall with smooth professionalism, lighting the way with the sunlight-bulb flashlights attached to their crossbows. They rotated positions whenever the group came to an intersection, with men covering the intersecting passageways, while others moved up to take point as the group passed by.

"Where did you get these guys?" Val whispered to Padraig. They walked together in the center of the group of killers, with Hillary and Malcolm right behind them.

"Mercenaries-R-Us," he replied with a tight smile. "They were having a close-out sale. Buy one, get one free."

"Well, let's hope you didn't get damaged goods then. We're screwed if these guys are past their expiration date." She winced as the words left her mouth. Some of these guys probably wouldn't make it through the night. Joking about their expiration date felt callous. "Sorry. Poor choice of words. No offense."

"None taken. In situations like this, gallows humor is the best kind."

Even though they had a sizable group, the narrow hallway restricted them to walking two abreast. Val worried about that. Would the vampires be able to bottle them up and keep them from getting out of the tunnel? Numbers didn't matter if you couldn't get your troops into the fight.

Troops. She started to laugh at the word, but the chuckle turned sour in her stomach. She was leading a group of professional killers into battle against a group of undead monsters. They really were troops. This really was a war.

She glanced at Malcolm and Hillary, trailing along behind her. Did they understand what they were getting into?

"I don't like having all these lives on my hands," she muttered under her breath. "I only want to be responsible for myself."

"It's a bit late for that, isn't it?" Mister E drawled. He floated on his back in front of her, languidly puffing on his candy cigarette and blowing smoke rings.

"I didn't ask them to come. In fact, I told them they should stay home."

"Poor Val. Why do other people insist on being independent creatures with their own motivations?" Mister E chuckled. *"You know that absolves you from responsibility, right? You told them not to come, but they chose to be here anyway. You are not responsible for what happens next."*

"Easy for you to say. You have no conscience."

"Not true. I'm just a law-and-order kind of cat. I believe in free choice, consent, and owning one's own actions. Your friends are consenting adults who made an informed decision to risk their lives. What happens next is on them, not you."

"Yeah, well you also think the consent of a six-year-old girl is good enough for a lifetime contract. Forgive me if I don't subscribe to your point of view."

"You say tomato, I say tomahto. Again, free choice. If you choose to feel guilt or responsibility for other people's freely chosen actions, that's on you."

Val shook her head. "Talking to you is like banging my head against a wall."

"It's a good thing you have such a hard head then, isn't it?"

The man in front of Val stopped abruptly, holding up his hand for a halt. After a few seconds, she understood the reason why. The faint sound of chanting drifted down the hall. The ritual had begun.

Val tightened her grip on her knife. Though magic was her best defense, the blade felt reassuring in her hand. Despite all her power, she was a physical girl at heart. Punching, kicking and stabbing felt like the proper way to defend herself. Using her power always felt a bit like cheating.

Of course, when facing vampires cheating was pretty much her only hope of survival. They were too fast and too strong. If she tried going toe-to-toe in a fist fight, she'd be dead in seconds.

So. Cheating it was. She filled herself with wild energy, keeping it barely in check, ready to unleash in the blink of an eye.

Looking around her, she saw others doing the same. Checking their crossbows. Gripping their sunlight flashlights as if they were light sabers.

That thought almost made her smile. Wouldn't that be nice. They could use all the light sabers they could get.

Beside her, Padraig caught her eye. His face was grim, and he had the stance of someone accustomed to violence. Poised on the balls of his feet. Ready to move. He winked at her, and she nodded back.

It was now or never.

"All right," he said quietly. "Just like we practiced. On my mark. Three, two..."

Screams erupted from the hall behind them and Padraig whirled, his eyes widening with shock. He never got to "one."

55

The vampires had been waiting for them. And rather than sit back and let Padraig's men attack, the vampires had brought the fight to them.

"Ambush..." a man yelled before ending in a cry of pain.

Val whirled around to find chaos. They'd moved through an intersection thirty feet back, and the vampires had waited for the entire group to pass before making their move. Flashlight beams swung crazily as men spun around, trying to get a bead on the attackers rushing in behind them.

Shadows danced in the crowded hallway, making it hard to tell exactly what was happening from her vantage point. She saw limbs flailing and heard cries of pain and the twang of crossbow strings. Through the mass of bodies, she saw one man simply disappear—the back of his close-cropped head there and gone in the blink of an eye.

She swore. There was no way she could get to the front line in such confined quarters. Their numbers were useless if no more than two or three of them could face the enemy at a time. Worst of all, Malcolm and Hillary were now between her and their attackers. She'd thought her friends were safely tucked away where she could defend them, but the vampires' ambush had turned everything upside down.

"Move. Let me through!" Val tried to push past them, to get to the front of the crush. But it was no use, they were too tightly packed. She was stuck in the middle. Powerless to help.

More screams. More bowstrings twanging. Another man disappeared.

Then there was a blur of motion and a pale face appeared less than six feet away. He hissed, exposed fangs glinting as someone hit him with a beam of sunlight.

Beam of sunlight. She wished that was the case. Unfortunately, the sunlight bulbs were a poor substitute for the real thing. They were designed to grow plants or help people living in dark places that didn't get enough sun in the winter. Their purpose was to put out UV rays to stimulate vitamin D production, not to match the intensity of the sun itself. Trying to kill a vampire with a sunlight bulb was like trying to melt an iceberg with a wooden match.

Still, they needed every shred of advantage they could scrape together, and though the sunlight beams weren't incinerating the vampires, Val could tell they didn't like them.

"Shine the lights in their eyes!" she yelled.

The men did as she said, and the vampire flinched away. It was only a momentary distraction, but a moment was all they needed.

Another blur and Hillary was there, launching herself at the blinded vampire. He never saw her coming. Hillary lashed out with her sharp nails. Flesh parted, and blood stained the walls. In the light of the flashlight beams, the vampire looked shocked as his throat spurted. Hillary didn't give him a chance to recover, driving a crossbow bolt into the wound, the tip exploding out the back of his neck. The vampire gurgled and went down.

"Great balls of fire," Val breathed. "Hillary's not fucking around."

Her new roommate surged forward, engaging another pale-faced attacker, and hope bloomed in Val. For once, the vampires didn't hold all the cards when it came to strength and quickness. They had someone on their side who could match the creatures blow for blow.

Then more screams filled the air behind her, and hope withered on the vine.

Whirling back to face the front of the group, she found a repeat of the scene she'd just witnessed at the back. Limbs flailing. Flashlight beams swinging around in desperation. Cries of pain and the twang of crossbow strings.

Val's heart dropped into her stomach.

The vampires had waited until they'd all turned to face the rear ambush, then they'd sprung a second ambush, rushing at them from the front. Now they were caught between two groups of attackers, penned into the hallway like livestock.

And, like livestock, they'd be slaughtered if they couldn't get out of the trap.

Worst of all, Val was stuck in the middle of the group. She couldn't fight the vampires on either front, and she couldn't use her magic for fear of harming her allies as much as she helped. She balled her fists, fingernails digging into her palms in frustration. She had to do something. If they stayed where they were, this fight would be over before it even began. They had to get to the ritual room where they could put their numbers to use.

Facing the front of the group, she shouted, "Get down!"

She called the wind, and let it roar past her, releasing the storm into the face of their attackers. In seconds, the hall was full of dust, streaming by in colored ribbons.

"This must be what the surface of Jupiter is like," Mister E commented.

Val ignored him and poured on the power.

The way in front of her was clear now. Her allies huddled against the wall, shielding their faces with their arms. She strode forward, borne along by the storm, letting it sweep her adversaries away. Their surprise attack wasn't surprising anyone anymore. She might as well make some noise.

Pale faces emerged from the dust as Val strode forward, lunging at her, their fangs bared. Each time she saw one, she increased the force of the wind tenfold, funneling the blowing grit directly at their faces in a tight focus, the same way she'd blasted the mortar from the wall in her SFPD cell. The wind and sand flayed the skin from their bones, peeling pale faces from skulls like wet paper. She strode forward, scattering vampires from her path like autumn leaves.

The tunnel opened sooner than she was expecting. Between one stride and the next, the pressure in her ears lessened. The fury of the storm dissipated as it spread out into the larger space.

The ritual chamber was full of dust and swirling wind. The chanting had stopped. The candles had all been blown out.

"Well, at least you interrupted the ritual," Mister E said. *"Though I don't think the Baron will be very happy about it."*

His words were proven true a moment later. Off to her left, Baron Blood's furious voice filled the chamber.

"Valora Keri! This time you have gone too far. This ends tonight." Through the dust, the ruby eyes of his skull ring began to glow.

56

Val didn't know what the Baron intended to do with his ring, and she wasn't going to wait around to find out. She charged toward him, funneling a narrow blast of wind at his chest.

She didn't make it three steps.

A flash of motion came at her peripheral vision, and only her fighter's reflexes saved her. She twisted away, bringing up her knife in an instinctive parry. The blade cut only cloth, but it put her attacker off-target enough that the vampire's nails scraped harmlessly against her collar. She breathed a prayer of thanks to the gods of leather.

"Right. Defense first." Val surrounded herself with a tight whirlwind, just like the last time she'd broken up this particular party, and started moving toward the Baron again. It was slower going this way, but there was a much better chance she'd make it across the room alive.

And she did make it farther this time. Four steps instead of three.

Something grasped her ankle, tripping her up as she tried to take step number five. Val stumbled and went down, scraping her knees on stone.

"What the frog?" Her eyes widened with horror as she saw what had tripped her. A skeletal hand reached out of the stone, finger bones wrapped around her ankle.

"Ah, the joys of necromancy," Mister E commented. *"Making new friends wherever you go."*

Val kicked at the hand with her other foot, but the bones refused to let go. The stone rippled beside her thigh, and another set of skeletal fingers reached for her.

"Oh, hell no," she growled. The only problem was, if she couldn't brute-force the bones, what could she do? Brute force was her number one trick. "A little help? How do I get rid of these things?"

"Well, I could think of any number of things, if your skill set wasn't so limited. As it is... let me think a minute," Mister E mused.

Crossbow strings twanged across the room as the first of Padraig's men finally made it into the chamber. At least one thing was going right.

The second hand latched onto her leg just above the knee.

"Think faster," she yelped, kicking and squirming. She hacked at the hand with her knife and managed to chip the bones. But the thing refused to let go.

"What about that trick you did at the jail?"

"Wearing away mortar with wind? I don't see how that's relevant. There's no mortar here."

Mister E gave a long-suffering sigh.

"Not mortar, you idiot. Bone."

Val's mouth made an O.

"You think that'll work?"

"It's worth trying. Unless you have a better idea."

The stone began to ripple again, and a third set of finger bones breached the surface.

"Nope," she gasped. "A wind saw it is."

She focused on creating a tiny, focused whirlwind, spinning the air hard and fast like the blade of a grinder. She pressed the wind against the ulna of the arm grasping her ankle. White bone dust exploded into the air.

Relief flooded her, but it curdled quickly as she saw the shallow impression her blade had left in the bone. At this rate, it would take minutes to cut through the bone. Too long.

A symphony of grunts and curses filled the chamber now, as Padraig's men joined the fight in earnest. Crossbows twanged. Sunlight bulbs flashed. Blood spurted. Men screamed.

Val saw all of this only peripherally. Her attention was on the bony hands locked around her leg.

"Find your discipline," Mister E admonished her. *"Focus. Make it sharper."*

She ground her teeth and narrowed the blade of wind, until it was no wider than the tip of a pencil. Bone dust fountained into the air, and the invisible blade pushed through the ulna like a shovel through dry sand.

"Yes!" Val exclaimed, turning the blade to the radius. It parted quickly.

Unfortunately, even with the arm severed, the grasping fingers did not release her ankle.

"Seriously?"

"I believe it has attachment issues."

"Har-har." Val focused her wind blade on the second arm, quickly severing it from the ground as well. She scrambled out of reach as the third hand tried to grab her.

"Give the lady a hand!" Mister E grinned. *"Or two hands, as it were."*

She stared down at the bony hands still clutching her leg. Now that she'd cut them from the ground, they didn't appear to be doing anything in particular, just holding on to her leg. Creepy, but currently non-threatening. Val decided to ignore them. She had bigger fish to fry.

She turned back toward Baron Blood, again preparing to lash out at him with a straight punch of wind. She stopped, appalled by what she found.

Standing between her and the Baron was a pair of skeletons. And they weren't just hands this time. These were fully formed human skeletons.

"Oh, for fuck's sake," she growled.

Val tried to blow them out of her way with a windstorm, but most of the wind went between the bones, and the skeletons did not move.

Except when she tried to go around them. Then they stepped directly into her path again.

"Afraid to face me yourself, Baron?" Val snarled.

He did not rise to the bait. "We use the weapons we have, Valora Keri. You use wind. I use bone."

"Goddammit," she murmured under her breath. "It's going to take forever if I have to keep cutting my way through a bone forest."

She flinched as a form appeared beside her, but relaxed as she saw it was Padraig. Then she did a double take. He was wielding a sword.

"What the hell is that?"

He grinned at her and held up the blade for her inspection. "This is Quicksilver."

Light caught on silver runes etched on the flat of the blade. Emeralds were set into the hilt.

She gaped at him. "Not only do you have a sword, but you named it?"

"I most certainly did not." He sounded offended. "This sword has been in my family for generations. She was named long before I first drew breath."

Long before he first drew breath? Val looked at him sideways. Who talked like that?

"Okay," she said slowly. "We'll let that go for the moment. The more pertinent question is: Do you think you can fight skeletons with a sword?"

Padraig's grin widened.

"Only one way to find out, isn't there?"

He leapt to the attack.

Padraig moved like no one Val had ever seen before. He wasn't lightning fast, like the vampires. Nor was his technique flawless, like some of the fighters she'd trained with. But he made every movement look smooth and easy. If she had to choose one word to describe his fighting style, it would be effortless.

His opponents, by contrast, were awkward and angular. Even if they hadn't been made of bone, no one who saw the skeletons move would have ever confused them with something natural. They stuttered and jerked like stop-motion animation.

Padraig flowed forward, bones shattering beneath the weight of his graceful slashes. He moved quickly, but never seemed to hurry. A calm smile rested upon his lips, as if he fought skeletons every day. As if the whole thing was nothing more than an amusing game.

"Who is this guy?" she whispered.

"I don't know. But there is more to your ally than meets the eye," Mister E said, his golden eyes narrowing.

They stood mesmerized as Padraig toyed with the skeletons. A flick of his sword removed one of the creature's hands at the wrist. Another slash took out a rib. He never hurried, and his smile never wavered. He seemed to be in no more danger than if he were lounging in a field of daisies.

"Any time you want to take on the necromancer," Padraig said. "Be my guest."

Val felt herself flush. Had she really just been standing and staring in the middle of a battle?

"On it," she said apologetically.

Baron Blood stood upon the platform he used to conduct his rituals, jaw clenched in concentration. His hands were outstretched before him, fingers moving as if he were playing an invisible piano.

No, not a piano. He was playing with undead puppets. No wonder the skeletons' movements were so jerky.

Val vaulted onto the platform. The Baron turned toward her, gesturing. She felt the skeletal hands still clamped on her leg twitch, the bony fingers digging painfully into her muscles.

But Val was already on him.

She took a full stride, allowing her momentum to shift her weight onto her forward foot, and drove the hilt of her knife into the bridge of his nose.

Baron Blood dropped like a stone, blood running down his face. His eyes rolled up until only the whites were showing, then his body went rigid as his heels drummed upon the planks of the platform.

"What's happening?" Val breathed. "Is he having a seizure?"

"I'm sure I don't know," Mister E replied. *"Do I look like a doctor to you?"*

Padraig stepped up beside her.

"We have to retrieve the ring. Put an end to this nightmare."

A new voice spoke behind them.

"I wouldn't do that, if I were you."

Val turned to find Melinda Pearl standing over the collapsed bones of Baron Blood's skeletons. She was immaculately dressed, as always, her sharp heels digging into the dust. Her smile was thin and blood-less. Rodrigo stood on one side of her, smirking. Jonathan Grey loomed on the other.

"Hand over the ring and nobody has to get hurt. Except this one, of course."

Val's blood ran cold as she followed the vampire queen's gaze. Hillary lay curled on the ground at Pearl's feet.

.

57

H illary whimpered. A crossbow bolt stuck out of her shoulder. Blood ran down her temple.

"Let her go," Val snarled.

"She is mine," Pearl said. "I created her. I own her."

"Slavery is illegal. Maybe you missed the memo."

Melinda Pearl's laugh tinkled like icicles in the wind. "Human laws do not apply to us. It's cute that you think they do."

Val surveyed the room. Behind Pearl and her two lieutenants, a woman lay chained in the center of the ritual circle. She was limp and senseless, which was probably a good thing. Hopefully the woman was unconscious and not dead. Val had only wanted to stop the ritual, not kill the poor woman who'd paid for what she believed was a longevity treatment.

Several other bodies lay scattered around the chamber, most of them wearing black tactical gear. Padraig's men. Three survivors huddled against the wall, a single vampire standing casual guard over them. Relief swept through Val as she saw that Malcolm was one. He sat on the floor, hugging his backpack to his chest. It looked like the vampires had taken their crossbows and other weapons but hadn't deemed the backpack a threat.

Or maybe it was Malcolm they didn't think was a threat. Her roommate's eyes were big and round, his expression rigid with terror. Val
sent him a reassuring nod, but he gave no indication that he saw her.
He just stared into space, the knuckles on his fingers nearly white as he
clutched something inside his pack.

Great. Add permanent psychological damage to her list of sins.

But she didn't have time to worry about that right now. Pearl was
speaking again.

"You've cost me a lot of aggravation, Val Keri. Still, you've brought
back my lost lamb, so all in all I think today has been a win. Give me
the ring, and I'll let you walk out of here alive."

"So you can turn all of the rich bastards in the city into vampires?
Not going to happen," Val snarled.

"I will own this city soon one way or another," the vampire queen
said coldly. "You may think you can stop me, but you are a minnow
swimming against the tide. You have no chance in this battle."

"No chance, huh? Tell that to Jack. I'm sure he thought the same
thing about my chances of stopping him from getting the Scepter of
Sutro. Tell that to Baron Blood. He didn't think I could stop him either."

Pearl bared her fangs. "I've tried to play nice with you, Val Keri.
You could be a very useful piece in the game of power. But if you
continue to set yourself against me, I will have no choice but to remove
you from the board."

"Try it, you bloodless bitch."

Rodrigo moved. In the blink of an eye, he was up on the platform,
reaching out to snatch the ring.

But Val was ready for it. She took a half-step to the side and
twisted, pulling in a blast of air as she did. The wind hit the vampire in
the back, driving him forward. He stumbled over Val's leg and
slammed face-first into the wall behind the platform.

While Val was busy congratulating herself, Rodrigo rebounded and
came at her again. Caught off guard by the quick turnaround, Val
barely had time to widen her eyes before the fangs of the vampire were
inches from her face.

Fortunately, Padraig was faster.

His sword flickered, and the blade materialized between Rodrigo's ribs, knocking him off course. The momentum of the vampire's attack carried him past Val again, and he skidded to a halt at the edge of the platform. He put his fingers to his side and scowled as they came away wet.

His eyes fixed on Padraig as he hissed, "That was a mistake."

"One in a very long list of them," Padraig replied calmly. "Starting with my misspent youth." He settled into a defensive crouch. "Shall we dance?"

To Val's shock, Rodrigo didn't immediately overwhelm Padraig. The vampire was clearly stronger, but the swordsman proved to be as fast as his undead foe, if not faster. He gave ground, his sword blurring in a defensive net. Half a dozen small wounds appeared on Rodrigo in as many seconds. The wounds might as well have been mosquito bites for all the reaction they garnered from the vampire, but they were better than the alternative.

"If we survive this, we need to have a little talk with Padraig," Val whispered. "He's been holding out on us."

"Agreed," Mister E said. *"Padraig is undoubtedly more than human. Though what exactly he is, I cannot say."*

Val watched the battle move back and forth across the platform, struggling to keep up with the action as the two men moved faster than she could follow.

Unfortunately, not everyone was as engrossed as she was. Arms like steel bands clamped around her ribs, and she yelped as she was lifted off her feet. Jonathan Grey chuckled against her back. He turned so they were both facing Melinda Pearl.

Pearl gave her an icy smile.

"Now. About that ring."

58

"Put me down!"

Val strained against the arms holding her. She kicked her heels into the shins of the giant. No reaction. Jonathan Grey might have been carved from stone.

On the other side of the platform, Padraig and Rodrigo's battle raged. Baron Blood lay motionless.

Melinda Pearl stepped forward.

"The ring." She extended her hand, palm up.

Val spat in it.

"Go to hell."

Jonathan Grey tightened his arms and Val groaned. The groan turned into a yelp as a sharp pain stabbed into her side. He must have cracked a rib. The vampire maintained the pressure for what felt like an eternity before letting up.

Val sagged in his arms, panting, sweat standing out on her forehead. She had to find a way out of this... But how? Hillary was lying on the floor, bleeding. Malcolm was sitting under guard, watching her with haunted eyes, his hands toying with his backpack. Padraig was barely keeping Rodrigo at bay. And as long as Jonathan Grey had her clamped tight in his thick arms, Val was helpless. There was no way she could break the massive vampire's grip.

She thought about calling up the wind blade she'd used to cut through the skeletal hands, but a glance at Jonathan Grey's arms told her that would be too slow. The vampire's arms were as thick as her thighs and would take several seconds to cut through. While that was happening, Grey would no doubt squeeze her again, only this time he'd use his full strength, not the tiny fraction he'd used to crack her rib. Val would be crushed like a grape long before her blade cut her free.

There had to be another way.

"Last chance, Keri. I can take the ring from your corpse just as easily. It really makes no difference to me." Pearl's smile was glacial.

Val shivered, casting her eyes around the room, looking for anything that could help. All she found were the corpses of Padraig's men and a couple of vampire bodies strewn across the cavern floor. Their assault had failed. They were all going to die.

Then she noticed what Malcolm was toying with. At the same time, her roommate caught her eye. She flicked her gaze to his hands and raised a questioning eyebrow. His tongue flickered over his lips, then he nodded. He looked terrified, but resolute.

"Get ready," she mouthed. Malcolm's jaw tightened.

Val flicked her gaze back to Pearl, who was frowning. The vampire queen could tell something was up. As Val looked back to Malcolm, the vampire queen turned, following her gaze.

"Disco inferno!" Val shouted, squeezing her eyes shut tight.

Malcolm's mobile spotlight came out of his backpack and blazed to life. Eight hundred thousand candelas of sunlight bulbs seared into the vampires.

Melinda Pearl shrieked. Jonathan Grey bellowed, dropping Val as his hands came up to shield his face.

Val didn't hesitate. She turned, knife in hand, slashing across the back of Jonathan Grey's leg. Tendons parted and the giant vampire's leg buckled. He toppled, rolling his face away from the light.

"The bigger they are," she muttered.

Across the platform, Rodrigo had also been blinded by the spotlight. Padraig took the opportunity to plunge his sword through his opponent's chest. The vampire lieutenant crumpled. She doubted the wound would kill him, but hopefully it would be enough to keep him out of the fight.

Val turned back to the vampire queen. One side of Melinda Pearl's face was blistered and burned. Tears of blood ran down her face. She kept her back turned to Malcolm's light as she glared at Val.

"Your time is up, Keri." The queen blurred into motion, fangs coming to rip out Val's throat.

Then Padraig's sword was there, the blade extended protectively before Val, forcing the vampire queen to pull up short.

"You've chosen the wrong side, fae," she snarled. "We are the new power in this city. I will crush you and your interests."

Padraig's blade never wavered. "I've heard that before. Many times over the years. I'm still here, vampire."

He circled left, trying to turn Pearl so she would have to face Malcolm's light. The vampire queen was even faster than he was, though, sidestepping to keep her back to the scorching light.

But that gave Val an opening.

She moved in the opposite direction, flanking Pearl. The queen tried to hedge, turning slightly to keep both Padraig and Val in sight, but Val got to where Malcolm's spotlight was at her back. Pearl hissed in pain and was forced to look away. Now, not only was the queen trapped between Padraig and Val, but she couldn't turn to face Val without getting blinded.

Pearl checked the room for help, but both of her lieutenants were out of the fight. Across the room, Padraig's men had put a bolt through the heart of the vampire who'd been standing guard over them. The queen was alone and outnumbered.

"This isn't over," she raged. "I will crush you both like the insects you are."

With a final shriek, she was gone, dashing up the stairs and through the doorway on the far side of the chamber.

Padraig and Val looked at each other, then whirled to make sure there weren't any more surprises waiting for them. There weren't. Rodrigo and Jonathan Grey lay curled on their sides, protecting their faces from the light as best they could. The other vampires were sprawled on the floor, dead or dying.

Val's gaze fell on Hillary.

"Shit," she whispered. One of the young woman's arms was a deep red, blistered and burned by Malcolm's light.

Val leapt off the platform and used her body to block the light. As she knelt next to the young woman, something tickled at the back of her skull.

It took her a few seconds to realize it was magic. She looked up to find Baron Blood staring down at her from the dais, his lips moving as he silently chanted the words to a spell. The eyes of the skull ring shone red, contrasting with the eyes of the necromancer, which were as black as the void. His smile was sharp and deadly.

He barked a guttural syllable and stretched his fingers toward Val.

Everything went black.

59

V al felt as if she were being pulled apart. Stretched like taffy.
No, not like taffy. Taffy didn't feel pain.

Val was being stretched on a rack. Drawn and quartered. Pulled through a cheese grater.

She screamed, but the sound disappeared in the wind.

The cavern was gone.

She floated in darkness, her body suspended in a lightless void.

Actually, it wasn't completely lightless. There were faint misting colors, drifting like a will-o'-wisp. Eddying like a living thing.

"That's because it is a living thing," Mister E hissed. *"That's your life energy. The necromancer is juicing you like an orange. Look there."*

She followed his glowing eyes and saw a stone portal. Baron Blood stood atop it, chanting, the eyes of his skull ring flaming embers in the dark.

The drifting mist was being pulled into the portal, swirling down into the void. Her soul being sucked into oblivion.

"No!"

Val struggled, fighting against the spell, straining to move.

She might have been trying to move Mount Everest.

Her body was heavy and unresponsive. A dead thing trapping her in place. It was like every nightmare she'd ever had, the disaster approaching in slow motion while she willed her body to move, to scream, to do something. But nothing happened. She could only watch her doom approaching through terrified eyes.

"He's pulled you into the spirit realm," Mister E supplied.

"And in this realm, he's stronger than I am," Val finished.

She watched as life energy rose from her body like steam. Watched it drift away toward the stone portal.

There was nothing she could do. Her magic simply wasn't strong here. She'd run into the same problem the first time she'd gone into Macy's realm. Only a tiny fraction of her power was accessible when she was outside her body.

Somehow, Baron Blood had known that. He'd bided his time and struck when she was vulnerable. He'd pulled her spirit here, where she was forced to play by his rules.

And whoever made the rules invariably won the game.

She drifted toward the portal, the stone arch looming up before her. She knew if she passed through it, she would be gone. Her soul wrung out of her like dishwater.

Val flailed, searching for a way to fight back. Anything that might help her.

Something pricked the skin of her finger. She looked down to find her hand closed around the stem of a red rose.

"Macy!" she shouted, her voice echoing in the void.

The mist eddied, disturbed by her struggle.

Nothing else happened.

Baron Blood smiled, bloodless lips exposing blocky white teeth. His eyes were pools of black.

"Macy!" Val tried again.

The Baron's chanting rose, thundering across the ether. Tendrils of mist wrapped tightly, cocooning her. She was an insect, wrapped in silk. Ready to be eaten.

The stone arch loomed over her. Her feet were just inches from the void.

She drew breath to call to Macy again. A last desperate shout.

Then the girl was there.

Macy appeared atop the arch beside Baron Blood. She was tiny compared to him, her head only reaching his chest. His eyes widened in comic surprise.

The little girl drew her fist back and punched him right in the nuts.

Baron Blood folded like a wet napkin.

The moment his chant faltered, the tendrils of mist around Val loosened. She stopped drifting toward the portal.

On the arch, Macy pounded the Baron, her small fists rising and falling. For a moment, Val thought the necromancer was done. Defeated by a girl who'd been dead for over a century.

Then a wave of energy pulsed out from the Baron's ring, knocking Macy onto the top of the arch. He loomed over her, raising his hand, a terrible fury twisting his features. The hellish light in his eyes matched the ruby glow of the skull ring.

There was no time for thought, only action.

Val instinctively spun a whirlwind, gathering the multicolored mist into a writhing funnel. But instead of wrapping the wind around herself, this time she twisted it around the Baron, trapping him inside the storm. She tightened the storm's grip until it tore at his clothes, ripping the very air from his lungs.

Baron Blood fought back, using the ring to create space around him, ruby energy crackling against the wind. Val convulsed as red lighting flashed through her. Her storm faltered. In this realm, he was just too strong.

Then Macy was back, launching herself at the necromancer again, tackling him down to the arch. Val gasped in relief as his attack faltered with the breaking of his concentration.

She hovered uncertainly, watching the girl and man grapple, and drifted below the arch, unable to reach the combatants. Her only way to help Macy was with her magic. But Macy and the Baron were too close together. She couldn't attack the Baron without hitting the girl as well.

She watched as the Baron's greater physical strength began to show. Slowly, he overpowered the girl, pinning Macy down on the arch. He raised his hand above her, power gathering in the ruby eyes of the skull.

"Now," Val whispered.

You don't realize just how much thinner finger bones are than other bones until you discover how easy they are to break. While the pair were struggling, Val had gathered grit from the arch into a tiny, focused whirlwind. Now she sliced this buzz-saw of stone fragments and pebbles into the base of the Baron's fingers.

Fingers are much thinner than the wall of a jail cell. Thinner even than skeletal arm bones.

In an instant, her whirling blade severed all four of the Baron's fingers. Blood sprayed.

The necromancer was too shocked to scream. He just gaped at the blood fountaining from the stumps of his fingers. Val punched him in the chest with a fist of wind, tumbling him off the girl.

"Macy! Get the ring!" Val shouted.

She didn't have to tell the girl twice. Macy snatched the ring with the Baron's finger still attached.

"Throw it here!"

The girl got to her feet and stared down at Val. Drops of the Baron's blood were splattered across her face.

"No." Macy closed her fist around the ring. "This ends here."

The girl set her jaw. Red light leaked between her fingers. She began to shake. Smoke rose from her fist. The light grew brighter, so bright Val had to shield her eyes. She smelled burning flesh.

The red light flashed brighter than the sun. Val had to clamp her eyes shut against the searing light. She could feel the heat burning her skin. Macy screamed.

The light winked out.

All that remained was darkness.

60

"Val? Val?"

She opened her eyes to find Padraig standing over her, his forehead creased with concern. He looked relieved when she opened her eyes.

"There you are. Are you OK? What happened?"

He helped her sit up.

"Baron Blood," she croaked. "That bastard pulled me into the spirit realm. He would have killed me if it weren't for Macy."

Padraig frowned. "Macy? Who's Macy?"

"A girl who lived here long ago. A spirit." She waved her hand at him. "I'll explain later. Where's the Baron?"

She turned to find Baron Blood lying on the dais. His eyes were open, and he was staring sightlessly at the ceiling.

"Gods, Val. What did you do to him?" Padraig asked.

"Not me. Macy."

Padraig bent over the necromancer. "Is he dead?"

Val wobbled over to stand next to him. Her legs felt like rubber. Apparently, being sucked into the spirit realm took a lot out of you.

"I don't know. Is he?"

"No such luck," Padraig said, pressing two fingers to the necromancer's wrist. "His heart's still beating. Doesn't appear to be anybody home, though."

Val remembered the way her wind blade had severed his fingers. The jets of blood spraying.

"It's probably shock. We fought. He was injured pretty badly in the fight."

She turned to survey the rest of the room, but Padraig's voice called her back.

"By the Ancients, what did you do to my ring?"

On the Baron's other hand, the skull ring had been slagged. The two small rubies that formed the skull's eyes lay in a pool of molten gold. The Baron's finger—which Val was relieved to see had not been severed in the real world—had been badly burned, the skin bubbled and scorched.

"Macy did it. Good riddance to that evil thing."

Padraig scowled at her. "That ring was the price of my assistance. You owe me, Val Keri."

Those words washed over her like cold water. Val shivered.

She gave him a sideways look. "I heard Pearl call you 'fae' during the battle. Care to explain that?"

"That would be telling, now, wouldn't it?" he snapped. His hazel eyes locked onto hers. "But you now owe me a favor, Val Keri. Do not forget it." He stalked off to check on his surviving men.

She shivered again as she put his words together with the way Padraig had moved during the fight. His uncanny speed and skill.

"Great, so there are fairies now too," she muttered under her breath. "And I owe one of them a favor."

"I believe they prefer to be known as the Fair Folk." Mister E floated at eye level, blowing lazy smoke rings. His grin widened as he noticed the direction of Val's gaze. *"He's got a great ass, too."*

Val's cheeks grew warm.

"I should have known. He's too pretty to be human." She thought of the perfect skin vampires had and remembered how beautiful the mad seraph Jack had been. "Why are all the supernatural beings gorgeous?"

The cat-demon shrugged. *"Natural selection? Camouflage? Maybe the only way they've been able to live amongst humans without getting burned at the stake is to dazzle you with charm and beauty."*

"That makes a certain amount of sense," Val mused. "And the ones who actually look like monsters are forced to hide, like the Morlocks. Though applying scientific evolutionary theory to supernaturals feels wrong."

"Science and magic are two sides of the same coin. Both are part of the natural world. Just because humans are more comfortable with one and not the other doesn't make magic any less natural."

"I suppose not," Val accepted grudgingly.

She squinted across the room at Malcolm's spotlight.

"Should I turn it off?" Malcolm asked.

"No," she said. "Keep it on. It'll keep Pearl from coming back to attack us again. We'll have to cover Hillary's skin up."

"You can use this." One of Padraig's men tossed her a black cloth bag.

"Seriously?" Val held the thing away from her like a snake. It was the kind of bag they put over prisoners' heads on their way to interrogation rooms. "Why the hell do you have these?"

He had the good grace to look embarrassed.

Padraig answered for him, "You have to be prepared to take prisoners."

"But black hoods? Where are you planning to take them? Guantanamo Bay?"

"You heard, Pearl. This is war, Val. You have to be prepared for anything. I know hoods have ugly associations, but prisoners are less likely to try to escape when they can't see where they're going. It saves a lot of hassle."

Val sighed. She didn't like it, but what he was saying made sense.

"Speaking of prisoners." She turned, then cursed. Rodrigo and Jonathan Grey had slipped away while their backs were turned.

Padraig came back across the room. "Sadly, things are never that simple. We're ready to go whenever you are. The sooner we get out of here, the better."

"Yeah. Can your men grab Baron Blood and give me a hand with Hillary?"

"Hillary can walk." The young vampire's voice came weakly from the floor.

Val turned to her in surprise. "You're awake."

"I'm not happy about it. Everything hurts." Hillary groaned as Val helped her sit up. She hissed in pain when Malcolm's light flashed across her face. "Can't he turn that thing off?"

"Yeah, I suppose so. There's not much point now that the vampires have all escaped." Val called out, "Malcolm, you can turn your spotlight off."

"But what if the vampires come back?" Malcolm's eyes were still wide with panic.

"Keep your finger on the switch, just in case," Val advised. "But I don't think they're coming back today."

Padraig smiled his perfect smile. "She's right. We've won the day. It's all over but the celebrating now."

"Well, we still have to patch up the wounded and collect the bodies," Val said soberly.

"All of which will be much more pleasant with a belly full of whiskey," Padraig insisted. He extended his hands and pulled Val and Hillary to their feet.

"OK, let's go." Val put her new roommate's arm over her shoulder, supporting her weight as they moved slowly toward the tunnel leading back to the O' Ceallaigh mansion.

61

Val left Padraig to his whiskey and slipped out into the night. It wasn't time for her to celebrate. Not yet. There was one more thing she needed to do.

She crossed the street, where fog was curling over the crest of the park like fingers scratching at a crown. Val pulled her leather jacket tight against the chill. Around her, the houses were silent and dark. She didn't know what time it was, but it was late. The city was asleep.

The fog muffled the sound of her boots. White tendrils licked her cheeks and left them moist. She fought back a yawn. Now that the battle was over, the adrenaline crash had left her exhausted. Every step was an effort. She wanted nothing more than to crawl into bed and sleep for a week.

But there was one more thing she needed to do first.

As she approached the Queen Anne, rapid footsteps approached from the dark behind her. She whirled around, her knife flashing out of its sheath.

"Whoa! I surrender!" Malcolm stood before her, hands raised.

Val blew out an exasperated breath. "Flying fish, Malcolm. Don't sneak up on me like that. Especially after the night we've had."

Her roommate gave her an uncertain smile. "Believe me, I was not sneaking."

"You can say that again. You sounded like a herd of ostrich pounding down the sidewalk." She sheathed her knife and cocked her head at him. "What are you doing here, Malcolm? Why aren't you drinking Irish Whiskey with Padraig and his crew?"

"I saw you sneak out, and I guessed this was where you were going."

"I appreciate the thought, but you can't help, Malcolm."

"I know. I came to say goodbye."

She held his gaze for a moment then nodded wearily.

"Come on then."

The lobby of the Queen Anne was deserted, the night clerk probably sleeping in the back room. A lucky break. Val had no patience left at the moment, and she had no idea what she would say if the night clerk had tried to stop them. Nothing polite, certainly. It was better this way for all involved.

The room was just as she'd left it. Minus the witches. It looked like the Sisters had returned for Paula—or her body—but they hadn't bothered to clean up the circle or the candles. Which suited Val just fine. She needed the circle for what she was about to do, and now she wouldn't have to spend time drawing a new one.

She wondered where the Sisters had gone. She wondered if Paula was alive or dead.

"If she's dead, the Sisters will definitely be coming after me," she muttered.

"Oh, they'll be coming after you regardless," Mister E assured her. *"Those witches know how to hold a grudge."*

"Thank you for that. Very reassuring."

The cat-demon grinned from ear to ear. *"Happy to set your mind at ease."*

Val checked the circle for breaks and filled in a couple of spots that had gotten scuffed. Broken circles were worse than useless: they were dangerous. Ritual magic had to be tightly controlled. If it got away from you, bad things were likely to happen. For an example, look no further than the explosion when she'd broken Baron Blood's ritual circle. She definitely did not want a repeat of that.

Finally satisfied the circle was intact, Val began lighting candles.

Malcolm cleared his throat. He'd been uncharacteristically quiet, watching her with solemn eyes.

"I want to go with you."

"Go with me? Go with me where?"

"Go with you to see Stephen."

Her head whipped around to stare at him. "Absolutely not. It's too dangerous."

"You said the same thing about fighting the vampires. And I helped." He stuck out his chin defiantly.

"That was different. There were a lot of us. Others who could protect you. In there, it's just going to be me. And I won't be at full strength. Without other witches to send me through, I'll just be a weak astral projection. If Macy still wants to fight, we'll be helpless."

"Stephen is my friend. My oldest friend. I want to see him one last time. Please, Val." Tears shimmered in his eyes. "Let me go with you. I need to say goodbye."

Val swore under her breath.

"Fine. But you really are taking your life into your hands. I have no idea what the spirit who has him trapped will do. Last time I managed to fight her off, but I was at full strength then. This time I'll only have a small fraction of my power. If she decides to keep us there, we may end up joining Stephen as permanent guests in her little tea party."

Relief flooded his face. "Thank you, Val. Whatever you need to me to do, I'll do it. I won't let you down."

"Just stay out of the way. Sit here. Don't smudge the chalk." She patted a spot inside the circle, and Malcolm stepped carefully over the white line and sat down, folding his legs under him.

Val joined him, lowering herself so they were sitting back-to-back. She could feel Malcolm's ribcage expanding and contracting with his breath. His body radiated heat through his shirt.

"Give me your hand and stay silent. You do not want to know what could happen if you break my concentration."

He obediently placed his palm over hers, his skin smooth and soft.

Academic's hands. Nothing like the wiry strength and torn up knuckles of Val's own. Still, his grip was firm. She took comfort in that.

She closed her eyes and began to chant, visualizing Macy's rose in her other hand.

This was her third trip there, and just like in the real world, the way got easier each time as she internalized the route. The rose helped a lot too, pulling her toward Macy like a lodestone. She found the glade almost immediately.

"This is not what I was expecting," Malcolm said.

She turned to find his astral projection still holding her hand.

"It's a velvet prison," she replied. "Macy keeps the spirits trapped in a perpetual present. They have no sense of the passage of time."

"Wouldn't that be the Buddhist's definition of Nirvana? I know my friend Jade is always going on about, 'Be here now'."

Val shrugged. "I wouldn't know. I'm not a Buddhist. But I'm pretty sure that if it's being done to you against your will, that means it's not Nirvana."

"True. So where is...?" His voice trailed off as he saw the picnic by the lake. Stephen was sitting on the blanket, sipping a glass of wine. Malcolm sucked in a breath, his fingers flying up to cover his mouth. "Is that really him?"

"It's his soul, yes. Macy grabbed it when he died and pulled him in here. She thinks she's protecting him."

Malcolm dabbed at his eyes.

"It seems pretty nice here. Where would he be otherwise? Maybe he wants to be here."

"Would you want to be stuck in purgatory? I don't know what happens after this, but I do know that, whatever it is, it's the way things are supposed to be. Our souls are supposed to move on. Being trapped here forever and not even knowing it? That's not Nirvana. That's hell."

"I guess you're right," Malcolm said softly. "Can I talk to him?"

"Sure, go ahead. Say your goodbyes. I need to find Macy and put an end to this."

Val watched Malcolm wander off across the grass. Stephen's shade jumped up and gave him a big hug. Tears sparkled on Malcolm's cheeks.

She sighed and rubbed the sudden pain in her chest. Goodbyes were hard.

Still, it was better than never getting the chance to say goodbye at all.

Val was just turning to look for the girl when Macy came stomping up to her.

"What are you doing back here? Didn't we fix the problem?"

She stayed calm in the face of the girl's anger.

"Yes, we did. It's safe out there now. It's time to go home, Macy. Time to let all of these people go home."

Macy folded her arms over her chest. The hem of her red dress rippled in the wind. She looked uncertain, her eyes young and scared.

"But what if the bad people come back? Who will keep them safe?"

"I will," Val promised. "You've been here too long, Macy. These people have been here too long. It's time to go."

The girl regarded her for a long moment, hope warring with suspicion on her face. Finally, she reached out and took Val's hand.

62

"That went better than I expected," Malcolm said. He gave a bittersweet smile and smoothed the blanket over his legs.

They were sitting in their living room, drinking coffee and watching the last rays of sunset paint lavender streaks across the sky. Malcolm had his feet tucked under him on the couch, a fuzzy purple blanket draped across his lap. Val sat across from him in the armchair, her feet wrapped in warm wool socks, heels propped on the edge of the coffee table. They'd both just rolled out of bed, having collapsed as soon as they got home in the wee hours of the morning and slept the entire day.

"Yeah, I was half expecting another fight." Val sipped her butterscotch latte and sighed. "But when you get down to it, Macy never wanted to fight. She only wanted to be safe, and to keep others safe too. She seemed almost happy to let the trapped souls go. I think she was tired, to be honest. She died a long time ago. It takes incredible strength to keep fighting for so long. That little girl was something else. Really powerful. Imagine what she could have done with her life if she'd been born in another time."

"Maybe she'll get the chance now," Malcolm said. "Maybe she'll get reincarnated as a kick-ass modern woman."

"Maybe," Val shrugged. "Like I said, I don't know what happens next. Where the souls go from here. I've seen too much magic in this world to discount anything. For all I know, every religion is right, and every person has a different path after death. Reincarnation is a comforting thought, at least."

"Is it?" Hillary came padding into the room, her hair mussed from sleep, a steaming mug cupped in her hands. "Would you want to come back to this over and over again?" She gestured vaguely at the window and the city beyond.

"We can't all be immortal blood suckers," Val said sharply.

"Fair point." Hillary settled on the other end of the couch. "Though I didn't have all that much of a choice."

"I thought you said you chose to become a vampire?"

"I did. But there were extenuating circumstances. Which I will not be going into." She held up a hand to forestall Malcolm as his mouth opened to ask the question. He pressed his lips together in annoyance, but let it pass. "The point remains, though: Is being reincarnated on earth over and over heaven or hell?"

"Neither," Val said.

Right on top of her Malcolm said, "Both."

"Exactly." Hillary nodded as if that proved her point. "Oh, this just came for you, by the way. It was sitting on the floor inside the mail slot." She tossed a small white envelope to Val.

Val turned it over in her hands. On the front, in beautiful gilded script, it said only: Valora Keri.

"Another fancy party invitation?" Malcolm's mouth quirked. "You're becoming quite the socialite, Val."

Val made a rude noise. "Hardly."

She turned the envelope over and slit the seal with her thumbnail. She withdrew a thick white card, then frowned at the words printed there.

"Well, don't leave us hanging," Malcolm said. "What is it?"

"You were right about it being an invitation. But a little off about the occasion." She tossed the card to Malcolm.

He read: "You are formally invited to the funeral of Andrei Vasilevski." The location, date, and time were below.

Malcolm raised an eyebrow. "Were you friends?"

"Vasilevski was a regular at the Alley Cat, and he strongarmed me into working for him a couple of times. I wouldn't call that friends."

"Then why the invitation?"

Val frowned and rubbed a hand over the arm of the chair. "It must be from his niece, Zoe. The one who introduced me to Padraig."

Malcolm and Hillary exchanged glances.

"Are you going to go?" Hillary asked.

"I don't know. Maybe. On the one hand, I'm not sure I want to strengthen those particular ties..."

"But on the other hand, you definitely do not want to offend the Vasilevskis," Hillary finished.

"Exactly." Val sighed and sipped her coffee. "Life was so much simpler when all I had to do was tend bar and fight the occasional monster. I don't like being noticed by the movers and shakers of this city."

"Afraid you'll get moved and shaken?" Malcolm smirked.

Val didn't return his smile.

"I don't like being pushed around by forces that are out of my control. My whole life I've been shoved this way and that. From the moment I was sent to live with my aunt in America, I've been running from one place to another. Do you know how long I've lived in San Francisco? Two years. And this is the longest I've lived in one place since I was six. Is it too much to ask for some stability for once?"

There was silence for a minute as they all thought about that.

Finally, Hillary said, "So, stop running."

Val puffed in exasperation. "And what? Play politics? Become a pawn in the game of power?"

"You're only a pawn if you let yourself be used. Powerful connections go both ways. Look at what we did last night. We couldn't have gotten that ring without Padraig's help."

"It put me in his debt," Val snapped.

"Having powerful connections does have its perks," Malcolm said thoughtfully. "I mean, your wardrobe has certainly been reaping the benefits."

"Ha-ha." Val rolled her eyes, but her expression became thoughtful.

Could she use her powerful connections to her advantage? As Hillary had pointed out, it had already worked once. And she did have powerful enemies. Melinda Pearl would certainly be trying to kill her. The Sisters probably would as well. She could use some muscle at her back.

But could she cultivate those allies without compromising her morals? That was a thornier question, and she was afraid she knew what the answer would be.

Still, Padraig had been nothing but helpful so far. And Zoe was a nice enough kid.

"What do I have to lose by trying?" she muttered.

"Famous last words," Mister E whispered from his perch on the back of her chair. *"You'd better let me train you if you want to play in the major leagues. Little fish get eaten."*

She scowled, but the demon-cat had a point. The last thing she wanted to do was bring a knife to a gun fight.

"Fine." She sighed and sipped her coffee. It seemed there were big changes ahead.

Her gaze flicked to Hillary. Who was she kidding? She had a vampire roommate. The big changes were already here.

The difference was, for the first time in her life she wasn't going to run from them.

<<<<>>>>

Thank you for reading Pale Midnight, the second book in The Keri Chronicles! Before you go, I have a small favor to ask.

Reviews are vitally important for book publishing, especially when launching a new series.

If you could take a minute to leave a review on Amazon or Goodreads, it would really help a lot. It doesn't have to be large: Even just a few words can make a world of difference.

Thank you so much.

Yours,
A.C. Arquin

ABOUT THE AUTHOR

A.C. Arquin lives in his own worlds. At least, that's what his teachers always told him when they caught him reading a book in class instead of paying attention to the lesson.

Now all grown up, he still prefers realms of imagination to reality. The only difference is that nowadays, he writes down his adventures and shares them with the world.

When not writing, he is also a very busy audiobook narrator, under the name J.S. Arquin.

He is hard at work on the next book in the Keri Chronicles.

Get a FREE KERI CHRONICLES PREQUEL STORY as well, as all the latest news and deals, by joining his Reader's Group at www. arquinworlds.com/

f 🐦 📷

ALSO BY A.C. ARQUIN

THE KERI CHRONICLES

Dead Wrong

The Itch (A Gaslamp Fantasy Thriller)

THE CRIMSON DUST CYCLE (A Dystopian Space Adventure. Published as J.S. Arquin)

Ascent (Book 1)

Slide (Book 2)

Peak (Book 3)

Twist (A Crimson Dust Prequel)

The Crimson Dust Cycle Box Set

`

www.ingramcontent.com/pod-product-compliance
Ingram Content Group UK Ltd.
Pitfield, Milton Keynes, MK11 3LW, UK
UKHW010710061025
8242UKWH00039B/1003